"I've avoided prying into your past, Cassandra,"

he said. "As long as you're serving a purpose here, I'm willing to let things stand."

"Serving a purpose!" Cassandra fought back a scalding surge of tears. "Is that the only reason you've allowed me to stay, so that you can *use* me?"

His eyes had gone cold. "You're getting what you came for, aren't you? You've got a roof over your head, food in your belly and, at least, the trappings of respectability. What else could you want?"

"I want to be *valued!*" She hurled the words at him, struck by their truth. In the desperate months following Jake's death she had thought that nothing mattered except having the means to provide for her child. But she'd been wrong. What she'd needed as much as food and shelter was to be of worth to the people she cared about…!

* * *

Wyoming Widow
Harlequin Historical #657—May 2003

Acclaim for Elizabeth Lane's latest books

Bride on the Run

"Enjoyable and satisfying all around, *Bride on the Run* is an excellent Western romance you won't want to miss!"
—*Romance Reviews Today* (romrevtoday.com)

Shawnee Bride

"A fascinating, realistic story."
—*Rendezvous*

Apache Fire

"Enemies, lovers, raw passion, taut sexual tension, murder and revenge—Indian romance fans are in for a treat with Elizabeth Lane's sizzling tale of forbidden love that will hook you until the last moment."
—*Romantic Times*

WYOMING WIDOW

ELIZABETH LANE

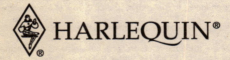

HARLEQUIN®

TORONTO • NEW YORK • LONDON
AMSTERDAM • PARIS • SYDNEY • HAMBURG
STOCKHOLM • ATHENS • TOKYO • MILAN • MADRID
PRAGUE • WARSAW • BUDAPEST • AUCKLAND

ISBN 0-373-29257-0

WYOMING WIDOW

Copyright © 2003 by Elizabeth Lane

This edition published by arrangement with Harlequin Books S.A.

® and TM are trademarks of the publisher. Trademarks indicated with
® are registered in the United States Patent and Trademark Office, the
Canadian Trade Marks Office and in other countries.

Visit us at www.eHarlequin.com

Printed in U.S.A.

Available from Harlequin Historicals and
ELIZABETH LANE

Wind River #28
Birds of Passage #92
Moonfire #150
MacKenna's Promise #216
Lydia #302
Apache Fire #436
Shawnee Bride #492
Bride on the Run #546
My Lord Savage #569
Christmas Gold #627
"Jubal's Gift"
Wyoming Widow #657

Other works include:

Silhouette Romance

Hometown Wedding #1194
The Tycoon and the Townie #1250

Silhouette Special Edition

Wild Wings, Wild Heart #936

Please address questions and book requests to:
Harlequin Reader Service
U.S.: 3010 Walden Ave., P.O. Box 1325, Buffalo, NY 14269
Canadian: P.O. Box 609, Fort Erie, Ont. L2A 5X3

To my mother, Beryl Washburn Young
1918–2002
The most valiant and beautiful heroine of all.

Chapter One

Laramie, Wyoming
June 10, 1879

"I know you're in there, girlie," the wheezy voice rasped through the thin planking of the door. "I heered you rustlin' them papers in there like a purty li'l red-haired mouse! Open the door, now, so's I won't have to get out my key."

Cassandra Logan huddled in the shadows beside the potbellied stove, her arms wrapped protectively around her bulging belly. Today was the first day of the month. The rent on the shack was due. The landlord, Seamus Hawkins, was here to collect.

And Cassandra had no money to give him.

Her stomach churned as her ears caught the jingle of his heavy key ring. In a moment he would be inside. Then what?

Things had gone from bad to worse in the seven months since her husband, Jake, had died in a gunfight over a pretty blond saloon girl. For a time, scrubbing floors in the Union Pacific Hotel had brought Cassandra enough money for food and rent. But finding work was impossible now. What employer would hire a woman whose apron strings were wrapped beneath her armpits?

As the key slid into the lock, she forced herself to move. Cowering in the corner would only encourage Seamus to bully her—the last thing she needed at a time like this.

Before he could turn the knob, Cassandra swung the door open and stood facing him, arms akimbo, trying to look as fierce as possible. Since the man was at least twice her size, it was a ludicrous effort. He leered down at her, fat and unshaven, reeking of whiskey and garlic.

"Well, where is it?" he demanded, clearly savoring his power over her. "You knew I'd be comin' 'round today."

Cassandra willed herself not to writhe beneath his gaze. "I'll have the rent by Monday," she lied desperately. "Surely you can wait that long. I've always paid you on time."

Seamus's eyes narrowed to slits. "I'll give you till this time tomorrow," he said. "Have the rent in full by then, or it's out you go. There be plenty folks needin' a roof an' able to pay."

He took a step over the threshold. Cassandra's stomach clenched as she sensed what was coming next.

"You know, girlie, there's more'n one way to pay

a man. You let me come 'round whenever I get a yen for somethin' sweet, an' you won't owe me a cent.''

''I don't think your wife would approve of that arrangement, Mr. Hawkins,'' Cassandra said icily.

''What my old woman don't know won't hurt her none.'' He winked slyly, edging closer as Cassandra battled gut-heaving panic. ''This could be a li'l private business deal, just between you an' me. I'd even buy you presents if you was nice to me. How about it, girlie?'' His breath was warm and damp, his gaze hungry. ''Twouldn't be so bad. You might even get to like it.'' He groped for her, but Cassandra slipped away, moving back toward the stove, one hand fumbling for the iron kettle.

''Give me a chance to come up with the money,'' she parried, stalling for time. ''The other—that wouldn't be a good idea with the baby—''

''Aww...I'd be careful. Truth be told, I'd take you over the money any day. 'Sides, 'twouldn't be the worst if somethin' did go wrong an' you lost the young'un, you havin' no husband and all. Why, a purty li'l thing like you, with no brat taggin' along, you could—''

The words ended in a gasp as Cassandra flung the kettle at his head. White-hot rage fueled the impact of the blow. Seamus reeled backward, blood oozing down his temple. He lunged for her, but she spun out of reach, putting the stove between them as she bent to snatch the hatchet out of the wood box.

''What'll it be, Seamus?'' she hissed, gripping the

weapon. "A finger? An eye, maybe? Take one step closer and you'll find out."

Seamus edged backward. Then, from a safer distance, he grinned at her. "So you like to play rough, eh, you little hellcat? Well, two can play at that game. If I didn't have my old lady waitin' down on the road in the buggy, I'd show you right now." He turned toward the door, then paused, dabbing at his temple with a dirty handkerchief. "I'll be back tomorrow to collect what's owed me. An' one way or another, girlie, you'd better be ready to pay, or you'll be out in the street. An' that'd be a damned, dirty shame, now, wouldn't it?"

Spitting on the handkerchief, he wiped the blood from the side of his face, then turned away and ambled outside. Cassandra slammed the door shut behind him and barricaded it with a spindly chair propped against the knob. Not that it would stop a big man like Seamus Hawkins. When Seamus wanted to come in, he would. His wife had been waiting for him this time. But what about tomorrow?

Racked by stomach spasms, she sank onto the edge of the bed and pressed her hands to her face. Her limbs felt watery. Her skin was clammy with sweat. She had to get out of this place.

But how? Where could she go? What in heaven's name would she do when the baby came?

Money—she would need money to get away. But she had so few treasures left to sell, and they were so dear—the garnet earrings that had been her grandmother's; her grandfather's fiddle; the gold locket with Jake's picture in it—the only image of him their child would ever know. How could she part with any of them?

A raw wind, rank with the smell of the nearby stockyards, whistled through the cracks in the clapboard walls. Cassandra shivered, her stomach still churning from the encounter with Seamus Hawkins. A cup of hot chamomile tea would do wonders for her body and spirit, she thought. There were only a few sticks left in the wood box, but what did it matter if she wasted them? Tomorrow Seamus would be knocking on her door, demanding payment. She could not afford to be here when he arrived.

Groping on the floor, she found the kettle where it had bounced off Seamus's head. Now for the stove— what a lucky thing she'd saved that discarded newspaper she'd found yesterday in the street. It would come in handy for lighting the fire.

Unfolding the paper, she ripped off the front page and began crumpling it to stuff into the stove. Suddenly her hands froze. Her eyes stared at the page.

There, smiling at her from beneath the headline, was the lean, handsome face of her late husband.

Cassandra's knees went watery. She stumbled back to the bed and sank down on the mattress, her hands smoothing the creases out of the page as her disbelieving eyes scanned the headline: Rancher's Son Missing, Feared Drowned.

She stared at the printed picture—a pen-and-ink drawing that some newspaper artist had copied from a photograph. Of course, it wasn't really Jake. She had seen Jake dead in his coffin. But it was someone who looked uncannily like him.

Straining her eyes in the scant light, she struggled to make out the small print beneath.

"Ryan Tolliver, son of Wyoming Rancher Jacob Tolliver, was declared missing and presumed drowned last week when a dory containing his possessions washed ashore on the banks of the upper Yellowstone River. Tolliver, 23, had been completing a survey for the United States Department of the Interior, and was last seen alive on…"

Cassandra held the paper to the window, squinting in an effort to finish the article in the fading light. But it was becoming too dark to read the fine print, and she was loath to waste her one precious candle. The picture, however, was still visible in the semi-darkness. Only as she studied the handsome young face again did Cassandra realize she had seen Ryan Tolliver before—right here in Laramie at the Union Pacific Hotel.

It had been last November, she recalled, just a few weeks before Jake's death. She'd been mopping the foyer when the tall young man strode in through the double doors, wearing chaps, spurs and a thick coating of snow and trail dust. Even then, Cassandra had been struck by his resemblance to her late husband. But she'd had no more than a few seconds to stare before he disappeared upstairs. Half an hour later he'd come down again, washed, clean shaven and looking even more like Jake than before. Whistling an airy tune, he'd walked out the front door and headed straight for Flossie's House of Blossoms across the street. That was the last she'd seen of him.

But now, as she studied the picture in the paper, Cassandra had no doubt that the man she'd noticed months ago was Ryan Tolliver.

Smoothing the wrinkled page, she laid it on the table, then turned to fill the kettle from the water bucket. She had not really known Ryan Tolliver, but the sense of his loss weighed on her spirit. He had seemed so happy that winter evening, so young and strong and vital. Cassandra could well imagine what the Tolliver family must be going through now as they waited for the news that would end all their hopes.

Crumpling a back page from the paper, she stuffed it into the dark belly of the stove, added two sticks of wood and lit a single match. Shadows danced on the moldering walls as the fire flickered to a steady blaze. Cassandra put the kettle on the open burner to heat. Then she turned back toward the open shelf to find the store of chamomile she kept in an old jelly jar.

Only then did she notice the way the fire flickered through the grate, casting a finger of golden light across the low table—a finger of light that pointed straight toward the smiling image of Ryan Tolliver.

Could it be a sign?

Cassandra stared at the picture, the tea forgotten as

a plan sprang up in her mind—a plan so audacious and risk-fraught that only a woman in her desperate state would have thought of it.

For the space of a long breath she hesitated, weighing the idea. It was dangerous. Worse, it was dishonest, even cruel. No, she resolved, her grandparents hadn't raised her to be a cheat and a liar. She simply could not do it. She would live on the street first!

And the street was exactly where she was headed.

Cassandra sagged against the table, her hands clenching into tight fists. Blast Jake Logan anyway! Why had he gone to the saloon on that awful December night? Why had he gotten himself shot in that silly fight over a dance hall floozy instead of just coming home to *her?*

But then, she'd asked herself that question too many times not to know the answer. She wasn't beautiful like the women in that painted and perfumed world. She was small and wiry to the point of scrawniness, with a rag-doll mop of cherry-colored curls and freckles that popped out at the barest touch of sunlight on her skin. Worse, she'd never known the right words to say to a man—words that would make him puff up his chest and feel like a hero. She was as blunt and honest as the grandmother who'd raised her, and if more vinegar than honey fell from her tongue, so be it. Pretense was not in her nature.

Maybe that was the reason Jake hadn't treated her better. When he wanted to, he could be sweet and tender. But sometimes, especially when he'd been drinking, he could be downright mean. Cassandra had hoped the baby would change things. But on the very night she'd planned to share her news, Jake Logan had died. He had died with his pants down in a tawdry upstairs room, never knowing he was to be a father.

Deep in her body Cassandra felt a little flutter kick, then a shifting motion as her baby turned and stretched in its warm, secret world. Wonder flooded her heart as she smoothed the apron over the growing bulge, feeling for the tiny life that pulsed and stirred beneath her hands. Soon she would have a child, a sweet baby all her own to love and care for. Heaven willing, she would never be alone again.

But what could she offer this child? A safe home with food on the table? The closeness and joy of a family? A secure future with the promise of a fine education?

Cassandra choked back a whimper of despair. She had nothing to offer her baby except love. To provide the rest, she would sacrifice anything—her own pride, her own life.

But even in her desperation, she could not imagine carrying out the wild scheme that had lodged in her mind. To take advantage of a grieving family would compromise everything she knew to be right and good. She would never be able to look at her own reflection in the mirror without a spasm of self-loathing.

No, it was out of the question.

All the same, the story of Ryan Tolliver's disappearance was intriguing. Cassandra could not resist wanting to know more.

The newspaper article lay on the table, begging to be read. Strangely agitated, she rummaged for another match and lit the candle she'd been hoarding. The story took up just two printed columns. She would only need a few minutes of precious light to read it.

Placing the candle where its light would fall on the open page, she finished making the tea. Then, cradling the chipped white cup between her hands, she sank onto a wooden box and began to read.

The room was a blanket of darkness around her, the tea warm and comforting in her belly. By the time she reached the second column of the news article the print had begun to blur. Cassandra's eyelids drooped lower and lower. She had been up since dawn looking for work, and she was tired. So very tired…

Startled, she jerked awake. The candle had guttered to half its original length. She had dozed off, Cassandra realized groggily. What time was it? What had awakened her?

As she leaned forward to blow out the candle, plunging the room into full darkness, she heard the low metallic click of a key sliding into a lock.

Instantly wide-awake, she sprang to brace the door. It crashed open, knocking her to one side as Seamus Hawkins lurched across the threshold.

"Awright, girlie." His voice was slurred, and his body stank of cheap whiskey. "I'm back t' finish what we started. No need t' fight me, now. You'll start likin' it once I git it 'twixt them sweet little legs o' yours."

Cassandra had been thrown back against the wall.

As he stumbled toward her, she groped for a weapon, anything she could use to defend herself.

Her hand closed on an iron bootjack with a weighted base—a silly extravagance, she'd called it when Jake had brought it home, as if a man couldn't pull off his boots with his own two hands. It was heavy and solid, but not long enough to keep Seamus at a distance. Her best chance lay in keeping away from him until she could reach the door and flee into the night.

Hoping to confuse him, she picked up a tin cup from the counter and tossed it across the room. It clattered in the darkness, bouncing against a table leg and onto the floor. Distracted, Seamus swung toward the sound, allowing Cassandra a split second to change her position. Not that it made any difference. He still stood between her and the door.

She shrank into a shadowed corner of the tiny cabin. The mica panes on the door of the stove glowed like little red eyes, giving the darkness a hellish cast. And it *would* be hell if he caught her. Being raped was unspeakable enough, but if he should hurt her baby, her darling…

Cassandra's grip tightened on the bootjack. She could hear the rasp of breath in her throat—the breath of a hunted, desperate animal.

Seamus must have heard it, too, for he suddenly turned, blocking the light of the stove as he lumbered straight toward her. "I got you cornered now, you little hellcat!" he wheezed. "Now, I won't mind if you put up a fuss. A good rasslin' match gits me as hard as a—''

Cassandra flung the bootjack at his head with all her strength. It glanced off his forehead, doing only superficial damage, but the blow was enough to throw him off balance. As he reeled backward, out of control, one foot landed on the tin cup that had rolled to the middle of the floor. For a split second his legs splayed wildly. His arms flailed like berserk windmills. With a shriek, he pitched backward.

Cassandra heard the awful crunch of bone as the back of his head struck a corner of the iron stove. Then Seamus Hawkins crashed to the floor and lay still.

Chapter Two

Morgan Tolliver stood on the porch of the sprawling log-and-stone ranch house. His raven eyes, a legacy from his Shoshone mother, narrowed as they studied the afternoon sky.

Virga. That's what they called the phantom rain that hung below the clouds, vaporizing in the heat before the drops could reach the ground. His eyes could see rain, his nostrils could even smell it. But he knew this ghost rain would do nothing for the sun-parched land. There would be no relief today from the searing drought that had turned the rich Wyoming grass to straw and the water holes to dust wallows.

Even the reservoir, which, two months ago had been filled with runoff from the spring snow melt, was getting perilously low. Once the water was gone, there'd be no way to irrigate the new hayfields he'd planted to keep the cattle fed over the next winter.

Everything, it seemed, had gone bad since the news of Ryan's disappearance. Morgan's long brown hands tightened on the porch rail as he thought of his spirited young half brother—laughing, reckless Ryan, the darling of the ranch and the apple of their aging father's eye. During his growing-up years, the boy had dogged Morgan's footsteps like an adoring puppy. It was Morgan who had taught him to swim and wrestle, Morgan who had put him on his first pony and helped him rope his first calf. Now Ryan had vanished, and it was as if his loss had sucked the life out of the earth itself.

Why in God's name did it have to be Ryan? Morgan asked himself for perhaps the hundredth time. *Why not me instead?*

He was turning to go back inside when a faint plume of dust on the far horizon caught his eye. Someone—or something—was moving along the road, toiling its way toward the house.

Morgan's heart contracted as he watched the dust materialize into a dark shape that looked more like a wagon than a single rider. Could it be someone with news about Ryan—or Ryan himself? Or would it turn out to be nothing more than a wandering stranger in need of a meal and a bed?

"Who is it? Can you tell?" His father had come out onto the porch, his chair rolling across the planks on silent wheels. Jacob Tolliver had aged in the three weeks since word of Ryan's disappearance had reached the ranch. His face was drawn, his hands and voice unsteady. He spent his days seated at the tall parlor windows, watching the empty road with his field glass, which he now thrust into Morgan's hand.

"Your eyes are sharper than mine. Take a look. Tell me what you see."

Morgan raised the glass to his eye and trained the lens on the road. He could make it out now—a weather-beaten buckboard that lurched through the ruts on its wobbling wheels, looking as if every yard gained might be its last. A single spavined mule staggered along in the traces, favoring a lame right forefoot. The whole sad conveyance was so thickly coated with dust that it looked like a ghost apparition emerging through shimmering waves of heat.

The lone driver was hunched over the reins, a small figure in a slouchy felt hat who looked to be either a boy or a shriveled old man. Morgan sharpened the focus of the glass in an effort to see more. Then, giving up, he shifted his attention to what might be inside the wagon.

In this, too, he was left unsatisfied. The rim of a barrel, probably for water, showed above the warped planking along the sides. Any other cargo on the wagon bed was hidden from view.

What could such a decrepit rig be bringing to the ranch?

A coffin?

With Ryan's body in it?

"Who is it?" Jacob Tolliver's voice crackled with impatience. "Can you tell? Is it your brother?"

"No." Morgan shook his head as he lowered the field glass. "It's someone else. A stranger."

Handing the glass back to his father, he strode down the steps and across the dusty yard toward the corral. If Ryan's body was in the back of that wagon, he needed to find out now, so he could do his best to cushion the blow for the old man.

The buckskin mare pricked her ears at his whistle and trotted over to the open gate. Morgan slipped the bridle over her head and buckled the throat latch. Without taking time for the saddle, he sprang Indian fashion onto her back and galloped out to meet the wagon.

The driver of the tottering buckboard straightened on the seat as Morgan approached but made no effort to wave or shout. Probably didn't have any strength left, Morgan groused. Who would send such a help-less little runt out here alone in a rig that looked like it was about to collapse? It was a wonder the mule and driver hadn't been picked off by coyotes along the way.

The wagon had stopped. Morgan slowed the mare to a walk as he approached, aware of the eyes that watched him intently from beneath the brim of the dusty felt hat.

"Don't come any farther, mister." The voice was small and throaty. A young voice. Just a boy, Morgan surmised, and the youngster was probably scared out of his wits.

But never mind, it was the contents of the wagon that concerned Morgan most. He edged closer, steel-ing his emotions against the sight of his brother's re-mains.

"I'm warning you, mister." The words held a

gritty edge. "I've got a Colt .45. It's loaded and pointed straight at your heart."

Morgan reined in the mare, wondering if there was anything behind the threat. The only sign of a weapon was a bulge beneath the outsized denim jacket. Probably nothing—but this was no time to be wrong, especially since he himself was unarmed.

"I won't hurt you, boy," he said quietly. "I just want to see what you've got in the back of that wagon."

"I've got nothing worth stealing, if that's what you're after." The youthful voice shook slightly. "Now get out of my way before I drill you like a grub-thieving possum!"

Morgan's lips tightened in a grim smile. "Big words from such a little man," he said, calling the youth's bluff. "Why don't you climb down from that wagon and show me how tough you really are?"

Silence.

"Then let me see that pistol you're so keen on using," Morgan demanded.

The huddled figure sat like a small, defiant lump of stone. Morgan felt the tension easing out of his body. But the dread remained like a cold knot in the pit of his stomach. If Ryan's body was in the back of the wagon, he had to face that reality and to deal with whatever came next.

"All right, we're going to play this my way," he said. "Tell me who you are and what you're doing on Tolliver land."

"This...is Tolliver land?" The husky voice carried a note of incredulity. "You work for the Tollivers?"

"In a manner of speaking, yes."

Morgan took advantage of the stranger's surprise to nudge the mare closer to the wagon. His heart leaped with relief as he glanced over the side and saw nothing but a tattered bedroll, a moth-eaten carpetbag and the water barrel he'd noticed earlier. His worst fears had not come to pass, thank God. But something strange was going on, and the young whelp in the wagon had some explaining to do.

"I've answered your question," Morgan said irritably. "Now you can damned well answer mine and tell me what you're doing here."

"I..." The youth seemed suddenly tongue-tied. Something about the small figure suddenly struck Morgan as odd—the set of the shoulders, the downcast face beneath the floppy old hat, the air of vulnerability that touched a long-buried chord of tenderness in him—a tenderness he swiftly masked.

"What the hell's the matter with you, boy?" he snapped. "You didn't come all this way for nothing! Stand up! Let me have a look at you!"

For the space of a breath there was silence. Then slowly the mysterious figure rose. Now, beneath the hat brim, Morgan could see the lower part of the beardless face—the narrow but firm chin, the full, disturbingly sensual mouth. The baggy denim duster hung like a tent on the slight body, hiding everything except for lower down, near the waist, where it was stretched tight, almost as if—

Morgan's jaw dropped. "What the devil—"

He had no time to say more as the stranger swayed for an instant, then, with a little moan, toppled headlong over the side of the wagon.

Reacting instinctively, Morgan grabbed for the falling body and managed to catch it beneath the arms. The sudden dead weight almost pulled him off his mount, but the mare, trained as a cow pony, leaned outward to compensate until he was able to balance the burden across his knees.

Only then did he have time to look down.

For a long moment he simply stared, cursing under his breath as his eyes took in the wild, impossibly red mop of curls that had spilled free of the old hat; the pale, heart-shaped face with its almost childlike features; the tiny freckles that sprinkled the porcelain skin like cinnamon specks on fresh cream.

Small and limp, she lay in his arms. Her eyelids, fringed with thick taffy-colored lashes, were tightly closed. What color would those eyes be? Morgan found himself wondering. Sky-blue? Green and sly like a bobcat's. He had known a number of redheaded women in his youth. No two had been the same.

He knew what he would see when he forced his eyes lower—his arms had already felt the ripe weight of her swollen body. How far along was she? Seven months? Eight? Lord, she looked so young, so helpless, more child than woman. What in blazes was she doing out here alone? How far had she come, and— an even more pressing question—*why* had she come?

She moaned, rooting against his chest like a young

animal seeking comfort. Morgan willed himself to ignore the swelling heat in the depths of his body. The woman appeared to be suffering from too much sun, compounded by her delicate condition. He needed to get her to the house and get some water into her. Any questions would have to wait until she'd had time to recover.

He paused an instant longer, weighing the wisdom of putting her back in the wagon to move her. No, he resolved swiftly, it would be faster to take her like this, on his own mount. He could send a couple of the hands out for the wagon and the mule.

Gripping the mare with his knees, Morgan shifted the young woman's body in his arms to balance her weight for the ride to the house. Her head fell back, lolling over his arm, revealing the small gold locket that nestled in the creamy hollow of her throat.

Driven by a strange impulse, Morgan lifted his free hand and brushed the gleaming heart with the tip of his index finger. The catch must have been weak or broken, because the halves of the locket parted at his touch, falling open to form two miniature hearts where there had been one.

In the section that bore the ring and chain, carefully cut and glued into place, was a miniature portrait. He bent closer to see it, painfully aware of the young woman in his arms, the warm, musky scent of her filling his nostrils, teasing his senses.

Was the man framed in the little gold heart the father of her child? Did she expect him to be here at the ranch, one of the cowhands, maybe? The fact that she wore no wedding ring suggested that, whoever he was, the bastard had done her wrong. Maybe a shotgun wedding was in order.

Morgan's eyes narrowed, squinting in an effort to focus the tiny heart-shaped image. Then the truth hit him with the force of a gut punch. The breath exploded from his lungs as he recognized the blurred but familiar face.

Ryan's face.

Cassandra stirred and opened her eyes. The first thing she saw was an expanse of whitewashed ceiling crossed by dark wooden beams. As her senses began to clear, she became aware that she was lying on her back, fully clothed except for her boots, hat and duster. A soft pillow cradled her head and a cool, wet cloth lay across her brow.

What had happened to her? Cassandra struggled to collect her thoughts but her heat-fogged brain refused to obey her will. Her mind contained nothing but the echoing creak of wagon wheels, the plodding of weary hooves, the blinding glare of the sun—and the dim awareness, now, of silence and cool shadow. Her limbs felt weightless, oddly detached from her body, with no power to move.

Was this how it felt to be dead?

As she lay staring into whiteness, something twitched below her taut navel. She felt a flutter then a resounding thump. Cassandra's eyes opened wide in wonder and relief. Her baby was moving. She was alive. They were both alive.

Her hands moved to her swollen belly, palms feeling the precious motion. As her memory began to clear, her thoughts flashed to that awful moment when she'd stood over her landlord's body, her heart pounding in helpless terror. She remembered the frantic rush to leave town, to be gone before someone opened the shack and set the law on her trail.

Her mind swept backward now, over days beneath the vast, open sky, over nights huddled in terror beneath the creaky old wagon she'd bought and paid for with her grandfather's fiddle…back to that point of decision when she'd abandoned every principle by which she'd ever lived.

This is for you, my sweet one, she thought, cradling the bulge of her unborn child between her hands. *The danger, the deceit, all of it. All for you…*

"You've got some tall explaining to do, lady."

The masculine voice, so deep it was almost a growl, caused Cassandra's pulse to jerk as if she'd been dropped in her sleep. When she turned her head in the direction of the voice, she saw the man sitting a scant pace from the bed, his rangy body overflowing the wooden rocker where he sat. His eyes were the color and hardness of cast iron, his hair as black as an Indian's. His grim, aloof face might have been handsome had it contained a modicum of warmth or humor. It did not.

She remembered him now—sitting bareback, like a warrior, on his buckskin horse, dust swirling around him as he blocked her way, demanding to know her business. She had not liked his manner then. She liked it no better now.

"What have you done with my rig?" she demanded, struggling to sit up.

"First you drink. Then we talk." He rose to his feet, picked up a tall pewter mug from the table beside the bed and tilted the rim to her mouth. The water inside was clean and cold, and Cassandra was bone-dry. Seizing the mug, she tipped it upward, gulping frantically as she spilled water into her parched throat.

"Whoa, there." He clasped her wrist, forcing her to lower the mug. "Take it slow, or you'll make yourself sick. Do you understand?" When she nodded, he released her and eased back into the chair.

Cassandra wiped her mouth with the back of her free hand. Her eyes glanced furtively around the small room. Its whitewashed walls were bare except for a tanned, painted buckskin hanging opposite the closed door. The only other furnishings were a washstand with a china pitcher and basin, a small side table next to the bed and the leather-backed rocker where the stranger sat, watching her every move. She emptied the mug in measured sips, then placed it on the side table.

"I asked you about my rig," she said.

"Your wagon broke an axle on the way in." His voice was brittle and strangely cold. "What's left of it is still in the road, waiting to be chopped up and hauled to the woodshed for kindling. As for that bag of bones you call a mule he's in the corral stuffing his belly with hay and oats—probably eaten more than he's worth already.''

Cassandra masked a surge of relief. She had grown attached to the surly old mule, her sole companion for the past six days. And even the news about the wagon was good. It lessened the chance that this self-appointed guardian of the Tolliver Ranch would simply show her the road and send her back the way she'd come.

''I suppose I should thank you,'' she said cautiously.

''You can thank me by answering my questions.''

''Which you have yet to ask me,'' Cassandra retorted. ''For that matter, you haven't even introduced yourself. Do you work for the Tollivers?''

His eyes regarded her coldly. ''Ryan didn't tell you about his family?''

Cassandra felt her heart drop. He was trying to trap her already, this grim, raw-edged man who had ''enemy'' written all over him. If she allowed him to outmaneuver her, she might just as well be back in Laramie fending off Seamus Hawkins.

Only then did it hit her that he had mentioned Ryan—speaking as if he already knew the story she'd planned to tell. Dear heaven, how could that be? Had he read her mind, or—

Her hand crept to her throat, fingers groping for the locket with Jake's picture inside.

''Are you looking for this?''

She saw the locket, then, dangling from his clenched fist. His narrowed eyes cut into her like flints. It would be difficult to lie to such a man, Cassandra thought. But that was exactly what she planned to do—*had* to do for the sake of her child.

''Give me my locket,'' she said. ''You had no right to take it from me.''

''I have the right to know what's going on here,'' he retorted. ''When was the last time you saw my brother?''

''Your brother?'' She blinked dazedly at the looming figure.

''I'll wager you don't even know my name. Do you?'' he challenged her.

Cassandra shook her head, mentally cursing herself for having missed this vital scrap of information.

''It's Morgan. Morgan Tolliver,'' he snarled. ''Now answer my question. When did you see him last?''

''In—in Cheyenne—last November.'' Cassandra stammered out the half-truth she'd gleaned from a clerk at the Union Pacific Hotel, who recalled that Ryan had paid him a generous tip to carry his bags to the depot, where he'd boarded the train for Cheyenne. Now, too late, she realized she should have tried to learn more about the Tolliver family. The newspaper article had mentioned nothing about a brother, only a father. And this forbidding man, with his black hair and mahogany skin, bore no resemblance to the laughing, golden-eyed Ryan.

Cassandra's heart sank lower. What else had she failed to learn? How could she cover herself long enough to play the single trump she held?

"Ryan didn't talk much about his family," she said, feeling the ugly weight as she crossed deeper into falsehood. "I…had the feeling there were things he didn't want me to know. But nothing would have made any difference. I was in love. And so was he— or so I thought at the time." Cassandra lowered her eyes artfully, writhing with self-disgust. "I fear your brother took advantage of me, Mr. Tolliver. He left Cheyenne without even saying goodbye, and I never heard from him again."

The man's expressive mouth scowled. His obsidian gaze never left her as he reached into his deerskin vest and drew out the battered newspaper page that Cassandra had kept in the pocket of her canvas duster. Slowly he unfolded it, taking his time before he thrust it toward her.

"So you saw this and decided to pay us a visit, did you, Miss—"

"Riley," she said, giving her maiden name. "Cassandra Riley. And yes, that's what happened. I don't know if Ryan's alive or dead, but I thought it right that this child be born here, among his family. Besides—" she cast him what she hoped was a poignant glance "—I had nowhere else to go."

"Very touching." His mouth twitched contemptuously. "Let me give you my own version of your story, Miss Riley. My brother liked his women, all right, but he liked them ripe and experienced, with no hidden snares. He would never have taken advantage of someone like…you."

"But he—"

"Let me finish. I don't believe you even knew my brother—at least not well enough to be carrying his child. Under circumstances that are none of my concern, you found yourself with child, saw the newspaper story and decided to take advantage of a grieving family." His dark eyes probed her soul, searching out the lies, the deceit.

"What about the locket?" Cassandra protested. "You saw the picture yourself."

"A photograph glued into a piece of cheap jewelry doesn't prove a thing," he snapped. "Tell me I'm wrong. I dare you."

Cassandra forced herself to meet those accusing eyes. Ryan Tolliver's brother had seen through her subterfuge. He had her dead to rights. Maybe if she confessed now he would let her stay. Surely a large ranch like this could use one more cook, laundress or housekeeper.

But no—his pitiless gaze told her she had already carried her gamble too far. If she told this man the truth, he would put her on the road himself, or, worse, have her arrested for fraud. She had no choice except to continue the dangerous game, no choice except to play the one trump card that remained to her.

Cassandra dropped her gaze to her where her hands lay clasped protectively over the roundness of her belly. Slowly, deliberately, she gathered her resolve. When she looked up again, her eyes were clear, and when she spoke, her voice was as calm as a frozen lake.

"Ryan had a scar," she said, "a jagged white scar,

running like a streak of lightning up the inside of his left thigh. He came by it, as I recall, at the age of fourteen when he was gored by a bull elk he'd wounded with his first rifle.''

Silence hung leaden in the small room as Morgan Tolliver rose to his feet and stood over Cassandra's bed. His wind-burnished features might as well have been chiseled from stone. But even he could not mask the emotions that flickered in those anthracite eyes.

Had she reached him? Had the information she'd taken precious time to buy from Yvette, the youngest and prettiest of Flossie's girls, been worth the price of her grandmother's garnet earrings? Cassandra's future, and the future of her child, hung on the outcome of the next few seconds.

Scarcely daring to breathe, she watched his face and waited.

Chapter Three

Her eyes were the color of violets in a spring meadow. Gazing down into their too-innocent depths, Morgan had to force himself to believe this child-woman was lying. Damnation, she *had* to be lying! It wasn't like Ryan to get mixed up with such a creature. He'd preferred his women ripe and voluptuous. Cassandra Riley was all eyes and freckles and wild red hair, with barely enough body to contain the child she carried. Even if they'd been acquainted in Cheyenne, Morgan couldn't imagine his brother would have given her a second glance.

Unless, against all odds, Ryan had fallen in love with her…

But no, even that didn't make sense. Ryan had a wild streak, but he was decent at heart. If he'd cared for the girl, he would never have run out on her.

She was lying through her pretty little teeth. That's all there was to it.

But how in blazes, then, did she know about the scar?

"What else do you know about Ryan?" he asked, his voice emerging rough and raw from the tightness of his throat.

"That he was kind and gentle and loved to laugh," she replied softly. "He never knew about the baby. If he had, things might be different now."

Morgan felt his jaw muscles tighten as her meaning sank home. If Ryan had known about the baby, maybe he'd have married the poor girl. Maybe he'd have brought her back to the ranch and settled down instead of signing up for that God-cursed government survey expedition.

But this line of thinking was crazy. He was staggering along the edge of believing her, and he couldn't afford to let himself step over the line. She was a fraud, plain and simple. He'd known it from the moment he set eyes on her.

But what if he was wrong?

What if this conniving little waif was carrying Ryan's child—the last, best hope that Jacob Tolliver's line would continue?

Morgan scowled down at the girl, weighing the elements of what he knew. Jacob had always wanted grandsons. When Morgan's own brief marriage had soured and ended, the old man had shifted his hopes to Ryan. Now those hopes were fading, and Jacob's life was fading with them. If Ryan failed to return, Morgan feared his father would die of grief.

Unless, woven amid the gloom, some bright thread of promise could be found.

Jacob had not been told about the locket. The old

man knew only that a young woman in a broken-down wagon had wandered onto the ranch, alone, pregnant and in desperate need of help. Morgan dared not risk revealing the rest of the story. Not, at least, until he knew the truth of it.

"I'm not asking for charity, mind you." Her small but determined voice broke into his thoughts. "I'm a hard worker, and I intend to earn every cent of my keep."

"And how do you plan to do that?" Morgan's gaze flickered downward to the swollen belly beneath the baggy plaid shirt, thinking that there hardly seemed enough of her to carry so much bulk.

"I can cook and wash with the best of them," she declared. "And while I'm resting up after the baby comes, I can always darn stockings and mend whatever else needs it. I'm a fair hand with a needle and thread." Her eyes moved to the front of his shirt. "That includes sewing on…buttons."

Morgan glanced down at his chest. He bit back a twitch at the corner of his mouth as he noticed the loose button, dangling by a single thread, halfway down his shirt.

"Did you happen to rescue my carpetbag from the wagon?" she asked. "I packed my sewing basket inside. Fetch it for me, and I'll give you a demonstration."

"Your demonstration can wait." Morgan edged backward, determined not to give the redheaded charlatan an opening, but she had already spotted her battered valise in the corner where he had dropped it.

"There it is. If you wouldn't mind—"

"Shouldn't you be resting?"

"I'm not an invalid," she said. "In any case I can't imagine that using my fingers will put too much strain on my delicate condition. Now, are you going to bring me that carpetbag and cooperate, or do I have to tie you to the bed and sew on that button by force?"

The mental picture her words painted was so ludicrous that Morgan could not suppress a smile. "All right," he sighed, reaching for the carpetbag. "You win this round. But I'm not finished with you, Miss Cassandra Riley. Not by a long shot."

"I'm sure you're not." She caught the bag as he tossed it, her small, freckled hands as deft as a boy's. "Now, please be kind enough to take off your shirt."

Cassandra's trembling fingers closed on the sewing basket, where it lay crammed in a corner of the hastily packed carpetbag. She struggled to avert her eyes as Morgan Tolliver slipped off his deerskin vest, laid it over the back of the chair, then began to unbutton his sun-bleached cotton work shirt. She had seen her share of half-clad men—Jake, of course, and a few hotel guests who'd startled her to flight when she'd come to clean what she thought was a vacant room. But this man's bearing was so aloof, his body so lithe and sinewy that she could not resist watching him. He lured her gaze like a cougar slipping out of its own pelt.

Most men she knew wore long johns even in summer. But Morgan Tolliver was bare beneath the shirt, his muscles stretching lean and taut beneath golden mahogany skin. The rose-brown dots of his nipples caught glints of light as he tugged the shirttail free from the waistband of his worn denim pants, stripped the shirt from his arms and tossed it on the bed. A leather pouch the size of a baby's shoe dangled from a thong around his neck. When he moved, light glinted on the delicate beading and quillwork that adorned the outside.

His eyes watched her every move as she opened the sewing basket, selected a spool of brown thread and snipped off enough length to sew on the button. Willing herself to ignore his open scrutiny, she found a needle and held it up so the light would fall on its eye. Her hands shook as she tried to force the thread through the tiny hole. Her sun-dazzled eyes began to water, blurring her sight as she wet the cut end to a point and tried again and again.

"Here." His callused fingers brushed hers as he took the needle from her hands and threaded it deftly. "You look like you could use some sleep. I can sew on the button myself."

"No." Cassandra snatched the shirt close to her body, as if challenging him to take it from her. "I'll do it. It's become a matter of principle. Give me that needle."

"Principle!" He dropped the threaded needle into her outstretched hand, then lowered himself into the rocker. His savage eyes seemed to burn through her, all the way to her deceptive little heart.

Cassandra knotted the thread and positioned the

button, forcing her fingers to perform the familiar task. ''I must say, you're nothing like Ryan,'' she said.

''Ryan's my half brother,'' he replied. ''My mother was the daughter of a Shoshone medicine man. Ryan's mother was a pretty blond schoolteacher our father brought home from Saint Louis. She died nine years later, trying to give Ryan a baby sister. Women don't seem to last long out here. Not white women at least.''

''I'm…sorry.''

''I take it you and Ryan didn't spend much time talking.''

The edge in his voice made Cassandra want to slap him. ''Whatever you're thinking, you can stop right now,'' she retorted hotly. ''I didn't come here to be insulted like—like—''

''Like what?'' he demanded when she failed to finish her sentence. ''Like a tramp? Like a whore, even? Is that how you came to know about the scar on Ryan's leg, Miss Cassandra Riley?''

Cassandra's fingers froze in midstitch. The shirt dropped unheeded to the quilt as she glared at him, masking her shame with fury. She was not what Morgan had just called her. But under the circumstances, she was certainly no better. At least whores were honest about who they were and what they did.

''I loved Ryan,'' she said, forcing the words through clenched teeth. ''And he loved me—at least I thought he did. He was the only one—the only one ever. As for you—'' She caught up the shirt and flung it at his exposed chest. "You can sew on your own damned button!"

Morgan did not stir. He let the shirt slide to his lap, his impassive granite features concealing his thoughts. An eternity seemed to pass before he so much as breathed—a weary exhalation that drained away the tension in his body.

"Do you want to stay, Cassandra?" he asked in a low voice. "Do you want shelter here, for yourself and your baby?"

Cassandra felt her jaw go slack. She stared at him. "Of course I do," she whispered. "Why else would I have come all this way?"

"Then listen to me," he said, placing the shirt on the bed, at a neutral distance between them. "There are some things you must understand—and some promises you must make."

"Promises?"

"If you stay, it's going to be on my terms," he said. "Otherwise, first thing tomorrow, I'll get a wagon with a couple of drivers to haul you back to Cheyenne, or wherever it is you came from. Do you agree?"

"I'll hold my answer until I've heard your terms, if you don't mind." Cassandra brushed back the damp tangle of her hair, her heart thundering. "You said there were things I needed to understand."

He leaned forward in the chair, his Shoshone eyes impaling her like flint-tipped arrows. "First of all, I don't trust you any farther than I can throw a full-grown buffalo. Is that understood?"

She nodded, struggling to hold her tongue.

"Until I have proof to the contrary, I've no choice except to assume you're lying—about Ryan, about everything."

"And if I'm telling the truth?" Cassandra met his gaze straight on even though she was jelly inside. "You've no proof either way, you know. Not until the baby comes, and perhaps not even then." Deliberately she picked up the shirt, located the dangling needle and resumed the task of sewing on the loose button. The shirt was slightly warm, its weathered folds releasing the subtle aromas of trail dust, horses and strong lye soap.

"That," he said, watching her, "is why I'm prepared to make a bargain with you."

"What sort of bargain?" She cocked a cynical eyebrow, knowing she could not let him see how desperate she was.

Morgan shifted in the chair, leaning toward her now. Through the half-open shutter, the late afternoon sun cast harsh, slanting lines across his face. It was not a gentle face, Cassandra thought, or even a particularly handsome face. Sharp bones jutted beneath his wind-burnished skin, hooding his eyes in deep shadow. He sat lightly, the open locket dangling from his fingers.

"Downstairs on the porch, there's an old man who's the heart and soul of this ranch," he said. "Jacob Tolliver came to this place as a trapper while the country was still wild. He married into the Shoshone tribe, bought land while it was cheap, and went on to build everything you'll see here. You were likely driving your wagon across the Tolliver Ranch all morning.

"Six years ago, out on the range, my father was struck by lightning. We found him in a gully the next morning, pinned under his dead horse with his back broken in three places. Since then he's been in a wheelchair, and hated every minute of it."

Morgan had turned toward the window, his profile craggy against the slanting light. "The one bright spot in my father's life has been Ryan. Now, with every day that passes, the old man's growing more frail. If Ryan doesn't come back, I fear he'll have nothing left to live for."

He'll have you! The words sprang to Cassandra's lips, but she bit them back without speaking. She had no business meddling in family relationships, she reminded herself.

But then, hadn't she done that already?

"I won't have him hurt again." Morgan had turned back to face her, his eyes challenging everything she'd told him. "If that baby you're carrying is really Ryan's, the promise of a grandchild could make my father's life worth hanging on to. But if you're lying—if you're nothing but a cheap little opportunist who's come to take advantage of a family tragedy—"

He swallowed the surging anger in his voice. "If that's the case, and my father learns the truth, the disappointment could kill him as surely as a bullet through the heart."

Cassandra forced herself not to cringe under the blazing scrutiny of his eyes. She forced her fingers to move, plying the needle with a steadiness that belied her galloping pulse. It was already too late for the truth. She had come too far, said too much. Nothing mattered now except providing a secure future for her baby.

"Ask yourself this," she said quietly. "If this baby weren't Ryan's, would I have come all this way, at such risk? Would I have traveled alone, for six long, miserable days in that rickety old wagon, just to find your family?"

"You're not the one asking questions here," he said. "I am."

Cassandra returned his stony gaze, her mind groping for some point of safety. Morgan would check out her story, that much was certain. But she had already laid a false trail to Cheyenne. As for the rest, she and Jake had married in Nebraska, arriving in Laramie only a few months before his death. Even as Cassandra Logan, her past would not be easy to trace. Barring the unforeseen, Morgan would find nothing to disprove her claim.

Unless Ryan Tolliver turned up alive.

But that was a gamble she had already resolved to take.

"You said you were prepared to bargain," she reminded him.

Morgan nodded grimly. "I'm giving you one last chance to come clean," he said. "Tell me the baby isn't my brother's. I'll see you safely back to Cheyenne, give you three hundred dollars toward a new start, and forget I ever laid eyes on you. No questions asked. Under the circumstances, I'd say that's a generous offer.''

For the space of a breath Cassandra weighed his words. Morgan's offer was indeed a generous one. If she accepted it, the money would take her anywhere she wanted to go and provide food and shelter until she could get on her feet once more. It would pay for the services of a midwife, buy warm blankets and clothes for the baby.

It would give her an honest escape from the deepening tangle of lies she had woven.

But she had not come here to be bought off. She had come here to secure a future for her child. Even now, as she studied Morgan's granite face through a haze of sunlight, she sensed he was testing her. Pass that test, and she might have everything she had hoped for.

''What if I refuse your offer?'' she asked softly.

''Why would you refuse?''

She steeled herself for the lie. ''Because whatever happens to me, Ryan's child deserves to grow up on this ranch, as a Tolliver.''

His dark eyes flickered. ''This is your last chance,'' he said. ''Stay, and you're on probation until I can check out your story. If I find out you've lied, you'll go to prison for fraud, and your baby will go to an orphanage. Do you understand?''

Cassandra gulped back the lump of fear that had congealed in her throat. Her fingers were so clammy with sweat they could barely hold the needle. The baby stirred, one tiny foot pushing upward in a solid kick beneath her ribs.

"I understand," she said.

"Until your story can be proved, you'll take your orders from me. My father's not to know anything about your claim until I say so. If you speak up sooner, I'll tell him you're lying and have you in the sheriff's office before you can blink. Is that clear?"

Cassandra nodded, feeling as if she had stepped into quicksand and sunk to her chin. The lies sucked her deeper, crushing her chest, cutting off her breath.

"I accept your terms," she said coldly, finishing the button and snipping the thread. "Here's your shirt. And now, if you don't mind, I'd like to have my locket back."

"A locket that falls open at a convenient touch?" He rose from the chair to loom above her, the locket chain dangling from his fingers. His lean-muscled body tapered upward from the loose waistband of his worn denims, revealing a glimpse of deeply shadowed navel. His skin was like polished copper, as smooth and golden as an Indian's—but then he *was* an Indian, Cassandra reminded herself—or, more correctly, a half-breed, the son of a white man and a Shoshone woman.

Towering over her now, with a thunderous scowl on his face, he looked every inch his mother's son.

"I'll hold this for safekeeping," he said, his fist closing tightly around the locket. "You'll get it back when I decide it's safe for you to have it."

Cassandra forced a bitter smile. "As you say, you don't trust me. That's something I'll have to accept—for now, at least."

His bare body rippled as he thrust the chain and heart into the pocket of his trousers. Picking up the shirt, he slipped it over his arms and shoulders and worked the buttons deftly through their holes. With no trace of self-consciousness, he unfastened the buttons at his waist to tuck in the shirt. Cassandra averted her eyes, fixing her gaze on the painted buckskin that hung on the far wall. Morgan Tolliver was clearly no gentleman, but her grandmother had raised her to be a lady, Cassandra reminded herself. No matter how trying the circumstances, she would remain so.

Only when she heard the faint clink of his belt buckle did she glance up and meet his gaze. For the space of a heartbeat his face appeared vulnerable, even concerned. Then his mouth tightened. The hardness slid back into his eyes so swiftly that Cassandra found herself wondering if she'd only imagined the brief change.

"My thanks for sewing on the button," he said coldly. "You'll be wanting a meal and a chance to wash. I'll send Chang up with some food and order his boys to carry in the tub and some hot water. Tomorrow, if you're feeling up to it, you can take your meals downstairs at the table. For now, you're to stay in this room and rest."

"As you wish, sir." Cassandra flung the words at him, rankled by his high-handedness.

His eyes narrowed. "You agreed to do as I say. And sarcasm doesn't become you, Cassandra Riley."

"I agreed to follow your orders," she retorted. "That doesn't mean I have to like them. Am I to consider myself a prisoner here?"

"Not a prisoner. Just an uninvited guest. And until I can check out your story, that's *all* you are." Picking up his vest from the chair, he turned and strode out of the room. Just beyond the doorway, he paused and glanced back over his shoulder. "You'll find a necessity under the bed. If you're worried about privacy, you can bolt the door from the inside. But nobody will come in without knocking. Whatever else you might think of us, you're safe here."

Before Cassandra could respond, he closed the door softly behind him. Her heart crept into her throat as she heard the key turning in the lock. Merciful heaven, was he locking her in?

But no—as if Morgan had changed his mind, the sound of shifting tumblers paused, then reversed its cadence like a sentence spoken backward. By the time Morgan's footfalls faded into silence, Cassandra was certain he had left the door unlocked.

Was it an invitation for her to leave? If she were to wait for darkness and steal out to the barn, would she find a wagon loaded, hitched and waiting with the blood money tucked beneath the seat? Was that Morgan Tolliver's game—giving her one last chance to go?

Cassandra swung her legs off the bed. Her bare feet

tingled as she lowered them to the floor and pushed her unwieldy body to a standing position.

Nausea uncoiled in her empty stomach. She felt oddly light, as if the room had filled with water and her head was detached and floating in it. Swaying dizzily, she sank back onto the bed. No, she would not be going anywhere tonight—nor any other night. She was bone tired, drained of every physical and mental resource she possessed. Ever more compellingly, a hidden instinct whispered that it was too late to set out on another adventure. She and her baby needed the safety of this house and the succor of this reluctant family.

Cassandra raked a hand through the tangled nest of her hair and, with a weary sigh, settled back onto the bed. Liar, cheat, whatever she might be, she had reached the end of her journey.

She had no other place to go.

Morgan stood alone on the porch, watching the stars emerge through the indigo twilight. The air smelled of rain—but Nature, the seductive witch, had tricked him before. The hint of moisture was only an illusion. There would be no life-giving storm tonight.

Upstairs, there was no sound from Cassandra Riley's room. Chang had reported that she'd wolfed down her supper and thanked him effusively for the tub of hot water his two sons had brought into her room. After her bath, she had wheeled the big tin tub out into the hall and closed her door. In the three hours that had passed since then, no one had heard so much as a whisper from her.

After the supper dishes had been cleared away and Jacob had retired for the night, Morgan had spread the ranch's account books on the dining room table, lit an oil lamp and bent himself to the tedium of entering the past month's bills and receipts. As the twilight deepened, he'd found himself listening, straining his ears for the creak of a floorboard above his head or the opening click of her bedroom door.

He had ordered her to stay put, Morgan reminded himself. But things were much too quiet up there. From what he already knew of Cassandra Riley, he would bet money she was up to no good.

Earlier he had been on the verge of locking her in for the night. But the woman was not a prisoner, he'd reminded himself. Neither, he sensed, was she a fool. More than anything, she needed a refuge for herself and her child. She would not risk her chances by defying his orders; not, at least, until her position was more secure.

But he could have been wrong. Even now, she could be prowling the house, looking for Jacob or anyone else who might believe her story and take her side against him.

Morgan had struggled to concentrate on the long columns of figures. But it was no use. As the silent minutes ticked past, another worrisome possibility had struck him.

What if she'd simply become restless and wandered off into the darkness—or worse, repented of the whole scheme and tried to leave the ranch on her own?

Good riddance, he'd told himself, blowing out the lamp and abandoning the books to darkness. If the woman was reckless enough to go running off alone, who was he to stop her? Until a few hours ago, he had not known Cassandra Riley and her wild scheme existed. As long as she didn't harm his family, why should he care what happened to her?

Now he stood at the porch rail, his thoughts churning as he stared into the darkness. Beyond him lay the barn, the sprawling complex of sheds and corrals and the long bunkhouse for the hired hands. From the time he was old enough to swing a hammer, he had labored beside his father to build this place. He had sawed logs, dug postholes and hauled the mortar for the stones that walled the first floor of the house. He had fought off locust swarms and cattle rustlers in summer; diphtheria and packs of hungry wolves in winter. He had poured a lifetime of sweat, pain, blood and blisters into this ranch, and he would protect its legacy with the last breath of his life—even from the schemes of a deceitful woman.

Morgan's eyes scanned the shadows for anything that looked out of place. There was nothing. But then, what had he expected to see? Did he think she was going to steal eggs, or maybe set the barn on fire? What a joke. The harm she could do went far deeper than mere physical damage.

Seething now, he turned away from the porch railing. There was just one way to find out whether Cassandra Riley was following his orders—go upstairs, check her room and see for himself.

If he found her there, he could stop stewing and get back to work. If the room proved to be empty…

But he would deal with that when the time came.

Squaring his shoulders, Morgan opened the door, strode across the landing and quietly mounted the stairs.

Chapter Four

Darkness enfolded Morgan as he reached the landing, but he needed no candle to find his way. The upper floor, built of hand-hewn logs above the original part of the house, was not large in area. Morgan's own bedroom lay at the far end of the hall with Ryan's room—now too silent, too empty—opening on the right. The rest of the space was taken up by two guest bedrooms. The smaller of these, originally planned as a child's room, was the one Morgan had chosen for Cassandra Riley.

He hesitated a moment in the shadows outside her door, then knocked lightly on the polished pine surface. One rap. Two. He waited.

There was no answer.

He knocked again, more forcefully this time. The door planks were thick, he reasoned, and she might not have heard the light rap. Again he waited. Again there was no response.

Morgan exhaled into the silence. He would try the

door, he resolved. If it was bolted, at least he would know she was inside, perhaps asleep.

The latch yielded to the light pressure of his thumb. Morgan's breath caught as the unbolted door swung open into the darkened room.

"Cassandra?" He spoke in a whisper, not wanting to startle her.

When she did not reply, he stepped soundlessly over the threshold. For the space of a breath he saw only shadows. Then a shaft of light from the rising moon gleamed through the uncurtained window, falling across the narrow bunk to illuminate the slight, lumpy form that lay beneath the quilt.

Morgan's throat tightened as he saw her. He knew he should turn and go, but his feet held him to the floor, refusing to budge. Unable to look away, his beauty-starved eyes drank in the sight of her.

She lay on her back, one pale arm flung upward, straining the fabric of her muslin shift against one tautly swollen breast. Her other arm curled protectively around the bulge of her unborn baby, cradling it as she slept.

Damp and fragrant, her freshly washed hair spilled across the pillow, rippling outward like the rays of the Madonna's halo in an old painting Morgan had once seen. Framed by that wild sea of hair, her face was as innocent as a child's.

His eyes traced the petal curve of her lower lip, pausing to linger on her small, stubborn chin. He should have known she would be asleep, he berated himself. The long, solitary journey in a jouncing wagon would have exhausted any woman, let alone one who was heavy with child. And how could she have managed to rest during those nights on the open plain, huddled alone in the darkness, at the mercy of any passing danger? No weapon and a baby on the way. She must have been out of her mind with terror.

What would drive a woman to take such a risk? Morgan asked himself. But he already knew the answer to that question. It was sheer, raw desperation.

The same desperation that would drive her to lie, to cheat, to do anything to secure a future for her child.

She stirred in her sleep, whimpering as her head tossed back forth and on the pillow. Beneath the patchwork quilt, her feet twitched as if she were dreaming of pursuit.

"No...Seamus, no..." Her body jerked and writhed, the words emerging between muffled sobs. "No..."

Her distress seemed very real. But shysters came in all shapes and sizes, Morgan reminded himself. And the ones who played on the sympathies of good people were worse than bank robbers and horse thieves. He could not afford to be touched by the girl's vulnerability. Not until he had checked out every last detail of her story. If the little witch proved to be lying...

"No...please..." Her body twisted frantically, small hands clawing at the quilt. "Please, Seamus, for the love of heaven, *don't*..."

Morgan felt his resolve crumbling. Cassandra Riley

might be a scheming little tramp, but right now something in her mind was scaring her half to death. Even though all the warning signs were up, he was no more capable of walking away from her than from a wounded bobcat cub.

His palm tingled as he brushed the damp hair back from her forehead. The feel of her cool, sweet skin made his throat ache. Only now did he realize how much he had wanted to touch her.

"It's all right," he murmured, his hand lingering on her hair. "You're dreaming, that's all. Rest, Cassandra."

As if she had heard him, she stopped thrashing beneath the quilt. Her whimpers subsided as, little by little, she relaxed in the bed, the rhythm of her breathing deep and even once more.

Had he contrived the whole reason for coming into her room? Had his far-fetched suspicions been nothing more than an excuse for him to be here, standing beside her bed in the breath-filled darkness?

Still looking down at her, Morgan forced his hand to withdraw. Yes, he could understand how Ryan might have fallen in love with this girl. She was no beauty, to be sure, but her spirit and vulnerability would tempt almost any man.

Almost. But not all. Morgan had sworn off love for good after the breakup of his marriage. For love to exist, there had to be trust. And this little flame-haired snip, with her bulging belly and her wild claims about Ryan was as trustworthy as a wagonload of rattlesnakes.

An old family friend, Hamilton Crawford, had recently retired from the Pinkerton agency and was living in Cheyenne. Tomorrow—no, tonight, Morgan resolved—he would write to Ham and ask him to check out Cassandra Riley's story. That way he could send one of Chang's boys to Fort Caspar with the letter first thing in the morning. Ham's reply might be slow in coming, but the mere knowledge that an ex-Pinkerton agent was checking her background could be enough to give the mysterious Miss Riley second thoughts.

But what if she was telling the truth?

Morgan's eyes lingered on her sleeping face as he pondered the idea, then brusquely dismissed it. Her story couldn't possibly be true. There were too many coincidences, too many holes. He owed it to his father, and to Ryan's memory, to uncover the lie and to send her packing before it was too late.

His knuckle brushed her skin as he reached down and tugged the quilt upward to cover her exposed shoulder. The satiny coolness of her flesh tingled all the way up his arm. Ignoring the sensation, he turned and walked quietly out of the room only to pause in the doorway, scowling back at her slumbering form as the thought struck him.

Who the devil was Seamus?

Cassandra awoke to the warmth of sunlight on her face. She opened her eyes, only to jerk them shut again as the morning glare jolted her senses through the bare window.

For the first few seconds she remembered nothing. Where was she? How did she get here? Her mind groped for a foothold on reason. Flinging her forearm across her eyes, she forced herself to lie still and take long, deep breaths.

The memory of the dream, in all its grotesque horror, came back first. Seamus had returned to the shack in Laramie, dressed in the brown suit that Jake had worn for his burial. Terrified by his vacant eyes, she had fled from him, running through the empty stockyards in a dreamer's slow motion, as if her feet were stuck in thick black tar. He had floated behind her, screaming the vilest names she had ever heard. *Bitch…filthy, lying whore…*

He had finally cornered her against a loading chute. His death-glazed eyes had glittered like a wolf's as he closed in on her, mouth smiling, hands reaching for her throat. She had cried out, begging him for her baby's life… *No, Seamus…no…*

You're dreaming, that's all. Rest, Cassandra.

The low, soothing voice had come out of nowhere, as had the gentle touch on her forehead. The strange thing was, she had known at once that the voice spoke the truth. She *was* dreaming. Seamus was gone.

She had caused his death herself, and fled, terrified, into the night.

Fully awake now, Cassandra curled onto her side and gazed around the little bedroom. The previous day was coming back to her now. Near the foot of her bed was the pine rocker where Morgan Tolliver—the enemy—had sat. Her sewing kit lay open on the bedside table, with her needle stuck into a spool of brown cotton thread. On the far wall, bathed in morning sunlight, the painting on the elk skin she'd barely noticed last night revealed itself as a swirling arrangement of horses, deer and buffalo, all pursued by mounted warriors in streaming, feathered war bonnets. So exquisitely drawn and positioned were these tiny figures that they seemed to be galloping over the creamy leather surface.

Cassandra sat up slowly, feeling the baby awaken and stir in its warm, secret world. ''Getting a little tight for you in there, is it?'' she whispered, patting the solid roundness. ''Don't worry, little one. You'll be out in the world soon enough.''

Carefully she stood up, wincing at the bone-deep soreness in her legs and buttocks. She sighed as her hands massaged the small of her back. How long would it be? she wondered. A month? More? Her menses had always been irregular, and with no experienced woman to guide her through the strangeness of it, she had only a vague idea of how far along she was or what to expect when the time came. She had helped her grandfather at lambing time, and she supposed the process would not be so different. Except this would be *her* baby, and she would be its mother. She could only pray that when the time came she would know what to do.

But why was she standing here muddling when it was time she got dressed and faced the day? The Tollivers wouldn't think much of her if she malingered in her bedroom half the morning. And it was essential that they think well of her, or at least that they care about her baby. She had made a poor start last night with Morgan Tolliver. But if she could find other allies here, even friends...

Impulsively Cassandra crossed to the window and peered out through the dust-streaked panes. Through the yellow-brown blur she could make out a vast maze of sheds and corrals, dominated by a weathered barn that jutted upward like a cathedral above a town. Behind the nearest fence, large, dark shapes swirled and shifted. Horses? Cassandra's impatient fingers fumbled with the window latch. Her soft push swung the sash outward.

A light breeze swept into the room, carrying with it a pungent blend of prairie dust, wood smoke, horse dung and fresh morning air. A tantalizing whiff of bacon drifted upward from the kitchen, triggering a growl in the pit of her stomach.

Feeling alive for the first time in days, she leaned outward into the sunlight, her breasts resting on the windowsill. The house was set on a slight rise, overlooking the rest of the ranch. Now she could see the sloping tin roof of the bunkhouse and the fenced enclosure around the coop, where bustling red hens and their fluffy chicks pecked at the earth. Horses milled in the spacious log corral, rearing and nipping in spirited play. Next to the feed trough, Xavier, her own dear mule, stood placidly munching hay. Poor old thing, he probably thought he'd died and gone to heaven. She would go out and visit him later. With luck, she might even be able to smuggle him a treat from the kitchen.

Beyond the dusty sprawl of buildings and corrals, the rolling prairie swept outward like the waves of a yellow sea. Most summers the wild grass would have been pale green, but the drought had left it so tinder dry that the threat of a prairie fire had haunted Cassandra all the way from Laramie. Like a land rising from a far-off shore, the Big Horn mountains jutted the length of the western horizon, blue in the hazy distance, the sunlight glinting on their snowless peaks.

The trill of a meadowlark echoed pure and clear on the morning air. Listening, Cassandra suppressed a little shiver of contentment. This was a good place, she sensed, a clean and honest place, like her grandparents' lost Nebraska homestead. She would give anything, *do* anything, to give her child the chance to grow up here, free from danger and want, free from shame.

If only there were some other way.

Below her window, a squat figure distinguished by a graying pigtail that dangled from beneath a blue cotton cap, hobbled off the porch and headed toward the chicken coop.

"Chang!" she said in a low voice. "Good morning, Chang!"

The startled Chinese cook glanced up, caught sight of her and grinned. "Morning, miss. Breakfast? I bring it up?" He motioned toward her with his hand. She had already come to like the small, lively man who'd served her a supper of roast beef and cloudlike buttered biscuits the night before.

"Breakfast, yes," she replied. "But please don't bother bringing it up to me. I'll get dressed and come downstairs."

"Good!" His smile broadened. "Mr. Jacob, Mr. Morgan, they can eat with you. Almost ready. Hurry."

"Give me just a few minutes." Cassandra felt her heart drop into the pit of her stomach as she spun away from the window and fumbled in the carpetbag for her only presentable dress. Once more it was time to begin the ugly game of lies and deception, playing her wits against the Tolliver men from behind the mask of Ryan's grieving sweetheart.

The mask she was prepared to wear for the rest of her life.

Morgan sat in the dining rooming, leaning back in his chair as Chang carried in platters of bacon, flapjacks and scrambled eggs to accompany the steaming pot of beans he had already placed on the table.

In the Tolliver household it was a long-standing custom not to eat breakfast before the morning chores were done. Morgan had risen at six, gulped down a mug of hot black coffee and gone outside to look after the stock. Most of the ranch's fifteen thousand head of Texas longhorns had been driven to summer pasture in the mountains, but there were horses to feed and water, cows to milk, orphan calves to tend and, this morning, a torn windmill vane to repair.

Morgan could easily have paid someone else to do the chores, but the truth was, he enjoyed them. He liked rising at dawn, watching the sky fill with light and hearing the morning chorus as each creature on the ranch welcomed a new day. He savored the slow rhythm of seasons, each one blending into the next, cycling like the spokes of the great medicine wheel. And he never lost his wonder at each new life that appeared on the ranch, from quivering foals to clutches of yellow-brown ducklings. Though he gave the matter little conscious thought, Morgan could not imagine his life without this work, without this land.

Earlier, he'd been on his way out of the barn when he'd glimpsed a figure in the upstairs window. Stepping back into the shadows, he had caught his breath at the sight of Cassandra Riley leaning into the sunlight, her creamy breasts straining the thin muslin shift where they thrust over the windowsill.

Her loose-hanging curls had caught fire in the morning sunlight, falling over the whiteness of shoulders and breasts to ring her delicate vulpine features with flame. Morgan had never thought her beautiful, but for one riveting instant, the sight of her in that sunlit window was almost enough to strike a man blind.

He would bet good money the little schemer knew exactly what she was doing.

For the space of a breath he had allowed his eyes to feast on the forbidden sight. Then, as Chang came out onto the porch, he had slipped back into the barn and made a discreet exit through a rear door. Cassandra Riley was looking for a protector, casting her web for any man within range, Morgan told himself. He would go straight to hell before he'd let her know he had almost stumbled into that trap.

The letter to Hamilton Crawford was already on its way to Fort Caspar, with wiry young Johnny Chang mounted on the fastest of the Tolliver cow ponies. How long would it take for Ham to come up with some answers? Two weeks, at least, maybe a good deal longer, Morgan reckoned. In the meantime he would be wise to watch Cassandra's every move—a challenge in its own right.

A light bump on the table's edge startled Morgan out of his reverie. His attention shifted sideways to where the elder of the two Chang boys had just moved Jacob's chair into its customary position at the head of the table. The old man looked more haunted than ever, Morgan thought.

"Rotten night." Jacob's eyes burned like embers in the hollowed pits of their sockets. "You've got a strange look about you this morning. Care to tell me what's going on inside that stubborn Shoshone head of yours?"

"Not much." Morgan poured the old man a cup of coffee from the pot Chang had just placed on the table and added a generous dollop of cream. "Just wondering if we ought to get some of those new white-faced Hereford cows, like the ones Alex Swan's been bringing in over on Chugwater."

"What's wrong with longhorns?" Jacob demanded, his gaze narrowing beneath the bristled crags of his eyebrows.

"Nothing." Morgan poured his own coffee and watched the steam curl upward toward the rafters. "Nothing, that is, if you don't have to put them in railroad cars. Got word last fall that a full third of the steers we shipped to Omaha were horn-gouged by the time they were unloaded. We had to lower the price for the whole lot." Morgan had given his father this information at the time, but now Jacob looked as if he had no memory of it. Ryan's disappearance had taken as much of a toll on the old man's mind as it had on his body.

"Humph!" Jacob cleared his throat and spat into his cloth napkin. "Longhorns are range bred—tough enough to stand the winters in these parts. Those short-legged bally-faced meatballs over on Swan's place will bog down in the drifts and starve to death. Take my word for it. Don't waste time and money finding out the hard way!"

"Want to wager on it?" Morgan speared two flap-jacks and dropped them onto his plate. Arguing was a long-established way of communication between the two of them. Now he used it deliberately, as a means to rouse the old man's interest and draw his mind away from Ryan. "I'll bring in a hundred head of Herefords this fall, early enough to season them to the cold. With that hay crop we're growing down in the bottoms—"

"Hay!" Jacob snorted. "Hell, that's another waste

of time! We've never had any trouble finding winter pasture for the longhorns.''

''But we always lose some,'' Morgan said. ''In a killer winter, we could lose the whole herd. A good supply of hay would keep us from being wiped out.''

''Bull.'' Jacob toyed with the scrambled eggs Thomas Chang had spooned onto his plate. ''These damned newfangled notions of yours are going to—''

He stopped speaking, his mouth, like his fork, frozen in midmotion. Morgan turned in his seat to follow the direction of his father's gaze.

Cassandra Riley stood, hesitating, in the doorway of the dining room.

She was modestly clad now, in a faded chambray gown with wrist-length sleeves, a high, crocheted collar and a shapeless waist, hiked up in front to accommodate her bulging belly. Her fiery mane of curls had been tamed into a coiled braid at the nape of her neck.

Eyes nervous, mouth fixed in a tentative smile, she walked toward the table. She looked as demure as a round little quail, Morgan thought, and almost as innocent.

''May I?'' She paused next to the empty place setting on the far side of the table. Morgan scowled, annoyed at himself for having failed to notice the third plate earlier. Warned, he would have been prepared for her entrance and he would have made more of an effort to prepare his father.

Rising swiftly, Morgan strode around the table to pull out her chair. Her downcast eyes avoided his as she moved into place. "Remember, we have an agreement," he growled in her ear. "My father's not to be told anything."

She nodded almost imperceptibly before lowering herself into the chair. She was every inch the proper lady now, hiding the siren he had seen in the upstairs window.

"Miss Cassandra Riley...my father." Morgan mouthed a curt introduction.

"It's an honor to meet you, Mr. Tolliver." Her voice was artificially bright.

"Ma'am." Jacob acknowledged her greeting with the lift of a bristled eyebrow. Even after all these years, he had the manners of a mountain man. But that hadn't stopped him from being the very devil with women in his day.

As Morgan took his seat, he shot her another warning glare across the table. Could he trust her to keep her mouth shut? Would she even care how much pain her lie could bring to a grief-stricken old man?

Glancing down, he realized he had lost all interest in breakfast. He could not venture to guess what the unpredictable Miss Cassandra Riley would do or say next. He only knew that if she so much as mentioned Ryan to his father, she would be one sorry woman.

Cassandra spooned a mound of scrambled eggs onto her plate, passionately wishing she'd chosen to eat in the bedroom. Were these two gloomy men all that was left of the Tolliver family? Were there no women and children to liven up this grim household?

"Flapjack?" Morgan passed her the stacked plate. She thanked him politely, took a warm pancake from the middle of the pile and drowned it in butter and maple syrup. He looked hard and angry, but at least he didn't seem bent on starving her.

Clearly, no one starved on the Tolliver Ranch. But she was already beginning to sense how easily a woman could fall prey to loneliness here. Maybe that was why there were no women in sight.

Determined to be cheerful, she cut off a bite-sized piece of flapjack with her fork and thrust it into her mouth. The batter was crisp and airy, almost melting on her tongue.

"Mmm!" she exclaimed, seizing on an excuse to break the silence. "Manna from heaven couldn't taste any better than these flapjacks! Did Chang make them?"

"Chang does all the cooking."

Morgan's cool answer reminded Cassandra that she had offered her services in the kitchen. Clearly her help was not needed.

Ignoring his rebuff, she turned toward the old man, who sat huddled in his wheelchair, toying with the food on his plate. His skin was gray tinged, his hollow cheeks etched with deep arroyos that flowed into the leaden tangle of his short beard. His flannel shirt was clean, his hair neatly trimmed and combed, but there was a wildness about Jacob Tolliver, a trace of the primitive that burned in his bloodshot yellow-green eyes.

She scrutinized his pitted features, searching for

some resemblance to his offspring. But she found none. Morgan could have passed for a full-blooded Shoshone, and there was no echo of Ryan's golden beauty in either of the two men. Jacob Tolliver's sons, she concluded, resembled their respective mothers.

"The beef stew and biscuits Chang brought me last night were delicious, as well," she said, pressing on. "Where on earth did you find such a treasure, Mr. Tolliver? Has he been with you a long time?"

For a moment Jacob Tolliver paid her no heed. Then the old man's hooded eyes flickered toward her, as if he'd finally realized she was speaking to him. He cleared his throat as if he were about to launch into a story. Then his knobby shoulders sagged wearily. "You can tell her," he said to Morgan.

Something flashed in Morgan's black eyes. Was it hostility or only relief, perhaps even gratitude, that she'd steered their conversation onto safe ground?

"My father stole Chang from the railroad," he said.

"Stole him?" Cassandra's eyes widened.

"Stole him as slick as whiskey." Morgan sipped his coffee, taking his time. "Chang came over from Canton in the mid-sixties to work as a dynamiter on the Central Pacific. When a rock slide crushed his leg, he was assigned to the kitchen crew. Chang had never cooked a meal in his life, but he took to it as if he'd been born in a stewpot. Before long, his reputation got around, and visiting railway bosses were coming by just to sample his braised mutton and biscuits."

Morgan had settled back in his chair, cradling the

coffee mug between his hands. Cassandra watched him, bemused by the discovery that this gruff, taciturn man possessed a hidden gift for words.

"My father owned title to some land in Nevada he'd won in a poker game a few years earlier. The railroad wanted to buy the parcel, so he traveled west to see the land for himself and negotiate the sale. The track boss made the mistake of inviting him to dinner. You can guess the rest of the story."

Cassandra took what she hoped was a ladylike nibble of her scrambled eggs. The moist, frothy clumps were exquisitely seasoned—wild onion, she speculated, with a bit of sage and other flavorings so subtle she could not venture to name them. She took another bite, savoring the rich but delicate taste.

"I would guess," she said, "that your father, the wily old pirate, found Chang, took him aside and made him an offer too generous to refuse."

At her words, Morgan's left eyebrow shot upward. The corners of his mouth twitched, threatening a smile—but only threatening. A real smile, she told herself, would probably crack that long granite face of his.

"Wily old pirate, am I?" Jacob growled. "That's a right brassy tongue you've got in that curly head of yours, Red."

"Well, *aren't* you a wily old pirate?" Cassandra challenged him, her heart racing. "Besides, what makes you think I didn't mean it as a compliment?"

He scowled at her. Then his thin lips stretched across his teeth in a skull-like grimace. "Right smart one we got here, Morgan. That's just what happened. But Chang was a mean negotiator himself. Before he'd agree to come, I had to promise we'd send for the wife and two boys he'd left back in China.''

"Thomas and Johnny?" Cassandra took another forkful of scrambled eggs. "I met them last night when they brought in my bath. I must say, they have excellent manners.''

"Good boys." Jacob nodded his agreement. "Weren't knee-high to a grasshopper when they come here, but their folks raised them fine. Thomas sees that I'm decently washed and dressed, and helps his father with the house. Johnny took to cowboyin' from the first time he laid eyes on a horse. Little squirt can rope any critter that runs on four legs and a few that don't.''

Jacob Tolliver chuckled humorlessly at his own joke. Then his eyes went hard. "That's enough talk about Chinamen. What I want to know, Red, is what brings a woman in your condition all the way to this godforsaken spot. Hell, it's a dangerous trip alone, even for a man. You and that old mule could've got yourselves drowned in a creek or picked clean by wolves…" His gaze narrowed and sharpened. "Did you come all this way to find your baby's pa? Maybe get the bounder to marry you? Is that it?''

Cassandra laid her fork on her plate, her appetite suddenly gone. She felt the old man's eyes drilling into her, felt the cold, silent threat in Morgan's gaze.

"I don't like secrets in my house," Jacob said. "Tell us, Red. Now.''

Chapter Five

Cassandra felt her stomach clench. A wave of cold nausea crept into her throat. Determined not to disgrace herself, she willed it back. It was panic, nothing more, she told herself. She could—and would—control it.

"Cassandra doesn't feel she owes us an explanation," Morgan broke in before she could reply to his father's question. "But, yes, she has reason to think her baby's father might be working for us—maybe up with the herd in the summer pasture."

The old man twisted a dangling strand of his drooping mustache. "Well, whoever he is, the damned fool ought to be horsewhipped, runnin' off and leavin' a young girl in a family way. Bring him in and I'll do the job myself. What did you say his name was, Red?"

Cassandra felt her stomach clench again. The flapjacks and eggs swam before her eyes. "Would you please excuse me?" she said, rising. "I'm afraid I'm not feeling well. I need some…air."

With as much dignity as she could muster, she strode out of the dining room and, once out of sight, bolted for the front door.

The morning breeze struck her face as she staggered onto the porch. She gulped it frantically, leaning over the rail like a seasick ocean passenger.

Little by little the urge to retch diminished. Cassandra closed her eyes, letting the wind cool her sweat-dampened face. It was all right—*she* was all right. But she could not make herself walk back into that dining room and face Jacob Tolliver's question.

What should she have told him? Not the truth, heaven forbid. And not the lie she had carried all the way to the Tolliver Ranch. Morgan was right—the old man was not ready to hear the shocking news that her baby was Ryan's.

If she'd had her wits about her, she could have given Jacob Tolliver the first name that came into her head. Then she could have made a dramatic show of searching for her lost sweetheart, bursting into tears when she learned he was not on the ranch. That, at least, would have satisfied Morgan. But it would have added one more lie to the sickening tangle she'd woven, a tangle that was already threatening to drag her down to eternal fire and brimstone.

Impulsively she stepped off the porch and wandered across the yard toward the corral. Waiting there, just beyond the fence, was her single true friend in this place—the one friend who had no need for lies.

"Xavier!" She held out her hand, wishing she'd thought to steal a biscuit from the table. No matter.

At her call the old dun mule pricked up his ears and trotted toward her, his limp noticeably better.

"How's it going, old boy? Are they treating you right?" Cassandra's eyes misted as she stroked the velvet nose, then moved her hand upward to scratch between the long, rabbity ears. The irascible creature had been her confidant, her protector and her only companion on the northward trek from Laramie. "It's a good thing you can't talk," she whispered, laying her cheek against the bony neck. "I'd have no secrets at all in this place, would I?"

The mule snorted, bobbing his massive head up and down as if sharing the joke.

"And what secrets would he be telling about you, Miss Cassandra Riley?"

The rough whisper, coming from just behind her ear, startled Cassandra into a fit of hiccups. She glared up at Morgan Tolliver, struggling to maintain her dignity while her diaphragm convulsed in painful spasms.

"Don't you ever...*hic*...do that to me again!"

His mouth remained as grim as a hatchet blade, but his eyes, Cassandra noticed, glimmered with sparks of amusement.

"Do you make a habit of...*hic*...sneaking up on people and scaring them? What if I'd had a gun, or a knife? You could be...*hic*...bleeding right now!"

The low, strangled sound in his throat could almost have passed for a chuckle. "Here," he said, lifting a burlap-covered canteen from where its strap was looped around a fence post. "You sound as if you could use a drink.'' His long brown fingers twisted out the stopper. ''I could probably find something stronger in the house.''

''This will do, thank you. Liquor isn't good for…*hic*…babies.'' Cassandra snatched the canteen away and tilted it to her mouth. The water that gushed down her throat was so unexpectedly cold that she choked on it.

''You could've warned me!'' Cassandra sputtered, wiping her mouth on the back of her hand. ''I was expecting that water to be lukewarm!''

''Old trick,'' Morgan said. ''You wet down the burlap and hang the canteen in the sun. The evaporation cools the water inside. Are your hiccups gone?''

''Why…'' Her eyes widened. ''Yes, they are. But I hope you aren't waiting for me to thank you.''

His left eyebrow tilted upward, exactly the same way his father's did, she realized. ''Since the words would likely stick in your throat, I'll spare you that,'' he said. ''Actually, I came out here to invite you for a wagon ride, if you're up to it.''

''You realize I just spent six days jouncing on a hard wagon bench.'' She eyed him suspiciously.

''I do. That's why I'm prepared to offer you a cushion to sit on and one of Chang's fried chicken picnic lunches.''

''Why?'' she asked, still distrustful.

''Because somebody needs to run supplies up to the men at the summer pasture. And since I've sent

Johnny Chang off on a long-distance errand, the job falls to me. I'd like you to come along.''

''Why? So you can keep an eye on me? Make sure I don't get into mischief?''

''That's part of it.'' His voice and face were expressionless.

''What's the other part?'' The mule, wanting attention, had butted its damp nose against Cassandra's shoulder. She reached up and scratched the big animal behind the ears as she waited for Morgan to answer. The sunlight was warm on her skin, the air sweet with meadowlark songs.

Why did she have to feel so ugly on such a beautiful day?

''After you rushed out of the dining room, my father still wanted an answer to his question,'' he said. ''I told him your baby's father was a cowhand, and that his last letter had come from this ranch. It was his suggestion that I take you up to the summer pasture to look for the man.''

So now Morgan was part of the lie. Cassandra tossed her head and forced herself to speak flippantly. ''Oh? And did you give my faithless sweetheart a name?''

He shook his head. ''Since I've taken over the hiring, my father doesn't know many of the men. A name wouldn't have made much difference.''

''Why didn't you just tell him the truth?''

''I don't know the truth. Not yet, at least.''

''So, for the sake of appearances, you want me to go through the motions of searching for my missing lover?'' She gazed across the corral, refusing to meet his eyes. Horses milled in the bright sunshine, their coats a gleaming mosaic of black, brown, pewter and sorrel.

''Would that be such a bad idea?'' he asked.

''Maybe not.'' Cassandra brushed away a blue-green fly that had settled on her arm. ''I could always pick myself out a good-looking cowboy, point my finger and say, 'He's the one!' Would that make things any simpler?''

''Don't be silly!'' he growled.

''You said you'd sent Johnny Chang on an errand.'' She swung around and looked directly at him. ''Did that errand have anything to do with me?''

His obsidian eyes did not waver. ''Johnny's carrying a letter to Fort Caspar—a letter to an old family friend, a retired Pinkerton agent who lives in Cheyenne. I told him about you and asked him to check out your story.''

Cassandra's stomach twitched and sank like a dying fish. ''You didn't waste any time, did you?''

''You knew I wouldn't.'' He exhaled raggedly. ''No danger you'll have that baby in the wagon, is there?''

''It's a bit early for that. But I didn't say I'd go with you.''

''You'll go.'' He turned away from the fence. ''The wagon's already loaded. Get whatever you need while I hitch up the team. Don't worry, we'll take it slow over the rough places. You'll be fine.''

Cassandra hesitated, but only for an instant. She

could not afford to defy this man who held so much power over her future. Besides, it was a beautiful, sunny day and she wanted to see more of the ranch. "Give me a few minutes to get ready," she said.

"Don't be long." He was already striding toward the barn.

Cassandra spun toward the house, then abruptly halted as a new thought struck her.

"Morgan!"

He turned expectantly.

"I'll go with you, but only on one condition."

Morgan's left eyebrow inched upward, his disdainful expression saying more than words. She had come to this place as a beggar and had no right to demand anything of him. But that was exactly what she was about to do.

"It's such a fine day," she said. "Promise you won't spoil it by making me talk about Ryan."

She saw the shadow pass across his face and knew she had touched pain. At once Cassandra felt ashamed of herself. Her own grief was a sham. Morgan's was real.

"Fine," he said. "We can talk about whatever you want. Hurry up now, and don't forget to bring something to keep off the sun."

"Yes. I know about the sun." Ignoring her skittering pulse, Cassandra turned and walked purposefully back toward the house.

The wagon was big and solid, not unlike the man who drove the team of massive brown draft horses.

Loaded with kegs of flour, oatmeal, beans and bacon, boxes of canned Arbuckle coffee, and smaller sundries such as sugar, salt and baking powder, it rumbled across the open prairie. Its wheels crushed the brittle grass, leaving in their wake a fine shimmer of yellow dust.

Cassandra had returned to her room to find her overalls and flannel shirt lying clean and folded on the foot of her bed. Blessing Chang's efficiency, she had scrambled into them and flung on her battered felt hat. Now, sitting beside Morgan on the wagon bench, she looked like a scruffy farm boy, albeit one who had just swallowed a watermelon.

True to his promise, Morgan had brought along a goose-feather pillow for her to sit on. He drove the team carefully, slowing over the rough stretches, of which there were many. Their conversation was sparse and self-conscious, largely confined to comments about the weather and the scenery.

Would he have grilled her about Ryan if she hadn't extracted his promise? Almost certainly, Cassandra realized. But he was a man of his word. She had already learned that much about Morgan Tolliver.

As they neared the foothills, the rutted trail began to climb. Sage, rabbit brush and occasional juniper crowded in amid the prairie grass, dotted here and there with clumps of brightly blooming cactus. The drought was less noticeable here, perhaps because the plant life was tougher. But even here the ground was parched, the sun a blinding ball of heat in the summer sky.

"Oh—" Cassandra gave a little gasp as a half-dozen pronghorns exploded out of a wash and bounded across their path a stone's throw ahead of the horses. They were all speed and dazzle, mouths open, drinking wind. Their white rumps flashed in the sunlight as they raced down the slope to vanish over a rise.

Cassandra had seen pronghorns from a distance but never at such close range. "Beautiful," she whispered. "And the two little baby ones—all legs—oh, Morgan, did you see them?"

"*Quaritz,* the Shoshone call them," Morgan said. "Fastest things on four legs, as far as I know. They can run circles around any horse and make complete fools of coyotes. But they have one weakness."

"What's that?" Cassandra asked, intrigued.

He shot her a sidelong glance, his black eyes reflecting sparks of sunlight. "Curiosity," he said. "That's how my grandfather taught me to get them within shooting range. You tie a piece of cloth to the end of a long stick. Then you find a herd, hide behind the rocks or in the brush and wave the stick in the air so that the cloth is moving back and forth. Sooner or later a pronghorn will get curious and wander over to see what it is. Even then they're not easy to shoot. I've known men to swear that a pronghorn can outrun a bullet."

Cassandra felt her baby stir as she shifted toward him on the seat. She remembered last night, when Morgan had stripped off his shirt, the glint of sun on the small beaded pouch. "You say your grandfather taught you. Was it your Shoshone grandfather?"

Morgan nodded. "I was only a boy when he died. If I could remember a third of what that old *bo ho gant* taught me, I'd be a wise man today."

"The pouch you wear…?" Her eyes fell on the slight bulge beneath his shirt.

"His medicine pouch. All he left me."

"You spent time with your mother's people, then."

"A long time." Morgan guided the wagon around a jutting, reddish boulder, his dark hands easy and skillful on the reins. "My father was living with the Shoshone when I was born. I was seven years old when he decided there was a better future in ranching than in trapping. His parents had died in Kentucky and left him their farm. He traveled back East to sell the house and land and to buy the first parcel of what became the Tolliver Ranch. He was gone for more than a year."

"You stayed behind? You and your mother?"

"He could hardly have taken us with him—an Indian woman and her wild little boy." Morgan's eyes followed the circling flight of a golden eagle. "That winter some white settlers brought measles to our camp. People died, young ones…old ones. My mother was one of the first. Then my grandfather."

"I'm sorry."

He ignored the platitude, continuing as if she had not spoken. "No one thought my father would return. I was taken in by Washakie, the great chief of all the Eastern Shoshone. Washakie would have raised me as his son, but that summer my father returned to take me with him. He wanted me to grow up on the ranch, as a white man.''

''And did you want to go with him?''

''Not at first. I was angry with him for a long time.''

''Are you still angry with him?''

''No.''

Cassandra glanced back over her shoulder, toward the ranch they'd left far behind. The house and out-buildings blended with the brown prairie, small now, like a handful of scattered pebbles on the landscape.

''You speak well for someone who grew up with Indians,'' she said. ''Your English is better than your father's. You must have had some schooling.''

''Thank Ryan's—'' He broke off, remembering their agreement. ''Thank my stepmother for that. She taught me to read and write and insisted I speak properly. And she brought a wagonload of books to the ranch, most of which I've read. But no, I never had the chance to go to school. My father didn't believe in it. He always said life was the best classroom.''

The wagon was climbing steeply now. Cassandra gripped the edge of the seat as the rocky trail wound its way upward through groves of bone-white aspens whose shimmering leaves dappled the ground with shade. The horses leaned into their collars, pulling against the slope and the weight of the loaded wagon. Morgan urged them forward, slapping the reins on their sweat-glossed rumps and muttering in what Cassandra judged to be Shoshone, since she could not understand a word of what he was saying.

She leaned forward, her heart pulling with the straining horses, willing the wagon to inch ahead. Muscles bulged and rippled; wheels groaned until, with a shuddering lurch, the wagon reached level ground.

The road stretched out before them across a high, grassy meadow ringed with thick stands of lodgepole pine and dotted with blue lupine, tiny golden buttercups and flaming spires of Indian paintbrush. Morgan halted the team with a guttural command. "Time to eat while we rest the horses," he said, swinging lightly to the ground.

Only then did Cassandra notice the wooden picnic hamper tucked among the kegs and boxes in the back of the wagon. And only then did she remember how little breakfast she'd had. Her stomach rumbled in anticipation.

Morgan lifted a faded patchwork quilt from the wagon bed, shook off the dust and spread it on the grass. Then he walked briskly around the wagon to where Cassandra stood waiting for him. His arms reached up reflexively; then he hesitated, a puzzled expression flickering across his face.

Cassandra broke into unladylike giggles as the realization struck her—faced with her jutting belly, he was unsure where to put his hands. "Here—" She reached out and clasped his hard brown fingers. "Just steady me. I'll do the climbing."

Stepping over the side of the wagon, she found the

front wheel with one boot. Her hands clasped his as she shifted her weight and swung her free leg upward to clear the sideboard. At that same instant one of the horses shifted in its traces. The wheel rolled forward, just enough to throw her off balance. Cassandra lost her grip on Morgan's hands. Her arms flailed as she tumbled outward into space.

Morgan grabbed for her, catching her low, around the hips. Her top-heavy weight sent him staggering backward. Instinctively she arched away from him, trying to balance, but it was too late. She heard him curse as they went crashing down together in a frantic tangle of arms and legs.

"Are you all right?" He had landed beneath her, deliberately breaking her fall with his body. Now she sprawled on top of him, bracing upward with her arms, his stormy black eyes inches from her own.

"Yes...I think so." Cassandra felt the reassuring jab of a tiny fist against her pelvis, and she sensed that neither she nor the child had been harmed. Morgan had seen to that. But what if she hadn't been so lucky? What if, in her carelessness, she had done something to hurt her precious baby?

She began to tremble, her chest jerking in sharp little spasms.

"Stop that!" His grip tightened on her arm. "Stop it, Cassandra. This isn't helping anything!"

"I...know." Cassandra fought for self-control. "I'm sorry." She forced herself to take long, deep breaths, one, then another. Little by little she felt her fear begin to evaporate. Her rocketing pulse settled into a ragged canter. *It's all right...it's all right...*

His sun-warmed body lay solidly beneath her own. Something stirred and hardened against her thigh. Cassandra knew what it was, but she had lost the will to move. She felt the swelling heaviness in her own loins, the slow, uncoiling liquid heat. Her heart had begun to race again. How could this be happening? How was it possible, when she was mere weeks from giving birth. This was wrong. All wrong.

"You'd better get up." His voice was a thick, self-conscious rasp.

"Yes." She scrambled off him, flushed with the heat of her response to his arousal. Both of them, Cassandra realized, were acutely aware of what had happened. But she knew they must not speak of it or run the slightest risk that it would happen again. She was Ryan's sweetheart, carrying Ryan's child. She had to make him believe that. She had to make herself believe it.

He was on his feet now, brushing the stickers from his clothes. "You're sure you're all right?" he asked gruffly.

"I'm...fine. Just fine." She took refuge in waspishness. "You don't have to mother me."

"You look as if you could use some mothering, Cassandra Riley." He reached into the wagon and lifted out the picnic basket. "But I don't suppose I'm the one for the job."

"So why did you really invite me along today?" She followed him toward the spot where he had spread the quilt on the grass. "It would have been a lot simpler for you to leave me at the ranch. Were you afraid to trust me alone with your father, afraid I'd tell him too much?"

He glanced back at her, scowling. "You already know I don't trust you. That was part of it. But I was also hoping to learn more about the woman who claims to be carrying the next generation of Tollivers."

"I thought that was up to your ex-Pinkerton friend."

"Sit down." He dropped to his knees, opened the picnic hamper and began lifting out covered baskets of food. The mouthwatering aromas of fried chicken and blueberry muffins wafted into the mountain air.

"I'll save you and your friend some time," she said, easing herself down on the blanket and reaching for a muffin. "I was born in Ohio. My father was killed at Gettysburg, and my mother passed away the next year from consumption and heartbreak. The neighbors sent me to live with my grandparents on their homestead in Nebraska. That's where I grew up." She took a bite of muffin, savoring its warm, buttery taste and congratulating herself that, up to this point, at least, she had told the truth.

"What part of Nebraska?" Morgan prompted her with the sharpness of a ferret scenting a fresh trail.

"A little north of Omaha." The muffin seemed to lose its flavor as she slipped into the half lie. In truth, if their homestead had been located much farther north, she and her grandparents would have been living in the Dakotas.

"Are your grandparents still there?"

She forced herself to wrinkle her nose and laugh at him. "Good heavens, Morgan Tolliver, you could at least be subtle about wheedling information out of me! You're as single-minded as a snake in a prairie dog hole!"

"Are they?" He did not even blink.

Cassandra reached for a golden-brown chicken leg. "As far as I know, there's nothing left of the old place except their graves. I hung on as long as I could after they died, but I couldn't manage the farm alone. I sold it to a rancher who wanted it for grazing land. By the time I paid off the liens on the property, there was hardly any money left."

Again it was a near truth. She had sold the land when she married Jake Logan, and Jake had burned through her money like wildfire through ripe wheat.

"Some distant cousins offered me a place with them in Cheyenne," she said, plunging back into the quagmire. "The ticket was expensive, and when I arrived, there was no trace of my relatives. An old man at the train station said they'd packed up and gone to California. I was stranded, with no money and nowhere to go."

She pulled a strip of chicken loose with her fingers and nibbled on it in silence. The morsel was perfect, its coating light and crisp, its meat succulent, almost flaky. But she was losing her appetite. Her grandmother had always said lies left a bad taste in a body's mouth.

"I finally found a place as a live-in housekeeper to a sick old woman. I worked for her until last month, when she died, and the bank took over her house."

Cassandra was up to her neck in lies now. But as her grandfather would have said, might as well be hung for a sheep as for a goat. Even now, Johnny Chang was on his way to Fort Caspar with the letter to the ex-Pinkerton agent. But any reply would be weeks in coming. Time, at least, was on her side.

Morgan cleared his throat. "Then you were living with the old woman when you met my—"

"No!" She cut him off vehemently. "You promised you wouldn't make me sad by talking about him, remember? And, look, it's such a beautiful day!" Her gaze swept the sunlit panorama of trees and mountains. The sky was a deep morning-glory blue, speckled with a scatter of clouds in the west. A cooling breeze blew down from the naked peaks of the Big Horns, passing with a ripple across the pale green meadow grass.

A stone's throw from the picnic blanket, a smallish black bird with a glossy brown head darted in and out of the long grass hunting for insects.

"What an odd bird!" Cassandra exclaimed, groping for a way to shift the conversation. "You must know a lot about the birds and animals in this country, Morgan. What can you tell me about it?"

Something dark flickered in Morgan's eyes. "That's a cowbird," he said, "so called because its kind likes to follow grazing cows and feed on the bugs that fly out of the grass.''

''Oh.''

An ungainly silence hung between them. Morgan frowned at the sky, lips pressed tightly together. ''Another thing about the cowbird,'' he said slowly. ''It doesn't build a nest or raise its own young. Instead it drops an egg in the nest of another bird. When the egg hatches, the baby cowbird demands most of the food the parents bring. As it grows, the other babies, the ones that don't starve, are crowded out of the nest. Meanwhile, the mother cowbird has flown off without a care.'' His eyes narrowed. ''I never did like cowbirds much for that.''

Cassandra stared at him, the taste of well-seasoned chicken turning to ashes in her mouth. Morgan was not just talking about a bird. He was telling her, in his own oblique way, exactly what he thought of her—that she'd chosen the Tolliver Ranch as a likely nest, a place to drop her baby where it could be fed and reared by caring strangers while she did as she pleased.

A tide of rage and shame rose from the pit of Cassandra's stomach, constricting her throat and stinging her eyes. She had hoped Morgan was beginning to trust her, maybe even to like her. But he felt nothing for her, she realized. Nothing but suspicion and contempt.

Chapter Six

By midafternoon, the eiderdown clouds of morning had multiplied and thickened. Now they boiled over the peaks of the Big Horns like wheat mush on a hot stove, billowing across the sky, dark and heavy with the promise of rain.

Morgan watched them, cursing under his breath as elation battled worry. This was not virga he was seeing. The roiling clouds carried every sign that an honest-to-God storm was brewing—a storm that would flood the parched grassland with life-giving water. One part of him wanted to laugh with pure savage joy, to leap out of the wagon and dance a Shoshone welcome to the coming rain.

The other part of him, the serious, sensible part, was mindful of the exposed wagon, the horses and the steep, narrow road that could turn to treacherous slime in a downpour. Most acutely of all, he was aware of the woman who sat beside him, a woman who was in no condition to endure a jolting wagon ride, especially in a thunderstorm.

Cassandra Riley had withdrawn since his remark about the cowbird. They had finished Chang's delicious food in awkward silence, avoiding each other's eyes as they ate. Then she had climbed back into the wagon on her own, confining her remarks to the mountain scenery as they wound their way up to the summer pasture and delivered the supplies to old Charlie, the grizzled range cook.

He probably should have kept his mouth shut, Morgan groused, thinking back on his words. But her question about the bird had left him an opening a mile wide and too tempting to resist.

Why had he done it? he asked himself now. Had he meant to test her? To wound her? To make it clear that he didn't believe a word of her story? Whatever the reason, his barb had clearly hit home.

He cast her a furtive glance, observing the way she sat like a proud little queen, her chin thrust high, her blazing curls fluttering in the wind where they'd worked loose from their long braid. She had taken off her shapeless felt hat when the clouds moved in. Now she clutched the hat tightly in one hand. The other hand was braced against the wooden seat, easing the motion of the wagon against the vulnerable parts of her body.

Unbidden and unwelcome, the memory of their accidental fall surged in his mind—Cassandra's womanly weight pressing the length of him, her ripe belly warm against his groin. He stared at the sky, fighting the memory of her jerky little gasps and the sweetness of her hair brushing across his cheek.

Morgan groaned inwardly, recalling the expressions that had flashed across her face when she'd discovered that he was aroused—an instant of surprise, then fear, then...

But he would be a fool to dwell on what he'd seen next—the softening of her mouth, the parting of her wet lips and the closing of her eyes. And he would be an even bigger fool to seek that response again. One of two things was true—this woman was carrying his brother's child or she was an unscrupulous fraud. Either way, she was nothing but trouble and he had no right to touch her.

"Are you all right?" He cast her a quick sidelong glance.

"Yes." Her cornflower eyes flickered nervously toward him. "But those clouds look as if they mean business. How much longer before we're ho—" She bit off the word and corrected herself. "Before we're back at the ranch?"

"A couple of hours at this pace." He chose to ignore the slip, although it had rankled him. She had not earned the right to call the Tolliver Ranch her home. Not, at least, until he had more proof than she'd offered him so far.

He thought of the letter that was already speeding its way to Fort Caspar in Johnny Chang's saddlebag. How long would it be before he heard from Ham Crawford? A month? Two? Cassandra Riley could be a mother well before then, he realized morosely. And unless that baby was the spitting image of Ryan—

"Can't we go faster?" Her husky little voice was

taut with anxiety. "We had terrible lightning storms in Nebraska. When I was fourteen, a bolt killed one of our cows fifty feet from where I was standing. I've been afraid of storms every since."

"Going faster will make the ride rougher. Do you want to risk that?" Morgan saw her wince as the wagon lurched through a dry streambed. What kind of idiocy had let him agree to bring her along today? He should have taken his chances and left her at the ranch with his father. Now he was faced with the prospect of a violent storm, a mud-slicked road and a hysterical, pregnant woman.

Thunder rumbled behind them, echoing across the shrouded peaks. The wind freshened, blowing tendrils of dark red hair across her freckled face. Her eyes were wide and frightened but her head was high, her mouth set in a stubborn line. "No," she said. "Take it slowly. I don't want to risk any more harm to the baby."

"I'm sorry." Morgan forced himself to speak the words she expected to hear. "It hasn't rained here since April. If I'd had any idea it would rain today, I would never have invited you along."

"'Invited' is hardly the word I'd use," she said coldly. "You didn't give me much choice. You were afraid to leave me behind, weren't you? Afraid I'd insinuate myself into your father's good graces, then tell him I was carrying Ryan's child. Deny it, I dare you."

"I told you I didn't trust you," he said, clenching his jaw as the wagon's rear wheel skirted a protruding boulder. The first drops of rain had begun to fall, plopping to the ground with a heaviness that raised small dust puffs where they fell.

"So what are you going to do?" she snapped, ignoring the rain that made thumbprint-sized blotches on her flannel shirt. "Lock me in my room? Follow me like a watchdog from morning to night? We made an agreement, one I intend to keep. There's no call for you to go around snarling at me, or telling me stories about silly birds that lay their eggs where they don't belong. You've made it very clear what you think of me, Morgan Tolliver, and I accept your reasons. But if you think I'm going to back down and throw away my baby's future—"

The rest of her words were drowned by the violent *whip-crack* of lightning that split the sky from horizon to horizon. The horses screamed and bucked as the shattering boom shook the earth beneath the wagon. Braced against the footboard, Morgan strained backward, struggling with the reins as he crooned to the team, half-consciously chanting the horse-soothing song his grandfather had taught him.

Glancing sideways, he caught a glimpse of Cassandra. She was clinging to the wagon seat, her fingers white, her eyes large in her frightened face. The rain had begun in earnest now, soaking her clothes and turning her hair into dripping red strings around her white face.

"Are you all right?" he shouted above the hissing roar of the storm.

She nodded grimly. "Please, can't we stop and get under something—the wagon?"

"Too dangerous here. We've got to get off this hill before the rain triggers a landslide. There's an old slicker under the seat. Get it out and put it around you. Then hang on tight!"

By now Morgan had managed to get the horses under control. He urged them gently forward, hands firm on the reins. Once more he glanced at Cassandra. She had found the black slicker and was huddled like a sparrow against the downpour, her nose catching the drizzle from the overhanging hood. "Don't worry about me," she said through clenched, chattering jaws. "I'll be fine."

The steepest part of the trail lay ahead. A zigzagging two-mile gash down the side of a long slope, it was bad medicine in any weather. Now, slimed with mud and runoff, it was a wagon-driver's nightmare. Thick reddish goo sucked at the massive hooves of the horses, exacting a toll of strength with every step. The wheels of the wagon alternately stuck and slid, defying the feeble force of the mud-slathered brake.

Rain streamed down Morgan's face and sheeted off his shoulders. He scarcely noticed it. All his efforts were focused on keeping the wagon stable, the horses steady on the treacherous road. Cassandra had not spoken a word of blame, but her very presence was a condemnation. After two months of blazing drought, he had given no thought to the chance of a storm today. His mind had been on other things. The wrong things.

He had invited her along on the pretext of mollifying his father. But had that been his true reason?

Morgan cursed silently as he remembered last night, standing beside her bed, battling the tenderness that threatened to shatter his resolve. Damn it, he had *wanted* to be with her today. He had wanted to see the sunlight on her hair, hear the lilt of her husky, boyish voice. He had wanted to pry open the lock she kept on her secrets, to know everything there was to know about this small, stubborn, infuriating woman.

But even that plan had failed, he reminded himself. Cassandra Riley had weaseled more secrets out of him than he'd told a woman in years. As for the few tidbits of information she'd given him, likely as not they were false leads, laid down to cover her trail. He would be a fool to believe anything she'd said.

Morgan's thoughts were wrenched back to the present as the wagon sagged sharply to the left and shuddered to a halt. He didn't need to look down to know that the road had washed out from under the left rear wheel and was in danger of giving way, spilling the wagon and its precious cargo down the steep slope below.

"Ha!" He slammed the reins hard right. The wagon groaned and lurched back onto solid ground. Morgan exhaled in relief. He could hear Cassandra breathing beside him, feel her leg resting against his own, thrown close by the motion of the wagon. Chain lightning flashed above the peaks, sending an avalanche of thunder across the roiling sky.

"Scared?" He spoke as if he were teasing her, but

the words came out hollow, echoing his own fear. Alone, he would be free to take his chances, to open up the team and go hell for leather, all the way to the bottom of the slope. But with Cassandra, even the thought of a bad bump or a fall was enough to make his blood run cold.

"Scared? Me?" She managed a nervous chuckle, but her voice was thin and shaky. "You should know better than to ask, Morgan Tolliver! Why, this is nothing but a drizzle. Show me a real thunderstorm, like the ones we had in Nebraska. Then maybe I'll be scared."

He grinned at her in spite of himself. "Spunky little thing, aren't you?" he said as the wagon fishtailed around a sharp bend.

"I've had to be." Her quiet reply was barely audible above the sound of the rain.

"Care to tell me more?" Morgan peered through the rain. Ahead he could see the huge craggy pine that marked the worst curve on the whole mountain road, a reeling turn that skirted the edge of a sheer, rocky slope. Get around that, and the most dangerous part of the ride would be behind them.

"Don't push me, Morgan," she said. "I've told you as much about my past as you need to know. The rest is none of your concern."

"Under the circumstances, I'd say it's very much my concern," Morgan retorted, his attention focused on easing the horses into the perilous turn.

"My baby is your concern," she said. "As for the rest, you can be satisfied that I'm not a criminal or a

whore. The rest may come with time and trust, but
for now please don't—''

The universe erupted in a blinding flash as lightning struck the huge old pine tree, splitting it to the
heart. Morgan felt the shock through the ground,
through the wagon wheels and the massive bodies of
the horses. Cassandra's white face flashed before his
eyes as the whole world exploded in ear-shattering
sound.

The tick of silence that followed was ripped asun-
der by the shriek of a horse. Then the wagon shot
forward like a bullet as the panic-stricken team bolted,
plunging down the muddy trail.

Both Morgan and Cassandra had been thrown into
the wagon bed. Scrambling back onto the seat, Morgan groped for the loose reins and managed to catch
them in his fingers. Cassandra remained on the floor,
clinging frantically to the side of the wagon. Her face
was bloodless beneath the black hood of the slicker.

As the horses approached the perilous curve, Morgan struggled for a grip on the reins. If he couldn't
slow the team they would never make the turn. They
would go flying off the edge of the road, spilling the
wagon down the slope. Alone, he might be able to
leap to safety. But the risk of such a jump would be
too great for Cassandra, and for Ryan's baby—

Lord, this was no time to start believing her crazy
story!

Lightning crackled across the sky as he yanked
frantically on the reins, fighting the downward plunge
of the team, wrestling twenty-five-hundred pounds of

fear-crazed horseflesh. What the big draft animals lacked in speed, they made up in sheer brute power. In their terror-crazed condition, they could barely feel the pressure of the bits in their mouths. They were out of control, plunging down the mud-slicked road to certain destruction.

As Morgan shifted forward, he felt the light press of the medicine pouch against his chest. His grandfather's most profound medicine gift had been the power over horses. Morgan had seen that gift work often enough to know that it was real. Now, almost as if the old man were beside him, he felt the peace of the gnarled hands on his own, felt the whisper of the ancient voice in his mind, and he knew that no other power could turn the racing team. He leaned hard left with the reins, willing his thoughts to reach out to the terrified animals. *Gwia-man.* Rest. Be at peace.

Had he spoken the words aloud or only in his head? There was no time to wonder. The horses were thundering toward the brink of the turn as if no power on earth could stop them. Morgan threw the full weight of his body into the reins. *"Gwia-man..."* He felt them respond to the pressure of the bit, felt them turn aside. Their massive hooves skimmed air as they wheeled, swinging the wagon behind them in a sliding arc. Morgan felt the rear wheels ride open space; then, as the horses slowed, they slammed into the bank. The wagon came to a shuddering halt, canted sharply over the slope with its rear end axle-deep in mud.

Rain drizzled into the gray silence, steaming off the backs of the gasping horses. Morgan exhaled, his pulse still hammering as he glanced around at his passenger.

"Are you all——?" His throat choked off the words as he saw her.

Cassandra was hunched in the bed of the wagon, arms clutched tightly around her belly. The face that she raised to him was pasty white through the soggy mass of her hair.

"Morgan…" Her bloodless lips moved with effort. "The baby…my baby."

Cassandra had felt the warm flood between her thighs the instant after the lightning bolt had split the great pine tree. The first pain had seized her as the wagon careened down the steep mountain trail with Morgan fighting to control the horses. *No!* her mind screamed now as a second contraction took her, squeezing with the power of a giant vise. *Please, God, this can't be happening! It's too soon…too soon…*

Morgan was clambering over the seat toward her. His face, looming above her through the rain, was wet and grim and strained. "We've got to get you out of the wagon now, before the road washes away," he said. "Can you stand up?"

Cassandra felt the pain pass, leaving her limp and shaking. "Yes," she muttered through chattering teeth. "But, merciful heaven, I can't have the baby here. You've got to get me home——" She caught her mistake again, then realized that words didn't matter.

Nothing mattered right now except the life of her baby, a baby that was coming into the world before its time, in a driving rainstorm on an isolated mountain road.

She had told Morgan she could walk, but clearly he was taking no more chances. He bent close, his hands working beneath her, scooping her against his chest. *Please, God,* she prayed as he lifted her in his arms. *I've lied and cheated, and I'm not worth a thought. But my poor little baby's done nothing wrong. Please don't let an innocent child pay for my sins!*

''We'll get you back to the ranch as soon as this wagon's out of the mud,'' Morgan said. ''Meanwhile, we've got to find you some shelter where you can rest and hang on. I thought you said you were in no danger of having this baby today.''

''That's what I thought.'' Her teeth were chattering violently. ''It must be happening early.''

''How early? When is it due?''

''I'm…not sure.'' Cassandra wrapped her arms around his neck as he climbed over the side of the wagon and jumped to the ground. She was aware that she sounded like a fool, and that her answer implied things about her relationship with Ryan that she might have to explain later, but for once, so help her, she was telling the truth. ''I've never been that…regular. Two weeks, maybe, or even a month, I just don't know—'' She was babbling, she realized. Dear heaven, how could she be saying such things to a man she barely knew?

Morgan made an impatient sound in his throat, then turned and caught up the picnic quilt with his free hand. Cassandra clung to him as he strode up the hill to where a rocky overhang jutted outward from the slope, sheltering a tiny patch of earth.

"Rest here," he said, dropping the quilt on the ground. "As soon as I've got the horses and wagon free I'll come back for you."

"Hurry. I—oh!" Her fingers dug into his shoulder as another contraction took her, squeezing and twisting until she wanted to scream. He held her as she writhed against him, gasping with pain, her face pressed hard into his rain-soaked shirt. Thunder broke across the sky, its wake spilling fresh torrents as the pain diminished. "It's all right," she whispered. "Put me down and go!"

He did as she urged, lowering her swiftly to the soggy quilt. "Hang on," he said. "I'll be back as soon as I can. Shout if you need me." With a final glance, he turned away and vanished into the rain.

Cassandra gulped air, bracing herself for the next contraction. How far was it to the ranch? she wondered. And what would she do for help once they got there. She'd seen no sign of a woman about the place, and men were useless at a birthing. That's what her grandmother had always said. Oh, why hadn't she thought this out and made better plans? If anything happened to the baby—

She pushed the idea from her mind, as if the very thought had power to create harm. Raising up on one elbow, she could see that Morgan had reached the wagon. He was busy with the horses, soothing and stroking them, checking their harnesses. The sight of him, blurred by rain and distance, gave her an unexplained sense of comfort. Morgan would take care of her as he took care of everyone and everything, she told herself. He would see that she got back to the ranch in time to have this baby in a safe, warm bed. She would be fine. The baby would be fine...

She gasped, clutching her belly as another contraction hit her like a doubled-up fist. This one was worse than the others, stretching her innards with a pressure that made her feel as if she were turning inside out. With no one to hear now, Cassandra gave vent to a shattering sob. This couldn't happen—she wouldn't *let* it happen.

Crossing her legs in the sodden overalls, she clenched her fists and prayed.

Knee-deep in mud, Morgan struggled to jam a thick log under the axle of the mired wagon. If he could keep the wheels from rolling backward, the horses might be able to pull the wagon free.

A string of curses burst out of him as the log slipped, costing precious inches. Swearing was a release, a mask for the cold fear that clawed at his heart. He had always considered himself a capable man. He could ride, rope and shoot with the best. He could dress a wound, nurse a fever and manage every detail of the ranch, from branding and herding to negotiating prices with Eastern cattle buyers.

But he was not equipped to deliver a baby. Not in

a storm with no medical supplies. Not when the mother was small and the baby was early.

Once more he thrust his weight against the log, fighting to release the wheels from the grip of the sucking mud. How much time did she have? No matter, he had only one option—to get Cassandra back to the ranch and into the capable hands of Chang's wife, Mei Li. He could not fail her. Not the way he had failed Helen.

It washed over him now in a bitter flood—the memory he'd kept at bay for so many years. A lump rose in Morgan's throat as he recalled the scant weight of the tiny wood coffin between his hands, the coffin he'd hastily fashioned to cradle the body of his stillborn son. He had promised Helen he would get her to Laramie in plenty of time for the birth. But he'd been out on the range when she went into labor almost five weeks early. He'd returned home late that night to find the baby dead and his wife behind their locked bedroom door. As soon as she was well enough to travel, Helen had left him. He had signed the divorce papers without protest.

The veins stood out on Morgan's neck as he strained against the log. Helen would probably have left him anyway, he thought. The daughter of a wealthy Eastern cattle broker, she had hated the harshness and isolation of ranch life. Morgan had hoped that a child might change things, but the loss of that small life had been the end of everything. She had not been able to forgive him. He had not been able to forgive himself.

And now, if anything were to happen to Cassandra Riley or her baby—

Morgan's thoughts snapped back to his task as he felt the end of the log grind into place behind the axle. He tested it with his weight to make certain it was braced. Then, with effort, he dragged his boots free of the mud and climbed back onto the road.

The horses stood with drooping heads, rain streaming off their massive bodies and down their sodden manes. Morgan hesitated for an instant, thinking it might be a good idea to go up the hill and check on Cassandra. No, he swiftly decided, the sooner he freed the wagon the better. If she needed him she would call.

Thunder boomed out of the angry black clouds as Morgan climbed into the wagon and picked up the reins. "*Nook!* Go!" he commanded, urging the big bays forward with light strokes of the leather on their backs. "Go!" He felt the wagon creak as the team strained against the dead weight, felt the grip of the mud give slightly.

"*Nook! Nam ish a!*" He leaped off the back of the wagon and flung his full strength against the log that braced the axle, using only his voice to guide the team. One inch, two inches the wagon moved. The mud hissed like a serpent giving up its prey as the wheels began to turn.

Clawing his way back into the wagon, Morgan seized the reins and drove the horses forward. The undercarriage groaned, threatening to snap under the strain. One more inch, two. The wagon shuddered and lumbered back onto the road.

Weak with relief, Morgan halted the team, climbed down from the wagon seat and hitched the horses to a thick aspen tree. Rain streamed off his face and body as he turned and ran up the hill.

Muddy water cascaded off the overhanging rock, hiding the place where he'd left Cassandra. Morgan felt his heart lurch as he saw one denim-clad leg thrusting out into the rain. He burst through the curtain of water to find her writhing on the ground in agony.

He reached out to her. She caught his hand and clasped it with such desperate force that Morgan could feel the grinding of his bones. "It's all right," he murmured, brushing the mud-soaked hair back from her face. "It's all right. The wagon's free. We can be back at the ranch in an hour."

"No!" Her face was ghostly white, her eyes wide with pain and fear. "There's no time, Morgan. The baby's coming. It's coming—now!"

Chapter Seven

Cassandra's fingers clawed the muddy gravel as another pain ripped through her, wringing her body like a piece of wet laundry. She was dimly aware that Morgan was unfastening her soggy overalls, working them down over the resisting bulge to reveal parts of her that no man except Jake had ever seen. Not that it mattered. Modesty was the least of her concerns now.

Morgan had covered the upper part of her body with the rain slicker. Its hem rode her bent knees, mercifully hiding what was happening below.

"Have you ever done anything like this before?" she asked him, gasping as the pain ebbed.

"I've helped birth calves and foals." His tone was carefully detached, hiding whatever emotions he might be feeling as he worked the wet denim down over her boots. "I don't suppose humans are much different."

"Oh, that's just fine." She managed a grimace.

''Pretend I'm a cow, and you'll have no trouble at all!''

Morgan didn't answer. As he bent low to peer beneath the slicker, Cassandra heard him curse under his breath.

''What is it?'' Sudden terror gripped her.

''Just wishing I had a damned light. Can't see a thing. There's a lamp in the wagon, I could—''

''No!'' She caught his wrist as the next pain slammed into her. ''Don't…leave me…Morgan.'' Her fingers dug into his skin as she felt the downward pressure. ''It's…''

Her words ended in a gasp as she felt the strain of parting flesh. Instinctively she bore down hard. The wet weight slid outward, leaving her raw and hollow and strangely alone. She waited for something more, but there was nothing but a terrible stillness, punctuated by the drizzle of the rain and the harsh rasp of Morgan's breathing.

No! Dear God, no!

Cassandra heard a sharp slap, another, followed by an eternity of silence as Morgan fought to clear the baby's air passages.

Please…oh, please…

There was a tiny but miraculous gulping of air, followed by a piercing wail.

''Oh, Morgan.'' Her heart was leaping. She struggled to sit up, but she was too weak even to get her elbows beneath her. He fumbled behind the slicker for a moment, then thrust a squirming bundle—all but lost in the folds of his deerskin vest—into her out-stretched hands.

"Congratulations, Cassandra." His voice was drained of emotion. "You have…a daughter."

The hours that followed were blurred by exhaustion. Later Cassandra would remember only bits and pieces—Morgan scooping her up in his arms, blanket and all, to carry her down to the wagon; the eternity of lying beneath the slicker on the jouncing boards with the baby cradled next to her bare breast. Such a ferocious little hunk of life, all kicking legs, long clasping fingers and squalling, sucking mouth. The hot, possessive love that had swept through Cassandra was the most powerful emotion she had ever known.

"Rachel." She'd whispered the name into her daughter's rose petal ear. "It was your great-grandmother's name, and now it's yours, my little love. You're going to be a beautiful girl, Rachel, and you're going to have a wonderful life. You'll never want for anything, I promise. I promise on my life…"

Morgan had driven the team full out to get the wagon back to the ranch as fast as possible. Even so, by the time they arrived she was chilled to the bone and whimpering incoherently. The baby, too, was fearfully cold. Morgan had taken the tiny girl and passed her swiftly to Chang. Then he'd lifted Cassandra in his arms once more and carried her upstairs to her bedroom.

Somehow he'd gotten her out of her clothes—it no longer mattered to Cassandra what parts of her body he saw or touched. She was spattered with mud and rain, her legs smeared with blood, but getting her warm was more critical than getting her clean.

"Where's my...baby?" She swayed dizzily, her teeth chattering, as he pulled the soft flannel nightgown over her head. "I want my b-baby."

"Chang's giving her a warm bath." Morgan's mud-streaked face swam in her vision. His eyes were bloodshot, his black hair glued wetly to his head. "Don't worry, you'll get her back soon enough. Right now you need to get into that bed and stay there."

He had already turned down the blankets. Cassandra reeled toward the bed and tumbled into it. By the time her head had sunk into the pillow, she was asleep.

Morgan felt himself shaking as he gazed down at her. Lord, it had been such a near miss. The baby could have died. *She* could have died, there in the cold mud beneath the rock, in a pool of blood and agony. It could have been two bodies he'd hauled home in the wagon, not a living mother and child.

His throat constricted as he remembered the feel of the tiny new life wriggling in his hands, his blessed relief at the sound of that wailing cry. Only now did the full impact of his fear catch up with him.

What if he'd lost her?

What if he had lost them both?

Cassandra whimpered in her fitful sleep, and Morgan became aware that he was dripping mud onto the bedroom floor. He didn't belong here, he reminded himself harshly. But then, *she* didn't belong here, and neither did her child. He had held her in his arms and touched her intimately to bring her baby into the world. But that didn't change the fact that Cassandra Riley was a liar and a fraud, or that, for his family's sake, it was his duty to unmask the woman.

Tearing himself away from the sight of her, Morgan turned and walked out into the hallway, shutting the door softly behind him. Ryan's closed room mocked him as he made his way past the landing. Was he wrong? Was it Ryan's child he'd delivered tonight? The space under the rock had been so dark, the circumstances so urgent, the baby so small and wet. There'd been no chance for even a brief inspection.

But he would have time, Morgan reminded himself. Time to study the baby's features, time to wait for Ham Crawford's reply to his letter. Meanwhile, Cassandra Riley had nowhere else to go. For the present, at least, she had found a home here on the ranch.

For the space of a long breath he stared at the closed door of Ryan's room, aching for his brother's ready laugh and teasing, reckless manner; burning for the answers that only Ryan could give him.

From the kitchen downstairs he could hear squalls of protest as Cassandra's daughter received her first washing. The baby was a scrawny little thing, all spindly legs and hands. But at least her lungs were strong. Maybe it would be a good thing, having a new life in this gloomy house. Maybe those strident wails would pierce the shadows and drive the ghosts away.

Morgan stood on the landing a moment longer, letting the lusty little cries wash over him, through him, like cleansing water. Then, turning aside, he went back downstairs to put away the tired horses.

Cassandra awoke to darkness. Her skin was wet and clammy, her nightgown drenched with sweat beneath the mound of blankets someone had piled on her bed. Her body felt as if it had been dragged through broken glass.

"My baby!" Her eyes shot wide open. She struggled to sit up, thrashing in panic beneath the weight of the covers. "Where's my baby?"

For a heart-stopping moment no one answered. Then the door opened, and her eyes caught the flicker of a candle.

"Where's my baby?" she demanded, kicking at the quilts in an effort to get her feet on the floor. "Please, I want my baby!"

"No. You are sick. You rest." The delicate voice was a stranger's, childlike in its pitch, lightly sing-song in its cadence. Small hands, astoundingly strong, pushed Cassandra back onto the pillow. "The baby sleeps. You sleep, too."

The candle had been set on the nightstand. In its flickering light Cassandra saw a doll-like face leaning above her, the eyes dark and almond-shaped, the graying hair brushed tightly back from an elegantly high forehead. Intricately carved jade earrings dangled from elongated lobes.

Thinking this might be a dream, Cassandra tried to blink away the strange vision. But the creature remained, hovering like an exotic fairy beside her bed.

"You sleep now. Be still and rest." The miniature hands pressed Cassandra's shoulders.

"Please!" Cassandra's head swam as she fought back. "Bring me my baby! I need to see my baby!"

The flare of delicate nostrils was followed by a sigh of resignation. The woman turned away and moved with tottering steps, toward a shadowed corner of the room, giving Cassandra a full view of her. She was a handbreadth under five feet tall, dressed in what appeared to be a dark high-necked jacket and full-legged trousers. Her slippered feet were no more than knobs, each one the size and shape of a small clenched fist.

Only then did Cassandra remember the conversation that had taken place over breakfast in the Tolliver dining room. This would be Chang's wife, she realized, the wife he had brought over from China when he first came to work for Jacob Tolliver.

She held her breath as the woman bent into a shadowed corner and picked up a blanket-swathed bundle. Her heart leaped as her eyes caught the slight movement beneath the wrappings. Everything was all right. Her baby was alive and safe. Nothing else mattered.

Her breasts were swollen and throbbing. Fluid seeped from her nipples as she opened the front of her flannel nightgown and gathered her daughter close. The pull of the tiny rosebud mouth sent a ripple of pain through Cassandra's body. It was the sweetest pain she had ever known. She closed her eyes, drifting in a cloud of strange new sensations.

Someone, she realized dimly, had washed the mud

from her skin and buttoned her into a freshly laundered nightgown. Had it been the doll-like Chinese woman who stood vigil beside her bed? Or could it have been Morgan? She had no memory of the hours that had passed. She did not even know what time it was, or what day it was, except that it was dark in the little room.

Where was Morgan now? Had he been here? Cassandra struggled to hold his image in her swimming mind. In retrospect, the thought of where he'd touched her sent a scalding red flush over the surface of her skin. But Morgan had only done what was necessary, she reminded herself. He had saved her baby's life, probably her own life as well. And she had not even thanked him.

Thanked him? The irony of that thought curled a corner of her mouth in a bitter smile. Morgan was the one who'd taken her on that wild wagon ride in the first place, then cut her down with that biting remark about the cowbird. If the man were here right now she would have his superior, self-righteous hide…

She floated back into dreams, soothed by the rhythmic pull of the strong little mouth at her breast. When she opened her eyes again, the Chinese woman was gone from the room, like a phantom from a dream. Cassandra's baby had fallen asleep in the crook of her arm, a trickle of milk pooling in the cleft of the dainty button chin that was a miniature version of her father's.

Cassandra's breath caught as she gazed down at her sleeping daughter. Rachel was a pretty baby, with delicate features set in a heart-shaped face and crowned by a nimbus of reddish-gold curls. Only her chin was truly distinctive, the deep dimple in its center unmistakably like Jake's...or like Ryan Tolliver's.

Dear heaven, was this a gift? Was her crazy scheme actually destined to work?

Overcome by a blazing surge of love, Cassandra clasped the little bundle against her heart. Yes, it would work, she vowed. She would make it work. So help her, if she had to lie and cheat all the days of her life, if she had to burn in hell for all eternity to provide for this precious little girl, she would do it without a moment's hesitation.

She glanced up as the bedroom door opened, expecting to see Chang's wife. However it was Morgan who stepped into the room carrying a lacquered tray with a celadon-glazed porcelain teapot and a matching cup. Cassandra fumbled with the open neck of the nightgown, just managing to pull the buttoned edge over her breast.

"I waylaid Mei Li in the hall," he said. "She told me you were awake." The candlelight cast his rangy form into a long shadow that danced across the surface of the painted elk skin. His cheeks glistened with moisture, and she realized he had just washed and dressed. A faint gray gleam through the windowpane confirmed that it was nearly dawn.

"We've been worried about you." Morgan set the tray on the nightstand next to the candle. "Mei Li's been here with you day and night. I just told her to go home and get some rest."

Day and night? Cassandra stared up at him, suddenly aware of her sweat-tangled hair and rheumy eyes.

"You've been out of your head for three days," Morgan said quietly. "Your fever broke just a few hours ago. Before that we feared we were going to lose you."

"The baby—" Cassandra mouthed the words, her throat parchment dry.

"Mei Li took care of her while you were sick." He glanced at the teapot on the nightstand. "She gave you her Chinese teas to fight the fever and keep you from losing your milk."

"I don't know what to say." Cassandra felt the hot trickle of a single tear on her cheek. So much kindness from the hands of a stranger. "I didn't even thank her."

"There'll be plenty of time for that." Morgan's own voice was weary. The guttering candle cast the creases around his eyes into stark relief, and she sensed that Chang's wife had not been the only person at her side, although Morgan would never volunteer that he'd been concerned about her. "I'm under Mei Li's orders to get this tea down you," he said. "Do you want me to put your baby back in her cradle?"

"Not just yet," Cassandra said. "And her name is Rachel, after my grandmother."

"Rachel." Morgan's eyes flickered, and Cassandra felt the widening of the gulf between them. Rachel Tolliver? No, he was clearly not ready to give the child his family name. Rachel Riley? Cassandra would not capitulate to that, nor would she fling away all pretense and use her daughter's true legal name, Rachel Logan.

The battle lines had been redrawn. For the present, young Rachel would be a child with no surname.

Morgan busied himself with pouring tea from Mei Li's celadon pot, his long fingers dark against the pale green glaze. Replacing the pot on the tray, he turned and reached out for the baby. "I'll take her while you drink. The tea's hot, and your hands are bound to be unsteady."

"Yes, you're quite right." Cassandra relinquished her treasure with a sigh. She had expected Morgan to be awkward and ill at ease with the baby, but he cradled the tiny bundle in a manner that was almost fatherly. The sight of Rachel nestled contentedly against his chest startled Cassandra for a moment. But then, she'd been ill for three days, she reasoned. If Morgan had been in the room, he would have had plenty of time to get acquainted with the baby. Surely, then, he would have noticed the cleft chin that was so like Ryan's.

Was that why his connection to the baby seemed so natural? Had he already begun to believe Rachel was his niece, a small, living part of the brother he had lost?

Cassandra picked up the exquisite little cup and, finding no handle, cradled it between her palms. Its porcelain sides were eggshell thin. She could feel the liquid heat against her skin and smell the pungent aroma of the tea as the steam curled into her nostrils.

"Look at you, Morgan." She forced herself to smile at him over the rim of the cup. "You're a natural with babies. Why haven't you ever married and had a family of your own?"

A shadow crossed his face. "I was married," he said. "We lost a baby before the marriage ended."

"Oh—" She stared at him, wondering how she could have ever thought she knew this taciturn man. There was a lifetime of knowing beyond what she had seen and heard. "I'm sorry," she said. "Truly sorry."

"It was a long time ago." He glanced down at the baby in his arms. "But I'm bringing it up now for a reason. My...wife left a small trunk full of baby things in the storeroom. I've asked Thomas to carry the trunk upstairs. You'll be welcome to take whatever you can use."

"You're sure?" Cassandra's pulse leaped. "Oh, Morgan, won't it make you sad, seeing those little things on another baby?"

His eyes hardened, making her want to bite her tongue. "As I said, it was a long time ago. And nothing in the trunk was ever used, because the baby was stillborn. It's just taking up space, like that cradle you see in the corner. Now stop fussing about it and drink your tea."

Cassandra tipped the cup and took a tentative swallow. Her eyes watered as the bitter liquid burned a scalding path down her throat. At least she hoped it was the tea that had triggered the dampness on her cheeks. This was no time to get emotional, not when her daughter's future was at stake. The fact that she had come to the ranch under false pretenses and lied at every turn, only to be repaid with kindness and generosity, could not be allowed to move her. She had set her course, and there could be no turning back.

Bracing herself against the acrid taste, she downed the rest of the tea in a single gulp. Her face contorted in a grimace.

"That's it, take it like the medicine it is." Morgan's chuckle brightened the room for the space of a breath. "When it comes to doctoring, I'll take Mei Li and her teas over any sawbones in the country. If you're feeling up to it, I'll have Chang make you some breakfast. You've been through a bad time. You need to start getting your strength back."

"I'm starved, thank you." Cassandra set the cup carefully on the tray. She might be a fraud, but at least she could be an appreciative fraud. "You've done so much for me—you, Mei Li, Chang and the boys. I want to make sure everyone knows how grateful I am."

"There'll be time for that." Morgan stirred, glancing restlessly toward the window where the eastern sky was paling to the hue of tarnished silver.

"Time?" Cassandra forced a smile. "Then you're not planning to dump us in the wagon and haul us back to Cheyenne anytime soon?"

She had spoken too boldly. She saw it in the hardening of the lines that framed his mouth. Leaning over

the bed, he placed the drowsing Rachel in her arms.
The crow of a rooster echoed from the yard below.

"The jury's still out on that question, Cassandra,"
he said in a low, taut voice. "And I've got work to
do."

Morgan finished the chores and scrubbed his hands
at the outside pump. The water gushed through his
fingers, clean and cold.

In the three days since the storm, the prairie had
begun to renew itself. Fresh shoots mingled with the
drought-parched grass, painting the landscape a pale
heathered green. Flowers, closed and waiting for water, had exploded in bright drifts of color—golden
buttercups and orange mallows, wild aster, forget-me-
nots and deep blue bird's foot violets. In a week or
so there would be sunflowers and blue-eyed grass.

Morgan stretched a sore muscle in his back. His
gaze followed a flock of cinnamon teal as they glided
in across the morning sky to settle on the reservoir
above the dam. The precious store of water had risen
since the storm. But there was not enough to sustain
the hayfields for the summer. They needed more rain.
Much more.

But it was hard to dwell on such gloomy thoughts
when the sun was rising and the air rang with meadowlark calls and shimmered with the hum of foraging
bees. New life was everywhere, and as he turned back
toward the house, Morgan thought of the new life in
the long-empty nursery upstairs, where tiny Rachel
slumbered in her mother's arms.

The baby, for all her scrawny size, had proved to be as tough as a newborn bobcat. But Cassandra had spent her strength bringing her child into the world. That, coupled with the exhaustion of the long wagon trip and the thorough chilling she'd suffered in the storm, had brought her to the brink of pneumonia. She would never know how many hours he had sat beside her bed, cradling the baby as he watched her fitful sleep. He would never tell her how he had spoon-fed Mei Li's medicinal tea into her mouth and wiped her face with cold cloths to keep down the fever. And she would remain unaware of the blessed relief that had washed over him when he'd learned that the fever had broken and she was awake.

Watching over Cassandra had given him plenty of time to study her daughter. His eyes had scoured every detail of the little puckered face and the incredibly long, clasping hands. The fine reddish curls were an unmistakable gift from her mother. The questioning eyes, their true color obscured by blue-gray baby irises, appeared to be no one's but her own. The cleft chin was remarkably similar to Ryan's, but that in itself proved nothing. A dimpled chin was a common enough feature, especially in babies.

Johnny Chang had returned from Fort Caspar, bringing a fresh pouch of Jacob's prime Virginia tobacco, a few pieces of mail and word that the letter for Hamilton Crawford had made the Cheyenne dispatch that very day. That meant Ham could be reading the letter within the week. Still, even with the best of timing, he couldn't expect a reply from the former

Pinkerton agent anytime soon. A thorough investigation could take weeks, even months.

Meanwhile, he had no choice but to continue the balancing act he'd begun the moment Cassandra Riley's locket had fallen open in his hand: to provide for her and the child yet hold back the measure of acceptance her every look and word demanded. To protect his father from the deception that would break his aging heart. To close his own heart and mind to the womanly sweetness that dangled just out of his reach. Was Cassandra his brother's abandoned lover and the mother of his child, or was she nothing but a common criminal? Either way, to lay so much as a hand on her would be to condemn himself to torment.

As he neared the house he saw that his father had come out onto the porch and was sitting alone in his wheelchair. In the past few days, the old man had become increasingly restless and moody. Morgan had blamed it on the weather, or some subtle change in his health. Then, the day before yesterday, Jacob had asked to see Cassandra's baby.

Weighted by dark premonitions, Morgan had fetched the child from her cradle, carried her downstairs and placed her on his father's lap. The old man had studied the tiny girl for a long moment, balancing her between his gnarled hands. Then he had returned her to Morgan without a word.

Only when she was back in her cradle had Morgan's sense of foreboding lifted. Jacob had been curious, nothing more. After all, there had not been an infant in the house since Ryan was small.

So many years without the sound of a child's laughter. What a long time it had been.

Approaching the porch now, he saw that Jacob was shifting in his chair, his hands pushing the wheels restlessly back and forth. Sensing that the old man might be needing something, Morgan doubled his stride, only to stop short as he caught sight of his father's face.

Jacob's eyes blazed beneath the hoary crags of his eyebrows. His mouth was a grim line of ill-suppressed fury. "You lied to me," he croaked. "Ever since that little redhead got here, you've been lying to me, both of you."

Morgan stared at him. "I don't know what you—"

"Don't play innocent with me, Morgan. You've got some tall explaining to do!" The old man's eyes narrowed to angry slits. "Why didn't you tell me that girl was carrying Ryan's baby?"

Chapter Eight

Morgan willed himself not to flinch under his father's condemning gaze. He had done his best to protect the old man from hurt, but the time for protecting was over. The only course left to him now was brutal honesty.

"You knew that Red was carrying Ryan's baby, didn't you?" Jacob growled. "Hell, I'd bet good money you knew it all along! Why didn't you tell me?"

Morgan weighed his words carefully. "I knew what she claimed. But I wanted proof before I said anything to you. I've asked Ham Crawford to check out her story. Once we've heard from him—"

"Blast it, that could take all summer!" Jacob snapped. "I'm an old man—don't have that kind of time. You want proof? *Here's* your proof!" The sun glinted on a shiny object that lay in the old man's lap. Jacob picked it up and thrust it into Morgan's hands.

Morgan had not seen the small silver-framed tin-type in nearly twenty years, but he recognized it at once. It was a faded portrait of Anna Claire, Jacob's pale and pretty second wife. She was seated in a velvet armchair, cradling her one-month-old son in her arms.

The baby, swathed in a lacy shawl, was Ryan. Morgan clearly recalled the day the photographer had come to the ranch and spent the better part of an afternoon taking pictures of the new mother and her baby. Now, as he studied the forgotten portrait, he knew what his father had wanted him to see. He knew it, even as his eyes resisted looking too closely at the tiny face.

Aside from a difference in the hair, the infant in Anna Claire's arms could have been Cassandra's daughter.

When he glanced up, Jacob was still glaring at him. "I may be a cripple, but that doesn't make me a doddering old fool. You should have respected me enough to tell me the truth."

"The truth?" Morgan forced himself to speak gently. "I don't *know* the truth. What if the woman is lying? What if you accept her child as your granddaughter and then find out you were wrong? You're so anxious to hang on to a piece of Ryan that you're grasping at any straw you can reach!"

He had wounded the old man. Morgan felt a stab of guilt as his father slumped in his chair. But the words had been necessary, he told himself. Better Jacob be hurt now than devastated later. "There's no need to jump to a conclusion," he said. "Give this a few months. We've got plenty of time."

"You've got time, Morgan. I haven't."

The old man's words penetrated like a shaft of ice. Morgan stared at his father, all pretense gone.

"The doctor told me when he was out here this spring," Jacob said in a flat voice. "Not that the news came as any surprise. A man knows when his body's giving out on him."

"How long?" Morgan reined in his emotions, knowing the old man would not welcome a show of grief.

Jacob shrugged. "A few months, maybe. No more. And the end won't be much of a picnic. Not that it matters. I pretty much stopped living when we got word your brother was gone."

"What's all this got to do with Cassandra Riley's baby?" Morgan had already guessed the answer to that question, but he knew where both their emotions would lead if the old man started talking about Ryan. "Why can't you just let things ride until we hear from Ham Crawford? The woman could be a fraud. Even a criminal."

"I know when I'm seeing my own flesh and blood." Jacob's jaw jutted stubbornly. "And as long as I know there's a new generation who'll carry on my line, if not my name—"

He broke off, scowling at Morgan. "Don't look at me like that. It's been damned near six years since Helen left, and I don't see *you* bringin' home any replacement to fill this house with babies. I can't count on you to carry on the Tolliver line, and now that Ryan's gone, that little mite of a baby girl is my best hope. My only hope.''

Morgan stood his ground, feeling as if he'd just been blasted by a sandstorm. Frustration welled up in him, heated by anger and twisted by grief. His fingers tightened on the oval edge of the little portrait. He had loved his stepmother and adored his baby brother, but right now it was all he could do to keep from flinging the silver-framed picture against the stone wall of the house.

He could not lash out at his father, he knew. Jacob was going to need all his patience and understanding in the weeks ahead. But there was someone else, someone whose arrival had turned a family tragedy into chaos.

Crossing the porch, he paused long enough to rest a hand on his father's sharp-boned shoulder. Then, still churning, he mounted the stairs.

Was he wrong about Cassandra? Should he accept her and her child into the family, as Jacob had? Even now, as he crossed the landing and paused outside her door, Morgan did not know what he was going to say to her.

Cassandra sat propped up in the bed nursing her baby. In the past hour she had eaten a hearty breakfast of ham, eggs and flapjacks, washed her face, brushed her teeth and combed the tangles out of her hair. If she rested today, maybe tomorrow she'd feel strong enough to be up and around. She hadn't come to the ranch to be waited on. She wanted to do her share of the work, and the sooner she started the better. Maybe today there would be some mending or darning she could do. She would ask Chang or Mei Li the next time one of them came to her room.

Snuggling into the downy pillows, she filled her gaze with the sight of Rachel's little flower face at her breast. Her eyes traced the doll-sized features— the crown of red-gold fuzz that seemed to blaze where it caught the morning sunlight; the wide, pure eyes and button nose; the puckered mouth, locked with such amazing strength around her nipple. So new and perfect. So hungry for life.

Love swept through Cassandra's soul with the force of a tidal wave. "You're mine, Rachel," she whispered. "And I promise I'll take care of you. As long as I have the strength to breathe, you'll never want for anything. Good food, a safe roof over your head, pretty dresses and ribbons in your hair, a fine education if that's what you choose. I'll do anything for you, little one. Anything."

She glanced up at the sound of a sharp knock on the door. That would be Chang or one of his boys bringing up the chest of baby clothes Morgan had so generously offered her. She mustn't forget to thank him, Cassandra reminded herself as she tugged the quilt over her shoulder, covering the baby and her exposed breast. "Come in!" she called.

She heard the click of the latch. Then the door swung open and Morgan stepped across the threshold.

It was as if a winter blizzard had blown into the room.

Startled by his icy gaze, Cassandra yanked the quilt up to her chin. An hour ago he had been friendly, almost warm. What could have changed?

"All right," she said, taking the offensive. "What have I done now, Morgan Tolliver? It must have been something terrible, to bring you storming in here like a—"

"Be still and listen," he growled. "I'm not in a patient mood."

"Just because you're out of sorts, that's no excuse to bark at me!" Cassandra snapped. "Why don't you turn around, go out that door and come back in like a gentleman? Maybe then I'll be more willing to hear you out."

"Cassandra."

Something in his voice, a thread of anguish that seemed too deep for words, stopped her tirade cold. Startled into silence, she stared at him.

"You've won," he said quietly. "You have everything you wanted."

Only then did Cassandra notice the small silver-framed picture in his hand. Moving deliberately, he laid it beside her on the quilt, where the soft morning light could fall across the photograph of the pale mother and her beautiful child. "Yesterday while you were still sleeping my father asked to see Rachel," he said. "Today he showed me this."

Cassandra gazed down at it, her throat tightening.

"Why, it's Rachel," she whispered. "At least, it almost could be, except for the blond curls."

"It's Ryan," Morgan said quietly. "Ryan and his mother."

"She's—she was a beautiful woman." Cassandra groped for words. "But you said I'd won. What did you mean?"

"He's dying," Morgan said softly. "That crusty old mountain man. He wants to believe that Rachel is his granddaughter. Under the circumstances, I have no choice except to let him."

"Morgan!" Cassandra clutched her baby beneath the quilt, her heart pounding.

Bitterness lay like a shadow across his stony features. "As I said, you've won, Cassandra. Congratulations."

She studied his grim face. "You don't believe me, do you? You never have."

He sighed. "It doesn't matter whether I believe you or not. We're in this conspiracy together now. And all I can say is, if you're lying you'd better do a damned good job of it. The old man doesn't have much time left, and I don't want him hurt."

"Neither do I." Cassandra knew there was more she should do—protest, weep, swear that Ryan had fathered her child. But she knew there would be no heart in it. She was trapped. Morgan was trapped. There was nothing to do but make the best of a bad situation.

Rachel had let go of the nipple and began to fuss, kicking at the quilt, threatening to push it off her mother's shoulder. Flushed and agitated, Cassandra struggled to hold it in place. Morgan averted his eyes, staring at the window as she maneuvered the baby out into the light and fumbled to close the front of her nightgown. By now Rachel was squalling. Cassandra gathered her up against her shoulder, rubbing her back until the crying ended in a lusty little belch.

"What about your ex-Pinkerton friend?" she asked on impulse. "There's no use pursuing that now, is there?"

"The letter's been sent, along with his fee. I won't stop Ham from doing his job, but as long as my father's alive, I'll keep the report to myself."

"And after he's gone?" Cassandra held her breath, wishing she'd bitten her tongue. Why did she so often seem to set her own traps and then walk right into them?

Morgan's eyes narrowed. "After that, all bets are off. If I find out you've played us false, we go back to our original agreement and you go to jail for fraud."

"And what if I haven't played you false? Or what if there's no proof either way?"

In the silence that followed her question, Cassandra could hear the baby sucking on the collar of her nightgown. She held her breath, her heart slamming her ribs as Morgan pondered the question.

His shoulders sagged as he exhaled. "No promises. We'll cross that bridge when we come to it. Meanwhile…"

"Yes, I know. We act as if nothing's wrong. Don't

worry, Morgan, I'll be on my best behavior. I won't
let you down.''

"No, you won't. You won't dare.'' He turned away
from the bed. ''I'll have Thomas find those baby
clothes and bring them up.'' He moved toward the
door.

"Morgan?''

He turned, a preoccupied scowl on his face.

"What do you really think of me?''

His eyes narrowed. ''You're sure you want to
know?''

"Yes. I need to know what I'm dealing with here.
Do you hate me so much?''

He sighed wearily. ''No one could hate you, Cassandra. But I don't trust you. You're like a feisty little
female bobcat with a newborn cub. You'll do anything—scratch, bite, steal, cheat and lie—to see that
your cub is provided for, and heaven help anyone who
gets in your way.''

"Is that so wrong?'' Writhing inside, she seized
the silver-framed portrait with her free hand and
thrust it toward him. ''Look at that little face! How
can you deny what you see? And how can you deny
what I've told you?''

Morgan took the portrait from her hand without
looking at it. Emotions warred in his obsidian eyes,
and she knew he was remembering what she'd said
about the scar on Ryan's leg and how he'd come by
it.

Cassandra studied the play of sunlight on his
craggy face, thinking of the burdens this man bore—

a lost brother, a dying father and a pushy, insensitive young woman who'd come out of nowhere to assert her claim on his family.

No one could hate you, Cassandra.

The words mocked her guilty heart. Dear heaven, how could he *not* hate her? It was all she could do to keep from hating herself.

Morgan tucked the picture under his arm as if to conceal it from his own view. "The truth—whatever it is—doesn't matter right now," he said. "I just want the time my father has left to be as peaceful and pleasant as I can make it. Meanwhile, you'll have everything you came for." Turning, he took a few more strides toward the door, then paused again.

"If the only clothes you own are the rags in that carpetbag, you'll need something to wear. Helen—my wife—left a trunk full of dresses she didn't want. They're a few years out of style, and she was taller than you are, but if you're a good hand with a needle…" He trailed off, letting the implications hang.

"You're sure?" Cassandra felt her heart leap. She'd had more urgent things on her mind than what she was going to wear once the baby came, but it had been such a long time since she'd had new clothes. Even the thought of making over someone else's hand-me-downs filled her with elation. "You won't mind?" she asked him.

"Mind?" He raised a bemused eyebrow. "Why should I mind?"

"Seeing me in *her* clothes? Was she beautiful, Morgan?"

He laughed harshly. ''You sound as if you were talking about a dead saint! Last time I heard, Helen was alive and well, living in Paris with her second husband! I'd have given her clothes away a long time ago if I'd remembered they were there. Take them with my blessing and put them to good use!''

''Thank you,'' Cassandra said, but she spoke to his back. In the next instant he had crossed the threshold and closed the door firmly behind him.

For a long moment she sat staring after him, pride and gratitude clashing inside her. What an infuriating man he was—challenging and surprising her at every turn, then walking away, leaving her a quivering wreck.

What had his wife been like? His *wife*—strange, the sting of the word when she thought of it. Almost as if she were jealous. But that was impossible. She and Morgan were enemies, united under a truce that was as fragile as an old man's body. Once Jacob was gone…as Morgan had said, all bets would be off. He was capable of throwing her and Rachel back into the world without a penny, or even sending her to jail, as he'd threatened to do.

She shuddered as the memory flashed through her mind—the darkened shack, the smell of rotgut whiskey, and Seamus Hawkins sprawled motionless on the floor. She hadn't meant to kill him, but no one else knew that. Even now, the lawmen could be looking for her. And if the ex-Pinkerton agent was sharp enough to find her trail, they would know exactly where to come.

If the worst happened, her one consolation would be the hope that Rachel would have a secure home here on the ranch. Ultimately, the key to that hope would be Morgan.

But for now Cassandra resettled the drowsing Rachel in her arms and snuggled back into the plump feather pillows. As Morgan had said, she had everything she'd come for—safety, comfort and the generosity of good people.

She thought of Chang and the gentle Mei Li, of gruff old Jacob who had accepted a stranger's child as his granddaughter. And Morgan. For all his declared distrust of her, Morgan had treated her with nothing but kindness.

She had deceived them all. And now she was trapped in a web of her own making. She could not leave. She could not tell the truth. She could only make the best of the debacle she'd created.

Bloom where you're planted. That's what her grandmother, that other Rachel, would have said. Now she, Cassandra Riley, had planted herself on this ranch in the middle of nowhere, with two stubborn, irascible men and their family of Chinese servants. Could she bloom here? Could she find a way to bless the lives of the people who had taken her in and treated her so kindly?

She had to try, but no, that wasn't enough. She had to succeed. Maybe then she would find a modicum of forgiveness for the terrible thing she had done.

The baby girl stirred in Cassandra's arms, her long fingers plucking the air as if she'd been an accomplished harpist in heaven. Her cloud-gray eyes opened wide, taking in the whitewashed ceiling, the morning sunlight and her mother's rapt face.

Jake Logan's daughter.

Cassandra brushed her lips across the rose-gold fluff of baby hair, her heart constricting as the ultimate truth struck home.

To secure her child's future, she would lie to the Tollivers. She would lie to the Changs. If need be, she would lie to the whole blessed Wyoming territory.

But what was she going to tell Rachel?

The midsummer twilight was cool after the long, hot day. The tall front windows, screened against the buzzing mosquitoes, had been flung open to welcome the evening breeze and the chirps of awakening crickets. Lamps had been trimmed and lit, transforming the cozy parlor into a glowing oasis of light.

Morgan sat in a leather-covered armchair, reading beneath the overhead lamp. At least he was pretending to read. In truth, if someone had asked him the title of the book in his hands, it would have taken moments of fumbling to bring it to mind.

Across the room, Cassandra curled against the arm of the matching settee, stitching a baby dress from the remnants of one of Helen's made-over gowns. The dress Cassandra was sewing matched the one she was wearing—an airy but practical creation in deep sage-green sprinkled with tiny embroidered flowers. Her hair was caught back in a crocheted snood, with a few mischievous tendrils escaping to fall around her face.

From time to time she paused to glance down at her baby, who slumbered in the laundry basket that had become her downstairs cradle. At such moments Cassandra's face took on a radiance that transformed her small, sharp features to heart-stopping beauty. Once, in Saint Louis, Morgan had seen a very old painting of the Madonna and child. The artist had been a master of color, suffusing the figures of the mother and infant with rich amber light. Now, bathed in the glow of the lamp, Cassandra and little Rachel possessed that same golden aura. Together they made a lovely picture.

If only he could frame them like that, Morgan thought. Frame them and hang them on the wall where they could do no harm.

He lowered his gaze to the book, not wanting her to glance up and discover him watching her. In the three weeks since her tumultuous arrival, it amazed him how she had settled in to life on the ranch, but then, ''settled'' was hardly a word that could be applied to Cassandra Riley. The woman possessed the restless energy of a small, darting hummingbird, along with a natural gift for meddling where she wasn't welcome.

Not that she didn't mean well. But there were some things a man simply didn't need—like the little bouquet of dewy-fresh wildflowers that appeared in a crock on the breakfast table every morning, or the crisp gingham curtains that now adorned the front and side windows of the house's upper story. She had even hung them in his own bedroom, insisting that all the windows should match. Only Ryan's room, which was on the back side of the house, had been spared.

And then there was Chang. That morning the cook had taken Morgan aside and begged him most humbly to find the missy some occupation that would take her out of his kitchen. Yes, he realized the missy was only trying to help, but the kitchen had been his domain for all his years at the ranch. Not even Mei Li, who prepared Chinese-style meals in her own small home, was allowed to cook in the place where her husband reigned supreme.

And there had been more. Even more irritating than Cassandra's intrusions into the kitchen were her efforts to teach Mei Li to read and write English! Again, Chang emphasized, he knew the missy meant to be helpful. But he preferred his wife as she was—Chinese! If he had wanted an American-style woman, he would have married one!

Finally Chang had taken a stand. He liked the missy, oh, yes indeed, she was a fine young woman. But if she was not made to stop interfering with his work and his home life, he would take his family and the money they'd saved and go back to China, where they could live in peace!

Morgan turned the page in his book, bracing himself for a confrontation. Tonight he would have to speak to Cassandra about the matter, and he knew she would not take kindly to what he had to say. She had more than her share of pride, coupled with a stubborn streak to match his own. Given the choice, he'd rather tangle with a cornered wildcat.

But there was no use putting it off. With a sigh of resignation, Morgan closed the book and placed it on a side table. Then, pushing himself out of the armchair, he rose to his feet.

"Cassandra, I've something to—"

"There you are, Red!" Jacob's chair thumped lightly as the wheels passed over the threshold and carried him into the parlor. "As long as her highness is asleep, what d'you say to five-card stud? And this time I'm not letting you beat me!"

Cassandra grinned impishly at him. "You didn't *let* me beat you, you old fox! I won fair and square!"

"We'll see about that. Are you game?" The old man's eyes danced as he flashed the deck of cards in his lap.

"Game. As long as Rachel doesn't wake up. Come on, I'll get the chips. Want to play, Morgan?"

"Not tonight." Morgan thrust his hands into his pockets. "You two go ahead. I've got a mare out in the barn who's due to foal, and I'll be needing to check on her."

"You could still play with us," she cajoled, but Morgan shook his head.

"My mind wouldn't be on the game. I've got some thinking to do."

"Hell, you think too much." Jacob followed Cassandra's swishing skirts into the dining room.

''Thinking's bad for a man. Rots his brains. Come on, Red, you can deal this time!''

''Sure you can trust me?''

''Hell, no! That's half the fun of it!''

Their banter faded as Morgan abandoned all pretense of reading and wandered out onto the front porch. For all Cassandra's meddling ways, he blessed what her presence had done for his father. They seemed kindred souls, she and Jacob—two naughty children, each as irreverent and outrageous as the other. And the old man doted on little Rachel. He had spent hours cradling her in his arms, watching her tiny, sleeping face with a tenderness that Morgan had not seen since Ryan was a baby.

Taking his time, he lit a lantern and carried it out to the barn. He found the mare drowsing in her stall, showing no sign that she might be in labor. Morgan checked her carefully, stroked her side and walked back to the house.

Extinguishing the light, he settled himself on the top step and gazed toward the mountains, where the evening stars hung in the indigo twilight. Strange how alone he'd felt since Cassandra and Jacob had formed their alliance, as if he were watching them from a distance, like a stranger-child, wanting to join their play but not knowing how to approach them.

Was he jealous of the old man? The very idea darkened Morgan's spirits. There was nothing unseemly between the two, he was certain. And he welcomed the spark that Cassandra and the baby had brought back to his father's eyes. But he envied their laughter, their easy camaraderie. Seeing them together only underscored how alone he was.

Not since his boyhood years with the Shoshone had he felt a sense of belonging. Even after his mother and his grandfather had died, Morgan would have been content to spend the rest of his life on the Wind River Reservation as Washakie's adopted son.

But then Jacob had returned to drag him into the white world—to cut off his hair, dress him in the confining clothes of a white boy and force him to speak only English. The day his father had taken away the medicine pouch containing his grandfather's sacred sage, Morgan had run away. Jacob had tracked his son down in a spring blizzard and brought him home, wrapped in his own thick sheepskin coat.

The battle of wills had continued for months. Only when Jacob had returned the medicine pouch and agreed to take him back to the reservation for yearly visits had life settled into a truce.

It had taken the gentle, cultured Anna Claire, Jacob's second wife, to bring father and son together. Ryan's birth, a year into the marriage, had made them a true family. Now Anna Claire was gone. Ryan was gone. And soon Jacob would be gone as well.

Morgan's fingertips brushed the slight bulge of the medicine pouch that hung beneath his shirt. He still made visits to the Wind River Reservation and always received a warm welcome from Washakie and his boyhood friends. But the place would never be home to him again. He had lived too long in the white man's world.

The twilight deepened around him, punctuated by the slap of cards on the dining room table and the silvery peal of Cassandra's laughter through the open window—Cassandra, who had blown into his life like a red-haired whirlwind, upsetting everything in her path. There was no hiding from her. No refuge where her face could not invade his thoughts.

He had even begun to dream about her—warm, sweet, achingly sensual dreams in which she lay beside him in the warm darkness, nestling spoon-style along the curve of his body, his hand cupping one milk-heavy breast, his groin stirring against the pressure of her silky little buttocks. In last night's dream, she had turned in his arms and kissed him. Her hands had raked his hair as her hot, ripe mouth opened like a flower beneath his own. Her darting tongue had teased and tormented him, challenging him to take what he wanted. Morgan had moaned in his sleep as he pulled her beneath him. Her cry of welcoming pleasure had quivered in his ears as he mounted and pushed his swollen erection into the warm, wet sweetness of her body. Her legs had wrapped around his hips, pulling him deeper as she met his urgent thrusts…

The memory of the dream was mercifully shattered by the sounds of a team and wagon approaching in the darkness. Morgan recognized the familiar jingle of harness, the creak of the loaded wagon and the sound of Johnny Chang's voice as he pulled the team to a halt outside the barn.

Catching the lantern from its hook above the porch, Morgan struck a match to the wick. He hadn't expected Johnny to return from buying supplies at the fort until sometime tomorrow. Was he bringing news about Ryan?

Morgan's fingers tightened around the lantern's wire handle as he strode across the yard to open the barn door.

By the time he reached the wagon Johnny had vaulted to the ground to unhitch the team. Johnny's big, silent, shaggy dog, who never barked, rose from the wagon bed, stretching and yawning.

"Everything all right?" Morgan asked, trying not to sound anxious.

"Fine." Johnny Chang was even shorter than his father, all sinew and lightning-quick nerves. Unlike his elder brother, Johnny had long since cut off his Chinese queue. He wore a Stetson and a plaid shirt, and his terse English bore only the slightest accent.

"Any news?" Morgan asked.

The young man shrugged, reached into his shirt pocket and pulled out two crumpled envelopes. He could not have known what they contained, but he had driven hard to get them back to the ranch tonight.

Morgan hung the lantern on a hook outside the barn, took the letters and held them to the light. One was addressed to Jacob and bore the return address of a Nebraska congressman who had once stayed at the ranch on a hunting trip. Condolences, perhaps, for Ryan's loss.

The second envelope was addressed to Morgan. He stared at it, his heart suddenly pounding as he recognized distinctive, slanting script.

The letter was from Hamilton Crawford.

Chapter Nine

As Morgan mounted the front porch, he could hear the echoing sounds of laughter—Cassandra's breathy peals punctuated by Jacob's hoarse bellow. He had not heard his father laugh like that since the last time Ryan was home.

Hamilton Crawford's letter, stuffed into the shirt pocket beneath his vest, seemed to burn through the fabric and into his flesh. He had promised he would keep Ham's findings to himself, whatever they might be. But what if the ex-Pinkerton agent had discovered something truly damaging? What if Cassandra Riley had turned out to be a criminal or, even more likely, a prostitute? Could he carry on this masquerade for the duration of his father's life? Could he even bear to look at her, knowing what she was?

The laughter ceased abruptly as Morgan walked into the dining room. Jacob and Cassandra had frozen in midmotion and were staring at his face.

"What is it, son?" Jacob asked, the cards quivering in his gnarled fingers.

Morgan forced an uneasy laugh. "Sorry, I didn't mean to look so grim. Johnny's back from Fort Caspar, that's all. I was hoping he might have some news for us, but he had nothing to report—only this letter for you, from Elliot Hainesworth."

Morgan held out the letter, but Jacob made no move to take it from him. "You read it to me," he said. "I don't have my glasses handy."

In truth, Jacob's glasses rarely left his dresser drawer. He was not illiterate, but the old mountain man read so poorly that he seldom made the effort. Morgan broke the seal on the envelope, unfolded the single page and began to read.

"First of all, old friend, allow me to extend my condolences to your family. I remember Ryan well from my visit to your ranch three years ago. Such a well-favored young man. His loss will be keenly felt by all who knew him."

Morgan glanced up from the letter in time to catch the glimmer of emotion in his father's eyes. "Go on," the old man said stoically.

"In light of your recent tragedy I hesitate to ask this favor. But remembering your gracious hospitality in the past, I wanted, at least, to give you, a chance to refuse my request. Senator Maxwell Call, General Sam Phillips and myself have been asked to represent the U.S. Government in some land negotiations with the Blackfoot Indians.

Since your ranch lies along our travel route, we were hoping to stop by for a day of hunting.''

Morgan glanced up again. ''There's more,'' he said.

''The congressman and his colleagues will be coming the first week in July. If you're not up to having them here, they'll understand and make other plans. You can send a reply to Fort Caspar, and they'll pick it up when they get there.''

Jacob did not reply. He appeared to be pondering the congressman's question. Morgan felt his protective instincts surge. The old man was too frail for visitors. The strain could prove too much for him.

''I can write the letter for you,'' Morgan offered. ''If we explain that it's only been a few months since Ryan's disappearance and we're not yet ready to—''

''Hell, no!'' Jacob exploded. ''This place could use some good livening up. It's been way too long since we had ourselves a real party on the place, with a barbecue and fiddlers and all the neighbors over. Havin' three government bigwigs here is as good an excuse as any. Right, Red?'' His gaze swung toward Cassandra.

''Are you sure you want to do this?'' To her credit, she looked concerned.

''Damned right I do. But we can't have a party

without a woman's touch,'' Jacob said. ''Will you be my hostess?''

Morgan saw her hesitate, then she gave the old man an affectionate smile. ''It would be an honor. First thing tomorrow, we'll start with the guest list, so we can get the invitations sent out. Then I'll talk to Chang about the food, and—''

A wail from the parlor interrupted her words. Instantly Cassandra was out of her chair, skirts flying behind her as she hurried through the open door that connected the two rooms. She returned a moment later with Rachel gathered against her shoulder. The baby was fussing hungrily, her little rosebud mouth chomping at her mother's lace collar.

''Supper time,'' Cassandra said. ''Game's over. I forfeit—unless you want to take over for me, Morgan. In any case, you two will have to continue this conversation without me.''

''Forfeit, my aunt Minnie!'' Jacob grumbled. ''I was holding three queens! I could've beaten you fair and square!''

''You'll get your chance. Tomorrow's another day—and another game.'' She flashed him an impish smile as she swept toward the stairs.

The room seemed far too silent after she had gone. Morgan sank into a chair across from his father, hoping the old man wouldn't ask him to take up the card game. He had no spirit for it tonight.

''Quite a woman,'' Jacob remarked, gazing toward the stairs where Cassandra had disappeared with the baby. "If I were your age, I'd find more interesting things to do than play poker with her."

"She's taken you in," Morgan said.

"Uh-huh. And I'm enjoying every minute of it." Jacob gathered up the loose cards and tapped the deck on the table to even the edges. "Too bad you're not enjoying her more yourself. That little baby needs a papa. And you could use a spunky young wife."

Morgan thought of the letter in his pocket and the promise he had made. "If what you believe is true, she's Ryan's woman, not mine. What if he comes back?"

"What if he doesn't?" Jacob asked sharply. "It's been almost three months. Nobody loves Ryan more than I do. But I've buried enough people to know that, when the worst happens, all you can do is take up whatever's left behind and go on."

"And if she's lying to us? If the baby isn't Ryan's?"

"Hell's bells, have you still got that bone stuck in your craw? All right, suppose she *is* lying. You marry the woman and sire a passel of boys to take over the ranch, and it won't matter whether her little girl's a real Tolliver or not!"

Morgan studied his father, seeing the fear in the old man's eyes, sensing his hunger to know that when he passed on some part of him would continue. That hunger had driven Jacob to believe Cassandra's story and accept her child as his granddaughter. But he wanted more. He wanted grandsons with his name and the indisputable stamp of his blood.

This was a time for patience, Morgan reminded himself.

"It's an interesting idea," he said guardedly. "But it takes two people to marry, and I don't think Cassandra fancies me, or even likes me. I'm too grim and stodgy for her taste. And probably too old."

Jacob chuckled. "If you believe that crock, then you haven't seen the way Red looks at you when you're not watching. Every time you walk into the room, it's as if a candle's been lit inside her. I haven't lived this long for nothing. I know the signs when a woman's interested."

"You're imagining things, old man," Morgan chided him gently. "You're seeing what you want to see. Cassandra Riley's not my kind of woman, and I'm not her kind of man, so put it to rest."

Jacob coughed and spat into the brass cuspidor he kept under the edge of the table. "Won't be too long afore I put everything to rest. Meanwhile I'm planning to kick up my heels and have myself a good time. And if you weren't such a damned stubborn fool, you'd do the same. Life is too short, and the grave's a cold, dark place. No sense buryin' yourself while there's a spark of life in your body."

Morgan reached out and laid a hand on the bony arm, thinking how unfair it was that Jacob and Ryan, with their roaring appetites for life, should be taken while he, who cared little either way, seemed destined for a long earthly existence. He would miss his father when the old mountain man was gone.

The appearance of Thomas Chang in the doorway

rescued Morgan from a flood of emotion. The elder son of the family was taller and more powerfully built than Johnny. His Chinese-style tunic and trousers matched the ones his father wore, as did the long queue that hung down his back. He spoke little and moved as silently as a shadow.

''Bedtime already, Thomas?'' Jacob glanced up as the young man slipped into the room. ''All right, let's get it over with.''

Thomas nodded a quiet greeting to Morgan as he positioned himself behind the wheelchair. He had spent years taking care of the old man and was genuinely devoted to him. What would Thomas do when Jacob was gone? He was such a gentle soul, so innocent and harmless. If he were to leave the ranch, the outside world would wound him at every turn.

So many things to think about.

Morgan rose from his chair, gathered up the cards and poker chips from the table and replaced them on the parlor shelf. Then he blew out the lamp and, surrounded by familiar darkness, made his way up the stairs.

The faint light of a candle flickered beneath Cassandra's door. As Morgan reached the landing, he could hear her crooning a soft, tender lullaby to her baby. He paused to listen, his mind conjuring images of what lay beyond the forbidden door. He pictured her nestled in the rocker, clad in her shift, the baby in her arms, perhaps at her breast. He imagined her dark red hair falling in a luminous cascade over her shoulders, her skin reflecting pale gold in the candle-light.

Marry her?

What a joke, Morgan thought. He and Cassandra were as poorly matched as a bull elk and a she-lynx. Aside from the fragile bond that had formed when he'd brought her baby into the world, they had nothing in common. Nothing at all.

The hell of it was, if he pursued the woman, there was a good chance she might accept him. But it would be for all the wrong reasons. Cassandra Riley needed a father for her baby. She needed a home and the security that being Mrs. Morgan Tolliver would bring. But she didn't need *him.* And she certainly didn't love him—not any more than he loved her!

The lullaby floated through the thick planks of the door, teasing his senses and tickling his imagination. Cassandra's husky little voice was untrained and slightly off-key, like the purr of a contented kitten. As its tenderness drifted into the dark recesses of his soul, Morgan found himself wondering how far she would go to provide for her child's future, as well as her own. What if he were to meet her unspoken terms, to offer her everything she wanted? Would having Cassandra—in his arms and in his bed—be worth the price of living without her love?

Morgan gazed at the door for the space of a long breath. Then, turning away, he drew Hamilton Crawford's letter from his pocket and walked softly down the corridor to his own room. The envelope was light, containing no more than a page or two, Morgan calculated. But then, Ham had never been one to waste words.

The gingham curtains Cassandra had sewn and hung fluttered in the night breeze as Morgan hesitated beside the narrow secretary desk, the letter in his hand.

What would he learn when he read it? That she was telling the truth? Morgan shook his head. It was far more likely that she was lying through her saucy little teeth. But right now, it didn't make a dime's worth of difference. Jacob needed her. He needed the hope that her baby had given him.

And he, Morgan, had become part of her game. He was trapped in the deception, just as Cassandra was, and his ongoing doubt served to make him a more convincing player. As long as he did not know the truth, he would not be forced to lie.

While the old man lived, the masquerade would have to go on. Afterward…yes, there would be plenty of time to open the letter and deal with what it contained. If Cassandra was truly the mother of Ryan's child, she and little Rachel would have a home here for the rest of their lives. If not…

For a long moment Morgan stared out the window at the rising moon. Then, turning, he slipped the sealed envelope into a desk drawer and closed it out of sight.

Rachel had awakened before dawn only to settle back into warm slumber after her first feeding of the day. Too restless to stay in bed, Cassandra had splashed her face with water, finger-combed her hair and pulled on a plain cotton dress. Her slippered feet made scarcely a sound as she stole out onto the landing and pattered down the stairs.

She loved the peace of early mornings when no one, not even Morgan, was up and about. She loved the sight of the last stars fading above the Big Horns and the first glimmer of dawn above the long sweep of the prairie. She loved the tranquility of the animals in these early hours, the easy shift and sigh of horses dozing in the corral, the dewy warmth of her old mule's coat when she reached up to scratch him between the ears.

Thinking of Xavier now, she stole into the shadowy kitchen and, ducking beneath a rack of hanging pots, snatched a ripe Jonathan apple from its basket on the counter. Clutching the prize in her hand, she tiptoed out of the back door and closed it softly behind her.

She had been careful not to disturb anything. Chang was very protective of his kitchen—she had discovered that the last time she'd invaded his territory and met with a wall of resistance. She would not be so pushy in the future, she resolved. But she was not about to abandon the idea of teaching Mei Li to read and write. This was America, not China, and Mei Li was an intelligent woman. She had the right to learn.

As Cassandra walked out into the yard, a roosting magpie took wing from the peak of the shed and flapped off into the dawn. The sky was a deep, glowing indigo, the moon a pale wraith above the rugged silhouette of the mountains. She turned slowly in place, taking in the full panorama of earth and sky and the house that seemed part of the land. *Please.* Her lips moved in silent prayer. *Please let us stay here forever…*

But what was she thinking? She had come to this ranch under an ugly cloud of deception. As a liar, she had no right to ask anything of heaven. She was alone in this scheme, with her future, and Rachel's, resting on her ability to maintain the falsehood.

Throwing off the darkness that had settled over her spirit, she wheeled and raced across the yard to the corral. Climbing onto the bottom rail of the fence, she gave a low whistle. The elderly mule in the far corner pricked up his ears and ambled over to greet her.

"Hello, there, boy," she whispered, stroking the wise old face. "Here, I've got something for you." She held out the apple on the flat of her hand. Xavier snatched it up in a single bite. His eyes closed with pleasure as the juice dribbled down his bewhiskered chin.

"You're happy here, too, aren't you?" Cassandra whispered into one rabbity ear. "Good thing I bought you from that run-down freight hauler, or you'd probably be buzzard food by now."

Xavier's massive head nodded vigorously, knocking Cassandra back from the fence. Laughing, she caught her balance, blew him a kiss and turned back toward the house.

Only then did she notice the faint glow of light coming from the crack beneath the barn door. And only then did she remember the mare that Morgan had mentioned was due to foal. Could something have gone wrong? Impulsively, Cassandra spun in her tracks and sprinted toward the barn.

The barn door was unbolted, the well-oiled hinges silent as Cassandra opened it far enough to slip into the barn's warm darkness. Surrounded by the rich aromas of hay and animals, she walked softly toward the glow that emanated from the roomy birthing stall at the barn's far end.

The lantern hung from a low cross beam, casting a pool of golden light onto the floor of the barn. Approaching from the shadows, Cassandra could see into the open stall. She paused in the darkness, transfixed by what she saw.

Stripped to the waist, Morgan knelt in the straw beside the newborn foal. His body gleamed with moisture, skin catching the light like burnished copper. The beaded medicine pouch dangled from its leather thong as he bent over the small, dark form in the straw, stroking it, chanting to it in a low, mystical voice.

The mare lay an arm's length away, alive but clearly exhausted. She struggled to raise her head, nickering softly as Morgan worked with her baby. Cassandra watched them from the darkness, holding her breath.

Suddenly a quiver went through the small wet body. The foal began to thrash. Morgan sat back on his heels, watching but not helping, still chanting softly under his breath. The mare, too, nickered her encouragement as the little creature gathered its legs beneath its body and lurched to its feet. For the space of a breath it staggered on spindly legs. Then it took a step, its nose and ears twitching.

"Oh," Cassandra gasped, unable to keep still. "He's beautiful!"

Morgan glanced up at her with calm, black eyes. "*She's* beautiful. She's a filly."

Cassandra took a tentative step forward. "May I touch her?"

He nodded, steadying the little creature as Cassandra edged forward and sank to her knees in the straw. His hands were long and beautiful against the foal's dark coat.

"Do you make a habit of this?" she asked softly.

"Of what?"

"Performing miracles—like this one, and the one you performed for me and Rachel."

"Life is the miracle. The mare was having a hard time. I had the luck to be here, that's all. The same as I did with you." His fingertips lifted her hand to the arch of the foal's neck. "Softly now. Don't startle her."

Beneath her palm, the brown coat was like coarse, damp velvet. As Cassandra stroked the little creature, her furtive gaze traced the outline of Morgan's craggy profile in the lamplight. How gentle he was beneath his gruff exterior, perhaps the gentlest man she had ever known. In his own quiet way he took care of everyone and everything on the ranch. He had even taken care of her, she realized, from the moment he'd ridden out to confront her and she'd tumbled out of the wagon into his arms.

"I'm going to need your help," he said, rising. "Hang on to the little one and keep her on the far side of the stall while I get the mother on her feet."

She nodded her understanding. The mare, weak as she was, would have to stand in order to nurse her baby. Wrapping her arms around the foal, Cassandra eased the quivering body into the corner of the stall. The filly struggled against her, already showing a will of its own.

"Spunky little thing," Cassandra said.

"She was bred for spunk. Just like her mother." Morgan crouched beside the mare, murmuring softly in Shoshone. The mare rolled her eyes, showing the whites as she struggled to raise her elegant head.

"That's it." Morgan moved behind the tired animal, nudging, and coaxing. Lamplight rippled over the muscles of his lithe, sinewy body. Here and there pale scars glinted against the coppery surface of his skin. One ran like a jagged streak of lightning from his collarbone to the back of his shoulder. Another formed parallel streaks along his ribs, like the slash of some great paw. And there were more scars, smaller ones, scattered like constellations against a bronze sky. Cassandra found herself wanting to know the story behind each and every one of them.

The mare was responding to Morgan's efforts. Her head was up now and she was straining to stand. Morgan strained with her, throwing his weight against her massive bulk, more as a means of encouragement than of force. Cassandra cradled the wriggling foal against her body. A little cry escaped her lips as the mare gave a sudden lurch and scrambled to her feet.

Morgan stroked and soothed the trembling mare until her agitated breathing slowed. Then he glanced toward Cassandra and nodded.

Cassandra released the foal. It tottered toward its mother on its long, spindly legs. The mare nuzzled her baby, snorting as her nostrils drew in its scent. Instinctively the foal found its way between the mare's legs and butted for the teat. Its little bottle-brush tail wagged furiously as it began to suck. The mare heaved a deep sigh and settled down to munching hay.

Morgan sank into the straw next to Cassandra, his back against the side of the stall. He looked as if he had been here for hours. His body was damp with perspiration, his eyes sunk into tired shadows that spoke of little sleep. But contentment lay in the relaxed lines of his face and the easy posture of his body.

"Will they be all right now?" She gazed at the mare and foal, yearning to hold on to the quiet peace that had settled over the morning.

Morgan nodded. "I'll watch them for a while to make sure. It was touch and go for a while, but I'd say the little one's off to a good start."

He closed his eyes, resting briefly. Cassandra found herself wanting to reach up and brush back the tangle of straight black hair that had fallen over his forehead, then to slip her hands downward and massage the weariness from the muscles at the back of his neck. She imagined the feel of his fine golden skin beneath her hands, the tautness of cord and sinew, the subtle beating of his pulse beneath her fingertips. She ached to touch him, but it was a touch he would not welcome, she reminded herself. Morgan would see it as a calculated move to win him, or even to seduce him. He did not trust her. He did not even like her.

Besides, she was Ryan's woman, allegedly in mourning for the father of her child. That was just one more mask she would have to wear. The most foolish thing she could do right now would be to let herself fall in love with another man.

Fall in love?

Merciful heaven, was that what she was doing?

The stillness in the barn was broken only by the twitter of sparrows in the eaves and the soft sucking sound of the hungry little foal.

Morgan cleared his throat in the stillness. "I've been meaning to talk to you about something," he said.

Cassandra's pulse leaped, only to settle back into its normal rhythm as he added, "It's about Chang."

She sighed, picking a bit of straw from her skirt. "I had a feeling this would come up," she said. "He doesn't like me messing with his kitchen, does he?"

Morgan gazed at a beam of awakening sunlight that fell through a needle-thin crack in the wall. "Chang likes you," he said. "But he's a proud man. The kitchen is his territory, and he doesn't like anyone interfering with his work, not even someone who's only trying to help.''

''I gathered as much,'' Cassandra said, trying to sound as if she didn't care. ''Did he complain about my interfering with his wife, too?''

''About your teaching Mei Li to read?'' A wry smile tugged at one corner of his mouth. ''Yes. He's threatening to take his family and go back to China if you don't cease and desist.''

''Even if Mei Li wants to learn? She does, you know, and I want to teach her. She was so good to me after Rachel was born, it's the one thing I can do to repay her. Besides, her husband and sons can read English. Why shouldn't she have the same right to—''

''Are you always this pushy, Cassandra Riley?'' He was gazing at her with a bemused expression on his face.

''Pushy!'' She scowled at him. ''Is that what you call standing up for what's right and fair?''

He nodded slowly, his eyes not quite concealing a twinkle. ''Pushy. And heaven help any poor soul who's not dancing to your tune.''

''Well, some people need pushing. Especially men.'' She turned to face him, remembering something else she'd meant to ask him about. ''Speaking of men,'' she said, ''what are you going to do about getting wives for Thomas and Johnny Chang?''

''Wives?'' He looked as if she'd dashed a pail of water in his face. ''They're only boys! And it's hardly my job to—''

"They're both past twenty. And their mother worries about them. She's afraid they'll get restless and leave if they don't have families to tie them to the ranch. Mei Li wants daughters-in-law and grandchildren around her in her old age. Family means so much to her, Morgan."

"And you want me to play marriage broker." He was leaning back against the side of the stall, regarding her with one quirked eyebrow. A shaft of silvery light fell across his rumpled hair.

"Not exactly," she said. "Mei Li's relatives in China can find suitable girls and make the arrangements. But the money—that's the problem. Chang and Mei Li have some cash put aside, but not enough to bring two brides across the ocean. They're too proud to ask for your help. I'm not."

Morgan gazed at the mare and foal, a thoughtful expression on his face. "To tell you the truth, I've been worried about the boys, too. Johnny's getting restless feet, and Thomas is going to be lost without my father to care for. Maybe your suggestion isn't as far-fetched as it sounds."

"Then you'll do it?" Elated, she seized his hand. The sudden contact with his warm flesh surged through her like a jolt of summer lightning. Heat flooded the surface of her skin, bringing a crimson flush to her cheeks.

His eyes flickered a warning. He made no move to withdraw his fingers from hers, but she could feel the tension as he waited for her to pull away. This man did not trust her, she reminded herself. He would see even the most innocent gesture as part of a scheme to bind her to him and his family.

Slowly and deliberately she slipped her hand from his and rose to her feet. When she spoke, her voice shook like a reed in the wind.

"Why don't you talk to Chang about the matter? He would never ask you on his own, but if you were the one to bring it up, I'm sure he'd welcome your help."

"Thank you. I'll do that." His eyes burned into hers, turning her knees to water. From somewhere outside the barn a rooster crowed, signaling the start of the new day.

"You still don't trust me, do you?" she asked softly.

Morgan regarded her with maddening calm. "I can't afford to trust you, Cassandra. The stakes are too high for that."

"And there's nothing I can do to change your mind?"

"Not unless you can change the truth." There was no anger in his voice, only a resigned sadness. Morgan had seen through her scheme from the beginning. The fact that his father's illness had forced him to play along didn't mean he had to like it.

Cassandra held back tears of frustration. "Excuse me, I've got to get back to Rachel," she said. Then, willing herself not to break and run, she turned and walked swiftly out of the barn.

Chapter Ten

The Chang house sat amid a grove of spring-fed willows, ten minutes by foot trail from the Tolliver Ranch house. Solidly constructed of stone and mortar, it was built in the Chinese fashion with its four sides arranged around an inner courtyard. To Cassandra, stepping through its round moon gate was like walking into an exotic and mystical world. She treasured every minute of the time she spent here with Mei Li.

The two women sat, now, on a low stone bench beneath the umbrella of a ripening plum tree. Cassandra nestled the dozing Rachel in the crook of her arm as Mei Li struggled to sound out the English words printed in charcoal on a piece of light-colored slate. The reading lessons had continued almost daily since Cassandra's intercession in the matter of the brides. Chang's grudging acceptance of these lessons was his way of showing gratitude. Even now, the letter and money were on their way to his brother in Shanghai, who would choose two suitable girls—sisters, perhaps—and make their travel arrangements.

''Enough lessons for now.'' Mei Li put the slate aside and reached for the celadon teapot that rested on a tray at the foot of the bench. With exquisite grace, she filled two tiny porcelain cups and handed one to Cassandra. ''Will you teach the wives of my sons also?''

The words should have gratified Cassandra's spirit. Instead they only weighed on her heart. With so many things to arrange by letter, it would likely be spring before the two brides arrived. And where would she be by then? Still living a lie, as she was now? Struggling for survival in some dingy, rented room? Locked away in prison? This ranch felt more like home than any place she had ever known. But she did not belong here. She had never belonged here.

''Of course,'' she said, smiling at Mei Li. ''I would love to teach your daughters-in-law.''

Mei Li sipped the clear Chinese tea and sighed her contentment. ''I am happy for my sons. It is not good to sleep alone. Not for men. Not for women.'' Her almond eyes flickered toward Cassandra. ''Not for Mr. Morgan. Not for you.''

Cassandra flushed to the roots of her hair, remembering the blurred, erotic dreams that had haunted her sleep since the encounter with Morgan in the barn. Dreams filled with sensations that left her damp and aching in the solitary darkness of her bed. Dreams so explicit that she could barely face Morgan across the breakfast table the next morning, knowing it was his touch she imagined in the night, his mouth nuzzling her erect nipples, his hands stroking flame along her thighs.

She gazed down at the lacy pattern of Rachel's white shawl, hiding thoughts that must never see the light of day. "I don't think Morgan cares a fig for me," she said. "If he could wish me back to where I came from, he'd do it in a minute."

Mei Li laughed softly. "You have not seen the way his eyes look at you when you walk away from him. It is the look of a man who wants a woman. And you…" She sipped her tea, letting the implication of her words hang on the shimmering afternoon air.

"You're imagining things!" Cassandra fussed with a fold of the crocheted shawl, knowing the wise Mei Li was reading her like a book. "Morgan doesn't even like me." There was every reason to believe that was true. Since that morning in the barn, he had gone out of his way to avoid her, scarcely speaking to her unless Jacob was present.

Mei Li's tiny hands were as graceful as butterfly wings as she set the cup on the tray. "It is one thing not to want. It is another to want but to resist wanting. When I look at Mr. Morgan, I see a man who is resisting, but wanting with all his heart."

Cassandra swallowed her tea, ignoring the tightness in her throat. "Did you know his wife?" she asked impulsively.

Mei Li nodded. "Mistress Helen was beautiful— tall with white skin, long brown hair and eyes the color of fine jade. But to me she seemed proud and cold. My husband told me that she and Mr. Morgan had angry words because he would not move away from this place and live in the city.''

''And the baby? Were you there when it was born?''

''Yes, I was there. Very sad. There was nothing to be done. Such things happen. But I believe that losing the baby gave Mistress Helen what she wanted—a reason to go away from here.''

''I see.'' Cassandra's fingers twisted a strand of fringe on the edge of Rachel's shawl. Mei Li's revelations stung like lye in a raw wound. But if they opened the door to understanding Morgan, she was willing to bear the pain.

''So how did Morgan take her leaving him?'' she forced herself to ask.

''He was quiet outside, angry inside, not so much with her as with himself. At night he drank whiskey, sometimes too much. We were all worried about him.''

Cassandra had never seen Morgan drink alcohol. ''What happened?'' she asked. ''What stopped him?''

''That fall, after the roundup, he left us and went back to his mother's people. All winter he stayed away. When he returned, he was as you see him— calm and gentle, but with no life in his eyes. And showing no desire for a woman. Not until you.''

Not until you. The words stabbed into Cassandra to strike a yearning so deep that, until now, she had not even known it was there.

But nothing she felt made any difference, she reminded herself sharply. And if Morgan were truly drawn to her, that would only make things worse. No matter how much she might want to, she could not offer her love to a man whose family she had cheated, deceived and possibly even endangered.

"Is everything ready for your party?" Mei Li asked.

"Yes, thanks to your husband and sons." Cassandra was grateful for the change of subject. "I've sent the invitations and planned the entertainment, but they've done practically everything else. So much work!"

Mei Li smiled. "In the days when Mr. Jacob could ride, we had many important guests at the ranch. Many fine parties. It pleases my husband to make a party again."

"I can see that." Cassandra had been wise enough not to interfere with Chang's preparations. She had watched in amazement as benches and plank tables emerged from storage to be set up in the yard. Long gingham tablecloths, freshly washed, fluttered like banners from the clotheslines, and the air swam with the mouthwatering aromas of breads and pies. A huge barbecue pit had been unearthed at the side of the house. There, beneath a covering of green willows, a prime, fat-marbled beef slowly cooked over a bed of glowing charcoal. Stacks of sturdy white porcelain plates and mountains of cutlery had appeared as if by magic from the innards of the kitchen. What grand times this lonely ranch must have known!

Congressman Hainesworth, Senator Call and General Phillips would be arriving that evening to stay in the guest rooms on the main floor. They would be rising at dawn to spend much of the next day hunting grouse and pronghorn, with Morgan as their guide. By late afternoon, when they returned, the guests from the neighboring ranches would be arriving for the barbecue and dance. In this sparsely peopled country, everyone from the wealthiest rancher to the poorest cowhand had been invited. It would be the grandest gathering the Tolliver Ranch had seen in years.

The very thought of playing hostess at such a lavish affair was enough to turn Cassandra's knees to jelly. Some women possessed a gift for putting people at ease and making them feel welcome. She had always envied such women. But charm, alas, had never been one of her strong points. Like the grandmother who had raised her, she was as blunt as a stone and as plainspoken as a crow. That was her nature, and it went bone deep.

But Jacob Tolliver was depending on her, and she could not bear to disappoint the old man. For his sake, she would do her best. She would wear the pretty, lacy dress she had remodeled. She would dance and laugh and see that everyone had a good time. She would be charming and gay if it killed her.

"Will there be music?" Mei Li's eyes sparkled as Cassandra nodded.

"Two fiddlers—the best to be had in these parts. You should come to the dance, Mei Li."

The tiny woman shook her head. "I do not dance. And even if I only sit and watch, people will stare at my feet. In China, small lotus bud feet are the mark of a proper lady. Here they are only a curiosity. No, my friend, I will stay here with your little Rachel and enjoy the music from my garden.''

As if on cue, Rachel squirmed herself awake and began to fuss. Cassandra lifted the crying baby to her shoulder and promptly wrinkled her nose. ''Ugh! You need changing something fierce, young lady! It's back to the house for you!''

Mei Li chuckled as Cassandra rose to her feet. ''You cannot know how this old nose has missed the odor of a smelly little baby! To me it is as sweet as jasmine!''

Cassandra flashed her a grin as she turned toward the moon gate. ''Heaven willing, you'll have a house full of babies. And if they all smell the way this little mischief does right now…''

Leaving the thought unfinished, she wheeled and rushed through the gate. Mei Li's laughter echoed behind her as she dashed along the willow-lined path, then dodged her way through the grid of benches and tables in the yard. The baby chortled, enjoying her mother's bounding run toward the house.

''Cassandra.'' Morgan stepped off the porch at her approach, as if he'd been waiting for her. Her pulse skittered as he strode toward her, his face looking as grim as a thundercloud. Cassandra stopped in her tracks, her heart sinking. What now?

''We're in a bit of a hurry,'' she said.

''So I gather.'' His nostrils flared as Rachel's aroma wafted upward. ''This won't take long.''

"It hadn't better."

He cleared his throat and shifted his stance as if not knowing quite how to begin. "On the off chance our guests arrive early, we need to clear this up now. How do you want to be introduced?"

The question struck Cassandra as trivial, and for an instant she was annoyed. Then the problem became clear. She could hardly expect to be presented to the visitors as Mrs. Ryan Tolliver.

"My father wants to show off Rachel as his granddaughter," Morgan said. "I think I've managed to talk him out of that, but it still leaves the question of what to call you. Miss Riley would at least be honest."

She glared up at him, stung by his superior air. "It would. But I'd have to put Rachel in hiding, or answer some embarrassing questions."

"That red hair leaves no doubt she's yours," he observed, frowning. "Would you settle for 'Mrs. Riley'? A widow who happens to be a houseguest?"

She winced as it struck her how close he had come to the truth. "Mrs. Riley it is. And for now, at least, the rest of the story is no one's business."

"No one's business." His eyes glittered dangerously. "So your reputation, such as it is, will be quite safe." With a curt nod, he turned and walked away, headed toward the barn.

"That wasn't necessary!" Cassandra flung the words after him, stung by his superior manner. Anger rose in her, hot and bitter, and for a moment she was overcome by the urge to put him in his place. After

all, she was not without power, not as long as Jacob
Tolliver believed Rachel was his granddaughter. To
support her claim, there was the locket, still in Morgan's possession. There was her knowledge of the
scar on Ryan's leg, and the amazing resemblance between Rachel and Ryan's baby photograph. As for
Morgan he had no evidence against her.

Or did he?

She stared after Morgan's departing figure, recalling the mysterious flicker in his obsidian eyes. What
had caused it? And why did she suddenly feel as if
the earth were dissolving beneath her feet?

What could Morgan be holding back from her?

Had the letter from the ex-Pinkerton agent arrived,
with enough evidence inside to send her to jail?

Somehow she had to find out.

Cassandra stood on the porch in the chilly dawn,
watching the hunting party ride out of the gate. Morgan led the way, mounted on a fleet buckskin mare.
Behind him, the congressman, the senator and the
general jogged along on their borrowed mounts, their
rifles and shotguns holstered and slung from their sad-
dles. Johnny Chang, trailing two packhorses behind
his mustang, brought up the rear with his big, silent
dog.

The three guests, accompanied by a bespectacled
clerk, had arrived by private coach the previous evening. After a late supper of Chang's beef stew, roast
potatoes and biscuits, they had spent some time visiting with Jacob, then retired to their rooms.

Morgan had awakened them well before dawn, except for the clerk, who did not hunt and wished to sleep. They had downed a hearty breakfast of bacon, flapjacks and eggs, then set out for a day's shooting in the foothills above the ranch.

Cassandra had met them last night, at supper, and liked all three of the men. They were charming and witty, each of them cloaked in an aura of importance. Never in her life had she expected to be sharing a table with such people.

Congressman Hainesworth was a few years younger than Jacob, fit and tanned from a lifetime outdoors. Senator Call was portly with bushy gray side whiskers and a jovial laugh. General Phillips was in his forties, lean as whip leather, with a drooping mustache and a long handsome face. It had come up in the conversation that he was recently widowed. Once Cassandra had glanced up from buttering her bread to find him watching her, not lasciviously but with undisguised interest. She had felt the color flash in her cheeks.

Now, however, as she watched the hunting party pass through the gate, it was Morgan's erect figure that held her gaze. Even in such distinguished company, his chiefly bearing set him apart. If she had come across the group of men without knowing who they were, she would have judged him to be their leader.

But she had not come outside to admire Morgan. She had only wanted to make certain he was safely away so she could go upstairs and search his room.

For a few minutes more she stood at the porch rail, shoulders wrapped in the rose-pink cashmere shawl that had once belonged to Morgan's wife. The sun's first rays glimmered above the horizon. Silver fingers of light flowed across the prairie, turning the clumps of sage and rabbit brush to the colors of winter frost. A red-tailed hawk, roosting on the peak of the barn, resettled its feathers and soared into the sunrise.

By now the five riders and their mounts were no more than a string of dots along the crest of the first hill. Still, Cassandra watched them, putting off the distasteful task that lay ahead of her. It was necessary, she told herself. She had to know whether Morgan had anything he could use against her and plan accordingly. But she didn't like herself very much this morning.

The first crow of a rooster stirred her to action. Soon Rachel would be awake, and before long the place would be bustling with preparations for the barbecue. She had to act now or not at all.

Turning, she strode into the house and mounted the stairs. When she looked down the hall from the landing, she could see that the door to Morgan's room was ajar. Despite his declaration that he didn't trust her, he had not bothered to lock it. Was it because, if he were to do so, she might believe he had something to hide?

Never mind, Cassandra lashed herself. If she stood here dithering, she would lose her courage altogether.

With a deep breath, she forced herself to step into the room and close the door softly behind her. For a moment she stood still, her heart pounding as if she had just stolen into a wolf's den. She had been in Morgan's bedroom before, but under very different circumstances. Now she felt the strangeness of her own presence here, as if she were seeing the place for the first time.

The room lay mostly in shadow, but the light slanting through the east window allowed her to see clearly. Could this be the room Morgan had shared with his wife? It was spacious, perhaps two or three times the size of her own small chamber. The heavy oaken bed, wardrobe and dresser appeared to be a matching set, factory made, most likely in the East. Aside from a few other odds and ends, the room was bare, as if he had stripped it free of memories. Only the ruffled gingham curtains, which he had so grudgingly allowed her to hang, lent any lightness to the room. This morning they struck her as silly and out of place.

The wide bed lay unmade, the quilts thrown back where Morgan had rolled out of bed in the hour before dawn. The bed would be a sensible place to start looking, she reminded herself. It would be natural for anyone, even Morgan, to slip a letter beneath the heavy mattress and consider it hidden.

The clean, lightly musky aroma of Morgan's body rose from the sheets as she bent over the bed. Dizzyingly sensual, it crept around her as she leaned close to run her arm beneath the mattress. Unbidden, the memory of last night's dream swept over her. Morgan's scent had been missing from the dream, but here in the bed where he'd slept, it was all around her. Inches from her face, near the center of the sheet, was a damp, transparent stain. Her loins contracted sharply as she realized what it was.

...*showing no desire for a woman. Not until you.* Mei Li's words echoed in her ears as she fought to keep her knees from melting beneath her. She knew she was seeing part of a common male function, one that, in itself, meant nothing. But the thought of Morgan's lean, bronze body lying naked and aroused between the sheets, shuddering as the dream carried him over the brink of physical release, was enough to make her mouth go dry. Her breath quickened as she felt the pulsing liquid heat between her thighs. Had she been part of his dream, as he had been part of hers?

But that was a useless question, and she could not afford to waste more time. Steeling herself against the assault on her senses, Cassandra ran her hands under both sides of the mattress. Her searching fingers found nothing but a loose feather and a few bits of lint.

Next she flew to the wardrobe, and from there to the dresser. Morgan's possessions were few. The search was swift and easy, revealing no hidden surprises.

Only then did her gaze fall on the narrow mahogany writing desk that sat next to the window. Chiding herself for ignoring the obvious, she strode to the desk and unfastened the brass catch at the top. The hinged writing leaf dropped down to reveal a complex of slots and pigeonholes, most of them empty. Cassandra discovered an inkwell, a pen with two spare nibs, some envelopes and blank sheets of vellum, and a half-melted stick of brown sealing wax. There was nothing else, and her tapping fingers revealed no sliding panels or hidden compartments.

She had almost abandoned the search by the time she remembered the small drawer in the front of the desk. Raising the leaf and latching it into place, she slid the drawer open.

The first thing she saw was her locket, dropped with its coiled chain into the drawer's front corner. She reached for it, then changed her mind. If the locket was discovered missing or disturbed in any way, Morgan would guess that she'd been snooping.

The only other object in the drawer was a long, envelope, webbed with creases, as if it had been stuffed into a pocket or saddlebag and smoothed out again. It had been postmarked in Cheyenne two weeks ago, and was addressed to Morgan in care of the quartermaster at Fort Caspar.

Cassandra's hand shook as she reached out for the letter. All her instincts told her this was the reply from the ex-Pinkerton agent. How long had Morgan had it? What secrets had he learned about her?

He had told her nothing, but then, from what she knew of Morgan, that was no surprise. He was a man who played his cards close to his vest. And right now she was serving a purpose. When that purpose was finished and Jacob was in his grave, then the reckoning would come.

Why had she ever come to this ranch and let its

people steal her heart? Why had she even thought of this desperate scheme, let alone had the audacity to carry it out?

But Cassandra already knew the answer to that question. She knew it every time she held Rachel in her arms and looked down into her sweet little pansy face. There was no gamble she would not take for her child, no price that she would not pay to give her a safe and happy life.

But what would that price ultimately be? Would she lose her gamble and end up in prison, with Rachel locked away in an orphanage or farmed out to some foster family?

The fingers that lifted the letter from its place in the drawer were icy cold. Holding her breath, she turned the envelope over…only to discover that the flap was securely sealed with a blob of dark red wax, bearing the imprint of an oval stamp with the initials, H.C.

Morgan had not broken the seal. He had not opened the letter.

Feeling light-headed, she steadied herself against the plain wooden chair that stood beside the desk. Her hand shook as she replaced the letter precisely where she'd found it and closed the drawer.

She crossed the bare floor on trembling legs, pausing with her hand on the door latch. For now, at least, Morgan appeared to be giving her the benefit of the doubt. But why? Given the chance, why in heaven's name wouldn't he want to know about her past?

The sound of Rachel's awakening cries shattered

Cassandra's musings. Turning swiftly, she paused to make sure the bedroom door was in its original position. Then, as her daughter's wails grew more demanding, she raced down the hall. There would be no more time for thinking today, and perhaps that was just as well. She could make no sense of what she had found in Morgan's room.

By the time the tired hunters trailed through the ranch gate, it was dusk, and the barbecue was well under way. Riding in the lead, Morgan sighed as his ears caught the sound of a lively polka. After a long day of riding, stalking and skinning, he would gladly have settled for a simple supper and an early bedtime. But that was not to be. Not tonight.

While the three guests of honor went into the house to clean up and change, Morgan stayed to help Johnny Chang unload the horses and take care of the game they'd bagged. Hainesworth had brought down a buffalo bull, and the others, between them, had bagged two deer, a pronghorn and a half-dozen grouse. The hides would need to be pegged for drying, the meat salted and hung. The three visitors had killed purely for sport, but Morgan had lived too long with the Shoshone to abide wasting any animal whose life he had taken. Everything would be used.

By the time the night's work was done, Morgan was sore, dirty, bone tired and as cranky as a mange-riddled bear. Even his appetite had faded. He wanted nothing more than a good scrubbing and the refuge of his bed. But he knew it was a useless wish. Out of respect for his father, he would clean up and force himself to spend several hours at the party, pretending to enjoy himself.

The strains of a waltz floated across the yard as he came out of the barn and plotted a course that would allow him to circle the festivities and enter the house through the kitchen. Even from a distance he could see the bright lanterns that decorated the tables and hung from the eave of the porch. Their flickering glow cast the dancing couples into gay patterns of light and shadow. Morgan paused to watch them, his hands thrust hard into his pockets. In a territory where men far outnumbered women, any single female under fifty was a belle. Cassandra, he reflected sourly, would be in high demand tonight.

From his place in the shadows, his eyes searched for her among the dancers. Even as he resolved to stop looking, he found her. She was whirling in the arms of General Sam Phillips, her head flung back, her mischievous eyes laughing up at him. Lamplight cast glints of fire on her untamed curls and washed her creamy shoulders with gold.

She wore a gauzy apricot-colored gown with short, puffed sleeves and a wide ruffled neckline—another of Helen's castoffs that she had cut down to fit her own petite frame. Helen had looked like a queen in that gown, as perfect and untouchable as a porcelain statuette. Cassandra, in the same dress, was a voluptuous little earth goddess, the tops of her milk-swollen breasts peeking like moons above the frothy lace. Morgan had thought her plain and scrawny when she'd first arrived at the ranch. Motherhood and Chang's cooking had changed all that. Tonight she looked delectable enough to devour on the spot.

As the general's hand tightened on the small of her back, Morgan felt a dizzying surge of fury. She barely knew the man. Yet here she was, flirting with him like a strumpet. And Sam Phillips was lapping it up like cream. Even now, he was probably wondering how far he could get with the dazzling Mrs. Riley before his visit ended.

Morgan battled the urge to bull his way through the crowd and wrench her out of the general's arms. The last thing he wanted tonight was to spoil his father's party by making an ugly scene with a guest, he reminded himself.

But the sight of her, so close to another man, her full mouth curved in an enticing smile, her breasts all but spilling out of her gown...

A flood of remembered images swept through his mind. Cassandra, sitting in the battered wagon, glowering at him from under her dusty hat brim as she tried to convince him she was a boy... Cassandra, sprawled on her back in the mud, rain soaked and exhausted, her face glowing as his trembling hands placed her newborn daughter in her arms... Cassandra, huddled in the straw, watching the little foal take its first steps, her eyes as wide and wondering as a child's....

His thoughts had been filled with such images over the past weeks, Morgan realized. Waking and sleeping, she had been with him—the womanly warmth in

her voice, the tenderness in her hands, the bright spar-
kle of mischief that played hide-and-seek in her eyes.

But had he been dreaming of the real Cassandra
Riley? Or was he seeing her true nature for the first
time tonight—the temptress, flaunting her wares,
sending a clear message that she was available to the
highest bidder?

Leave her be! a warning voice shrilled in his head.
*She's nothing but a redheaded bundle of trouble
who'll do anything to get what she wants! The devil
take her, and good riddance!*

But it was too late for warnings. Something had
erupted inside Morgan—a force so hot and wild and
reckless that he had no will to contain it. Unbidden,
he found himself striding into the swirl of dancers,
drawn like a moth to flame by a beacon of bright,
blazing hair.

Chapter Eleven

Cassandra felt her pulse jerk as she caught sight of Morgan through the blur of waltzing couples. He was trail-worn and haggard, his clothes and hair coated with dust. The look on his face alarmed her. Was something wrong?

She glanced swiftly toward the porch. Jacob was where she'd left him when the general had asked her to dance. He was laughing, balancing a drink in one hand as he joked with Congressman Hainesworth. Thomas Chang, ever watchful, hovered behind his chair.

What else could it be, then? Was it Ryan? Had someone found his body?

Dear heaven, had something happened to Rachel?

Cassandra had stopped dancing. She was barely aware that General Phillips had released her and was looking at her with a quizzical expression on his long, handsome face. The waltz played on, but she scarcely heard it. Her whole attention was fixed on Morgan as he made his way toward them.

''General.'' Morgan's manner was coldly polite. His voice rasped with weariness. ''If you would allow me a word with Mrs. Riley—''

Without giving the general time to respond, Morgan hooked her waist and swept her away, into the milieu of dancers. She stared up at him, stumbling over her own feet as she tried to recover her balance.

''Morgan, what is it? Is Rachel—''

''I haven't seen your baby all day. As far as I know, she's fine.''

''Then, what? Is it Ryan? Have you heard some bad news?''

He made a rough sound that might have been a laugh. ''There's been no news. And nothing else is wrong. Can't a man ask you to dance without your thinking the world's come to an end?''

She gazed up at him, bewildered. ''But you aren't dressed for the party. You haven't washed or changed. You look terrible, and you smell worse than a wagonload of buffalo hides! Morgan, what on earth—?''

A pained expression had come over Morgan's face as if something were gnawing at his insides. ''Dance or talk,'' he said. ''You choose. I've never been much good at either, let alone both at the same time.''

When Cassandra hesitated, he took a firm grip on her upper arm and steered her toward the edge of the straw-covered circle. She did not resist, but as they passed out of the light and into the shadows of the yard, she began to sputter.

"What do you think you're doing, Morgan? I can't just walk out on your father's party. I'm his hostess!"

He propelled her deeper into the shadows. "Then maybe as hostess, and as the bereaved Mrs. Riley, you ought to show a little more...decorum."

Quivering with the impact of his words, Cassandra waited until they had rounded the corner of the barn, where they could not be seen or overheard. Then she wrenched herself out of his grip and spun around to face him. "Is *that* what this is all about? That *you* don't approve of my behavior?"

His features had turned to stone.

"How do you expect me to behave?" she demanded. "Should I wear black from head to toe? Should I sit in the rocker on the porch with my knitting? Your father wants his guests to enjoy themselves. I'm just trying to make certain they do!"

"So I see." The edge in his voice could have drawn blood. "The general seemed to be having a very good time."

Cassandra felt the sting of his words as if he had struck her across the face. Wounded to the quick, she glared at him. She had made every effort to be charming to Jacob's guests, and she'd hoped Morgan would be pleased that his father's party was going so well. Instead he had lashed out at her with a vehemence that left her reeling.

"I've avoided prying into your past, Cassandra," he said, turning her thoughts to the unopened letter in his desk. "As long you're serving a purpose here, I'm willing to let things stand."

"Serving a purpose!" Cassandra fought back a scalding surge of tears. "Is that the only reason you've allowed me to stay, so that you can *use* me?"

His eyes had gone cold. "You're getting what you came for, aren't you? You've got a roof over your head, food in your belly and, at least, the trappings of respectability. What else could you want?"

"I want to be *valued!*" She hurled the words at him, struck by their truth. Times had gone from bad to worse when she'd lost her grandparents and married Jake Logan. In the desperate months following Jake's death, she had thought that nothing mattered except having a secure home, meals on the table and the means to provide for her child. But she'd been wrong. What she'd needed as much as food and shelter was to be of worth to the people she cared about.

"Your father has been very gracious to me," she said. "He's accepted me as a friend, even as a member of the family. But you, Morgan, you treat me like the dirt under your feet. You treat me the way you'd treat a—a—"

"A whore?" His eyes were slits, his voice a leaden whisper. "Isn't that how you knew about the scar on my brother's leg? And isn't that how you came to be carrying his child?"

For the space of a breath, shocked silence hung on the air. Then Cassandra slapped him. Her right hand flew upward in a long, true arc to strike the left side of his face with a blow that stung all the way up her arm. The force of the impact wrenched her shoulder.

But Morgan did not move. He stood like a granite pillar, the imprint of her hand blazing on his cheek.

The waltz had ended. From the far side of the barn, the strains of a lively polka beat a crazy-quilt counterpoint to the drumming of Cassandra's heart. He had hurt her terribly, and she wanted nothing more than to hurt him in return, to fling a verbal lance that would wound him to the heart. Her staggering mind groped for words that were cruel enough to say.

"I'd wondered about it all along," he said in a low, quiet voice. "But the idea didn't make sense to me. You seemed so innocent, so...soft. But tonight, seeing you out there in a man's arms, laughing, flirting with him—I knew, Cassandra. I knew that had to be the answer."

"You *knew?*" She would have slapped him again if she'd thought it would reach that cold, judgmental place inside him. "You don't know anything! Not about me, not about women! You keep your heart locked up in a little iron box where nobody can touch it. You'd never admit to needing anyone. You're too proud for that." She paused, letting her fury build. "No wonder your wife left you! If I'd been in her place, Morgan Tolliver, *I* would have left you, too!"

She saw him flinch, saw the tightening of his mouth. "I thought we were talking about you," he said in a flat voice.

"All right, let's talk about me!" Cassandra battled the impulse to tell him everything—her miserable marriage to Jake Logan, her struggle after Jake's death and the desperation that had driven her to commit this shameful crime against the Tolliver family. She could not tell Morgan the truth, she reminded herself. Not now, not ever. To do so would give him the power to destroy her.

"You're wrong about me, Morgan," she said coldly. "And you've no call to be my judge. There was nothing improper in my behavior tonight. General Phillips is a gentleman in every respect, and we were enjoying a friendly dance. Anything beyond that took place in your own mind and nowhere else."

"General Phillips is a soldier. And I'd wager there was nothing gentlemanly on his mind while you were in his arms. No man could look at you in that dress tonight and think like a gentleman. Not even me."

Cassandra's mind was piecing together a response about the bodice of Helen's dress being too large, and the fact that there'd been no way to remake it without ruining the lace, when the words he'd spoken suddenly sank home. She stared up at him, knowing there was only one meaning that made sense.

"You're jealous." The words emerged slowly, each syllable forced through a throat that was so tight she could scarcely breathe. "For all your self-righteous posturing, you're *jealous!* Deny it! I dare you!"

He glowered down at her, almost as if he hated her, she thought. For the space of a breath she expected him to hit her, as Jake might have done. But Morgan's hands did not stir. A muscle twitched in his clenched jaw, as if he were biting back an army of demons. She had gone too far, Cassandra realized.

Now she had only herself to blame for the consequences.

"Jealous?" His voice was a low rasp. "Hell, yes, I'm jealous. I'm jealous of every man who looks at you, let alone touches you. I'm jealous of my own father, when I hear the two of you laughing over your poker game. I'm even jealous of Ryan, because he knew you in a way that I have no right even to think about! I'm jealous of the ground you walk on and the bed you sleep in!" He loomed above her in the darkness, his eyes hooded in shadow. "There, you've ripped out my soul and nailed it to the side of the barn. Another damned trophy for your collection. Are you satisfied, Cassandra Riley?"

Cassandra gazed up at him, her legs trembling beneath her petticoat. Morgan was wrong about so many things, her past, her apparent ease with men, her alleged conquests. She had every right to hurl a slashing retort, turn on her heel and stalk back to the party. If she were wise, that was exactly what she would do. To leave him in anger would save face for them both.

But wisdom had never been one of her strong points. Looking at Morgan now, Cassandra saw only a man in pain, his pride laid as bare as the wound of a lead-tipped lash, and she could no more turn away from him than she could stop the beating of her own heart.

Unbidden, her hand stirred and drifted upward. He didn't flinch as her fingertips touched his cheek, but she felt the tension beneath his smooth, cool skin. She felt the resistance in him as the edge of her palm brushed the tightness of his jaw.

"Oh, Morgan," she whispered. "Morgan, you proud fool..."

She felt him break, felt his resolve shatter as his arm caught her waist. Cassandra exploded against him, her body arching upward to meet his strength. Her fingers raked his dust-stiffened hair as he lowered his head to hers.

He kissed her savagely, almost brutally at first, as if he'd expected her to fight him. When, instead, she responded with a darting flick of her tongue, a shudder passed through his body. A low moan escaped his throat.

She melted against him as he gathered her close, his wind-roughened lips grazing her mouth, her face, her throat. She strained upward, her eager hands pulling his head down to her breasts.

From somewhere in her mind a voice shrilled that this was the most foolhardy thing she could do, that loving this man would bring her nothing but danger and heartbreak. But the heat that blazed from the pulsing core of her body burned away all reason. She wanted him, wanted to feel his hands, his mouth on every part of her. She yearned to open herself to his need, to flood his parched soul with all the warmth and tenderness she had held back for so long.

She moaned as he buried his face in the hollow between her breasts. He inhaled deeply, his breath hissing inward against her skin as he filled his senses with the odors of her aroused body. Through her skirts, she could feel the jutting ridge of his erection. Aching, she curled inward and felt the leap of sweet fire from the point where his body pressed her through the layers of cloth.

His breath caught as he felt her move against him. He groaned. ''Cassandra, don't...''

Easing away from the intimate contact, he straightened and stood looking down at her. His mouth was a bitter line in the moonlight. His eyes were lost in pits of shadow.

''We can't do this.'' His voice was raw and husky, as if he'd just awakened from sleep. ''It's not right.''

Why? the question shrilled, unspoken in the silence as she stared up at him, her lips damp and swollen from his kisses. Morgan was right, she knew. But reason seemed a feeble thing when her body was on fire.

''You know why,'' he answered as if he had heard her speak. ''You know the reasons as well as I do.''

''Yes. Of course.'' She stood there twisting one of the little satin bows that decorated the skirt of her gown. Such a beautiful gown—she had looked forward to wearing it tonight. But it didn't belong to her. Except for Rachel, nothing in this place belonged to her, including this man she had no right to love.

The polka had ended. The sounds of talk and laughter drifted with the smell of tobacco smoke on the evening air. ''You'd best be getting back to the party before the general comes looking for you,'' Morgan said in that leaden tone that made her want to scream.

She glared up at him, her heart aching. "Yes, I suppose I had—"

"Miss!" Johnny Chang appeared around the corner of the barn, carrying a small, flickering lantern. Cassandra and Morgan both turned at the sound of his voice.

"Miss—" He hurried toward them, out of breath from running. "My mother sent me to find you. Your baby—"

"No!" Cassandra's world quivered on its axis. Her hand crept to her throat. "What—?"

"She woke up crying, hot with fever. My mother is doing her best." Johnny shot Morgan a quick sidelong glance. "But she told me to ask if anybody who's here tonight is a doctor."

Morgan shook his head. It was an answer Cassandra already knew, but it struck her to the heart.

"Please, God…" She muttered an incoherent little prayer as she plunged into the darkness, racing for the path that wound through the willows to the Chang house. She was barely aware of the bobbing lantern and Morgan's pounding footsteps, echoing close behind her in the night.

Moonlight washed over Cassandra's sweat-tangled hair as she sat on the stone bench beneath the plum tree, cradling Rachel in her arms. Her face was pale, her eyes bloodshot from exhaustion and tears.

Morgan watched her from the shadow of the overhanging porch, his own emotions worn raw by the ordeal of the past two hours. They had arrived at the

Chang house to find Mei Li sponging Rachel's tiny body with a cloth soaked in one of her medicinal teas. The baby had been whimpering and feverish, refusing even to nurse. Along with the fever had come racking bouts of diarrhea. Now little Rachel was becoming more and more dehydrated. Earlier, when Morgan had briefly held her, the baby had felt as insubstantial as a ghost in his arms.

Mei Li had boiled some rice, and Cassandra had used a teaspoon to force the rice water between her squirming daughter's clenched gums. More liquid had spilled on the once-beautiful peach gown than down Rachel's throat. She was wet, disheveled and dirty from head to toe. But Cassandra was clearly beyond caring about her appearance. Nothing mattered except the small, feverish bundle in her arms.

Mei Li had delved into her store of Chinese herbs and concocted a saffron-colored tea, said to be excellent for easing fevers in children. But no medicine could be of any use to a baby who refused to swallow it. What little did go down Rachel's protesting throat was swiftly spat up again. Cassandra's precious little girl was growing weaker by the minute as the tiny candle of her life burned down to its guttering wick.

Morgan ached, now, as he watched her cradling the baby in her arms, adjusting the damp blankets, singing a nonsensical little song in her whispery, off-key voice.

"'Hush a bye, don't you cry…go to sleep little baby. When you wake, you shall have…all the pretty little horses…'"

He had known, of course, that Cassandra loved her daughter. But to see the ferocity, the desperation of that love stirred a deep sense of protectiveness in him. He wanted nothing more than to gather them both into his arms, to keep them safe and sheltered and close to him forever.

But that idea was nonsense, a fantasy born of moonlight and hunger and the memory of Cassandra's willing body in his arms. The reality was here and now—a failing baby and a woman who would go back to her old life when this masquerade was finished.

And what had her old life been? The names he had called her came back to haunt him now. Did he really believe she'd been a whore? Or had he spoken rashly, from a well of jealous rage?

And did he truly believe Ryan had fathered her child? He had told her as much, but at a time like this, what did such questions even matter?

The party had long since ended—the fiddles silenced and shut into their cases, the dishes carried back to the kitchen, the guests sleeping or on their way back to their own homes. Chang and his sons were still cleaning up in the kitchen. Even the tireless Mei Li had fallen asleep in a chair, her hands small and pale against her dark cotton trousers.

Cassandra sat silent now beneath the moonlit plum tree, her head drooping over the tiny bundle in her arms. The night's eerie stillness was broken only by chirp of crickets and the distant echo of frog songs from the reservoir. Aching for her, Morgan moved out of the shadows and walked quietly across the flag-stones. She did not appear to notice until he stepped behind her and rested his hand lightly on her bare shoulder.

He felt the taut muscle quiver beneath his palm as she drew in a ragged breath.

"How is she?" he asked softly.

"Asleep," she whispered, "but otherwise no better. I can't get her to keep anything down, not even the rice water. And she's so hot. Like a little furnace. Oh, Morgan, I can't lose her! She's got to grow up. She's got to learn to walk and talk and dance and go to school and wear pretty dresses. She's got to fall in love and get married and have children. She can't end her life like this, as a sick little baby…" Her words ended in a tightly restrained sob.

Morgan battled a growing sense of helplessness. If Cassandra and her child were threatened by some terrible danger, he knew he would fight to the death to save them. But what could he do now, against an invisible enemy that was sucking the life from Rachel's little body?

Nothing, he realized. Nothing except hope and pray with her mother. Nothing but mourn with her if the worst came to pass. And none of it would be enough to make any difference.

"What would your grandfather have done?" Cassandra suddenly asked. "What kind of Shoshone medicine would he have used?"

"My grandfather wasn't that kind of medicine man," Morgan replied. "He had the gift of speaking with horses and the magic to drive away evil spirits. But he wasn't a doctor, not in the sense you mean.''

''But surely someone took care of sick children!'' She had turned to look up at him, the moon shining full on her grief-ravaged face. ''Who was it, and what did they do?'' Her free hand seized his wrist. ''Please, there's got to be something we haven't tried!''

Morgan exhaled, searching his memory. ''It was just the women, the mothers. And they used whatever plants they could find growing near the camp. Sage, rabbit brush...peppermint—''

Cassandra's fingers tightened on his arm. ''My grandmother used peppermint! She made peppermint tea and gave it to me when I was sick to my stomach. Sometimes it was the only thing I could keep down! Morgan—''

''It's worth a try. There's plenty of peppermint along the stream that runs into the reservoir.'' He strode toward the moon gate, then paused and glanced back toward her. ''You're sure it's safe? She's so small—'' He fell silent as her eyes met his, and he guessed what she was thinking. Given the baby's fragile condition, they had precious little to lose.

''Hurry,'' she whispered.

Cassandra sat listening as Morgan's footfalls faded into silence. The nighttime breeze was cool through the damp fabric of her gown, but she scarcely felt the chill. She felt nothing except the heat of Rachel's weightless body against her breast, nothing but the weakening pulse, like the flutter of an injured moth against her hand.

She had seen babies die this way on lonely Nebraska farms and in the clustered shanties that ringed the Laramie stockyards. She had witnessed the fever, the diarrhea and the awful dehydration that drained the life from bodies too small and weak to resist. She had heard the thud of dirt clods on the lids of doll-sized wooden coffins and walked away with tears blurring her eyes. When she'd discovered that she was with child, she had sworn that, somehow, she would find a way to protect her baby from this horror. But she had turned out to be no more diligent nor luckier than any other mother. Like so many before her, she had simply failed.

Rachel stirred, whimpering in her fever dream. Cassandra lifted the tiny bundle to her shoulder. The hot little head lolled like a wilting flower against her neck. Shifting the baby back to the crook of her arm, she dipped her hand into the basin beside her and patted cooling moisture on her scalp. The thick, russet baby hair lay in flat, wet curls beneath her fingers. "Little pansy face," Cassandra whispered, and her voice shattered as she spoke.

Only a miracle could save her darling now. But she'd given up the right to ask for miracles when she'd chosen to lie to the Tollivers. She was a sinner through and through, and now heaven was demanding the ultimate penance. *It isn't fair!* her mind screamed to the pitiless stars. *It should be me, not Rachel. Me! Do you hear?*

Rachel's eyelids drooped. A droplet of water clung to the pale gold lashes, holding in miniature the image of the crescent moon. From the depths of Cassandra's heart a desperate prayer stirred, forming words that rose into her choked throat.

"Please, God...I'm not asking for myself. I don't even deserve to be heard. But Rachel's never done anything wrong in her life. Don't punish me by punishing her. That wouldn't be fair." Cassandra paused, rethinking her words. Who was she to tell God what was and wasn't fair? That wasn't what he wanted to hear. He wanted a broken heart and a contrite spirit. That was what her grandmother would have said. Well, her heart was surely broken. But as for being contrite—how could she possibly regret coming to this ranch, even under the cloak of a lie? How could she not be richer for the people she had known here— Chang and Mei Li and their two stalwart sons? Crusty old Jacob whose surly manner hid a heart of gold? And Morgan, whose rough tenderness had stirred emotions she'd thought she would never feel again?

What would her life be like if she had never come here? Cassandra thought of the shack by the railway, the stink of the cattle pens and Seamus Hawkins's groping hands. How could anyone blame her for what she'd done?

A cloud drifted across the face of the moon, deepening the shadow beneath the plum tree. Rachel stirred and whimpered again, her fragile body as weightless as one of the corn-husk dolls Cassandra had played with as a child.

Cassandra dipped her finger in the basin and moistened the parched rosebud mouth. This was no time to justify the past, she chided herself. Not when her baby's life was trickling away like the sand in an hourglass. Rachel needed a miracle. And miracles did not come cheaply.

"Forgive me, Lord," Cassandra whispered into the darkness. "I've been proud and selfish and deceitful. I've told myself that my lie was no sin. But I know better. I need to make things right, and there's just one way to do that."

She cradled her baby, trying to imagine the look on Morgan's face when she told him the truth. She pictured his stoic features as he struggled to mask his emotions—surprise first, then hurt, then a gathering storm of outrage, bursting upon her in full fury. When his anger had spent itself, there would be nothing left but cold indifference. Morgan would never want to set eyes on her again.

No, she could not tell him tonight. Not while Rachel was so sick and she needed him so much. "But I'll tell him first thing tomorrow," she promised, taking up her prayer again. "No matter what happens tonight, Lord, I'll come clean, and I'll tell him everything…"

Again her thoughts veered away as she caught the sound of Morgan's rapid footsteps in the darkness. A moment later he appeared through the moon gate, clutching something dark and leafy in his fist.

"How is she?" He was slightly out of breath, and she realized how he must have hurried.

"The same. There should be hot water on the stove. I can steep the tea."

"Stay where you are. I'll do it." He strode past her toward Mei Li's kitchen, the clean, sharp aroma of mint lingering behind him.

"Don't make it too strong. She's never had peppermint tea. We don't know how she'll take to it." Cassandra tried to speak calmly, but the voice that emerged was raspy with fear and exhaustion. "And not too hot—"

"I'll cool it off at the same time I water it down." Morgan spoke from the kitchen, his words accompanied by the light scrape of metal across the top of the iron stove. "Rest, Cassandra. Wearing yourself out isn't going to help anything."

He spoke gently, almost tenderly—this man who, just a few short hours ago, had called her a whore. Morgan still believed those terrible words, Cassandra reminded herself. And the fact that she'd behaved like a wanton in his arms only served to strengthen that suspicion.

The ironic part was, she had won another victory tonight. For the very first time, Morgan had voiced his belief that Rachel was Ryan's child. Now it was only the circumstances, and her own character, he questioned.

But then, Morgan's opinion of her no longer made much difference. Tomorrow morning she would look him in the eye and tell him the whole sordid story—how her husband had died in a whorehouse brawl; how she had struggled to live through the months that followed; how at last, alone, great with child, fearing the law and desperate for refuge, she had carried out this heartless scheme against his family.

Morgan would never forgive her, that much she knew. But she could not predict whether he would send her packing at once, turn her over to the law or force her to stay and continue the pretense for his father's sake.

Only one thing was certain. Whatever had passed between them earlier tonight was at an end.

Tearing her mind away from the memory of his kisses, she laid Rachel across her lap, dipped her fingers into the basin and began smoothing water over her daughter's burning skin.

As the smell of steaming mint wafted from the kitchen, she began to pray again.

Chapter Twelve

Dawn came gently, stealing across the prairie to brush the clouds with pale hues of peach and lilac. A cool breeze rippled the dry summer grass, rousing a chorus of meadowlarks to warbling song. From the coop behind the Chang house, a rooster stretched its neck and coaxed the first crow of the morning from its sleepy throat.

Bleary-eyed and dirty, Morgan stood in the court-yard, watching the sky. His mouth felt raw, and his head ached from the long, sleepless hours he'd spent helping Cassandra tend to her sick baby. But now the night was over. It was time he went back to his room to wash, change and start the new day.

Around him, the small stone house lay silent. Chang and his boys had come in late, slept a few hours and risen before first light to begin their morning chores. Once they had gone, Mei Li, who'd been up most of the night, had excused herself and tottered off to bed, leaving Morgan alone beneath the tree with its weight of ripening plums.

Yawning, he stretched his arms and rubbed the stiffness from the back of his neck. Common sense told him that he should leave now and avoid the risk of waking Cassandra. But something drew him back toward the house, to the open doorway of the sitting room where he had left her.

Bracing a hand against the door frame, he stood for a moment, looking down at her where she slept in a nest of pillows on a low, quilted couch. Rachel lay curled in the crook of her mother's arm, wrapped in a downy pink shawl. Her small rosebud face was relaxed in sleep.

Morgan was not religious by white men's standards, but as his eyes lingered on the two of them, he breathed a wordless prayer of thanks. Miraculously, the peppermint tea had soothed Rachel's irritated system. Over the course of several hours, they'd gotten enough of it down her to ease the dehydration and cool the fever. Toward morning, she had taken some milk from Cassandra's swollen breasts and settled into a deep, healing slumber.

Morgan had offered to help Cassandra carry the baby back to the ranch house, but she'd been adamant about not wanting to disturb Jacob or their guests. Insisting she and Rachel would be fine in Mei Li's parlor, she had settled herself among the pillows and tumbled over the edge of exhaustion.

She slept now, with both arms clasped fiercely around her slumbering child, as if she were prepared to fend off the Grim Reaper himself. Her damply tangled hair spilled across the patchwork cushions, catching a glimmer of the sunlight that had crept through the open doorway. Deep mauve shadows pooled beneath her golden lashes.

The frothy peach gown, so provocative on her the night before, was streaked with stains and reeked of stale peppermint tea and sick baby. The left side of the bodice had slipped off her shoulder, exposing— ever so innocently now—the creamy upper curve of her breast.

Wherever the sun had touched her, Cassandra's fair skin was dotted with tiny golden freckles. Morgan battled the urge to bend over her and lightly brush each one of them with his lips.

When had he begun to love her? Was it only last night, while they were struggling to spoon mint tea down a squirming, squalling, choking baby, one of them holding her, the other plying the spoon? Was it that moment in the small hours of morning when they'd realized that Rachel's fever had broken, and Cassandra had flashed him a smile that had flooded her tired face with blinding beauty?

Had it been earlier last night, when the sight of her in another man's arms had triggered a burst of rage that had rocked him to the depths, or the moment when her stinging blow had struck his face?

No, Morgan mused, it had begun much sooner, creeping over him so slowly and quietly that he had not even realized he was trapped until it was too late.

Trapped.

He cursed under his breath, remembering the feel of her eager body pressing his, the staggering heat of his response. Loving this woman was a sure recipe for disaster.

If her crazy claim was true, then she was Ryan's sweetheart and the mother of Ryan's child. While any hope remained that his brother was alive, he had no right to touch her.

If she was a fraud or a whore…Morgan thought of Ham Crawford's letter, lying unopened in the drawer of his writing desk. He should do it now. He should walk back to the house, march up to his room, take the letter out of the desk, break the seal and read what his friend had to tell him about the woman.

And then what?

Cursing again, Morgan tore his eyes away from her disheveled beauty and turned back toward the moon gate. Cassandra Riley was too near, too much in his thoughts. She had clouded his reason.

His hand moved to the medicine pouch where it hung against his skin. His fingertips felt the crumpled stem of the sacred sage inside, and suddenly he knew that he needed time away from the ranch. He needed the solitary trails and the clean skyward sweep of the Wind River Mountains. He needed the rough honesty of his mother's people and the wisdom of his adoptive Shoshone father, Chief Washakie.

He would leave this morning, he resolved, before she could awaken and call him back. The journey would not be a long one—he would be gone no more than ten or twelve days. Johnny Chang could handle the business of the ranch, and Thomas would see to Jacob's every need.

If he found the peace he sought among the Shoshone, he would return with clear eyes, able to look at Cassandra and see the truth. Then, perhaps, he would have the will to open Ham Crawford's letter and act on what he learned.

Cassandra stirred, yawned and forced her eyes open. Her head throbbed dully and her neck muscles ached from sleeping in an awkward position. Her side was damp with sweat where Rachel's warm little body had pressed against her in the night.

Jerking herself fully awake, she checked the small bundle in her arms. Yes, everything was all right. Rachel was sleeping like an angel, her lips puckering and twitching as if speaking some secret dream language.

Transfixed, Cassandra gazed down at her slumbering child, remembering how terrified she had been last night as she and Mei Li and Morgan had battled to get fluids into the tiny, burning body. She remembered how she had prayed…

Her breath caught as the memory slammed home. Last night she had made a bargain with heaven—the truth, or what she dared tell of it—in exchange for her baby's life. God had kept his part of the bargain. Now it was time for her to keep hers. She would keep it quickly, before her courage failed.

Aching in every joint, she forced herself to stand. Her hair clung in damp strings to her face and shoulders. Her mouth felt as if she'd just swallowed a cattail. Her eyes felt gritty, and her once-beautiful gown was a mess of splotches and stains. But she would not let her appearance serve as an excuse for putting off a painful confrontation. She would find Morgan now and—

Rachel's hungry wail broke into her thoughts, shattering the moment's resolve. Her little one's breakfast was the one thing that could not wait. With a sigh, Cassandra sank back onto the cushions, covered herself with the shawl and put the baby to her breast. Rachel clamped on hungrily and began to suck. Cassandra's heart swelled with gratitude. Last night's terror was over, and the sun had risen on a new day, a day in which she had resolved to reclaim her integrity and face the consequences.

She knew well what that truth would cost her. The Tollivers were a proud family. Morgan would not forgive her for duping them. But her grandmother had taught her that promises to heaven were not to be taken lightly. She had made a vow and she would keep it.

She glanced up, startled, as a shadow fell across the doorway. But it was only Mei Li, tottering into the room on her tiny, bound feet. Her hands balanced the lacquered tray that held the steaming celadon teapot and two cups.

Mei Li's quiet smile lit the dim parlor. "I see your little one has her hunger back," she said. "Did you sleep well?"

"Like a stone."

"My elder son brought a clean dress from your room. When you are ready, you can change here. That way you can return to the big house without losing face.''

''Thank you!'' Cassandra blinked back a surge of tears, thinking how unfairly she'd deceived this good family and how hurt they would be when they learned the truth. ''You've been so kind to me, Mei Li. I don't know what I would have done here without you.''

''Whatever small kindness I have done is nothing compared to what I have received in return.'' Mei Li set the tray on a table and lowered herself to a stool. ''For so many years, with only men around me, I have been lonely for a friend in this place. You and your baby have brought me so much joy.''

Her voice choked with emotion. Unable to meet the sincerity in those dark almond eyes, Cassandra lowered her gaze to her baby.

''I am nothing but a foolish old woman,'' Mei Li said with a little laugh. ''Are you hungry? I have rice and eggs in the kitchen. When you have finished feeding your small one, I would be honored to prepare your breakfast.''

''At any other time, I would be honored to share your meal.'' Cassandra glanced up and forced a reassuring smile. ''But I need to be getting back to the ranch house. There's something I need to discuss with Morgan, and it can't wait.''

A startled look crossed Mei Li's face. ''But did he not tell you?''

''Tell me what?'' Cassandra stared at her, her heart creeping into her throat.

''Mr. Morgan rode out of the gate this morning,

trailing a packhorse,'' Mei Li said. ''My younger son told me he was going to visit his mother's people in the Wind River country.''

Morgan came up over the last rise and paused to rest the horses. Below him, the Wind River snaked a silvery path across a broad green valley rimmed by jagged peaks. Along the river's far bank, the summer camp of the Eastern Shoshone spread across the open ground. Morgan estimated that there were more than a hundred tepees. They were fashioned of buffalo hides spread over towering lodgepole frames, their open tops blackened from the smoke of many fires. Children and dogs raced along the river, splashing in the shallows. Buffalo meat hung on racks, smoking over fragrant coals.

Morgan's spirits began to lighten as he wound his way downward through stands of pine and aspen. For three solitary days he had been torn by thoughts of Cassandra. The desire had gnawed at him to push his conscience aside and simply take her, as he had dreamed of taking her from the first night he saw her.

Ryan was dead, the voice of temptation had whispered. It would be almost biblical in its rightness for a man to take the wife and child of a deceased brother, wouldn't it? In the lonely hours of the night, with the cold stars looking down, the argument had almost made sense. It had made so much sense Morgan had been on the verge of turning around and galloping back to the ranch to sweep Cassandra into his arms and his bed.

But reason had won out. Neither he nor Jacob was ready to abandon the hope that Ryan was alive. And in any case, Cassandra was not Ryan's wife. What was more, aside from her own word and a striking resemblance, there was no solid proof that Ryan had even fathered her child. Only Ryan could provide such proof, and if Ryan failed to return...

The tangle of unanswered questions had kept Morgan awake for the past three nights. But now, as he smelled the smoke from the cook fires, saw the grazing ponies and heard the shouts of welcome, he knew that coming here had been the right thing to do. He urged the horses forward, filled with the bittersweet awareness that he had not truly come home. He could never return to life as a Shoshone. But he loved these people, and he savored the gladness in his own heart as he rode to meet them.

A shout of greeting rose in Morgan's throat as a stately, white-haired figure appeared on the riverbank. Chief Washakie had passed his eightieth year, but his back was straight, his mind clear and his step firm. Morgan was not in the least surprised when the old man returned the cry, sprang onto the back of the nearest pony and galloped it into the swift-moving current of the river, riding to meet him.

Years ago, as a young chief, Washakie had seen the wisdom of an alliance with the whites. His shrewdness had spared his people many of the hardships that had crushed other tribes and won, by treaty, the right to stay on their ancestral land, here in the Wind River country.

Still, life had not been easy for the Shoshone. No treaty could protect them from diseases such as measles and smallpox, from the ravages of hunger and poverty, from dishonest traders or from overbearing do-gooders who were determined to destroy their culture and make them white. Washakie had fought against many enemies in his lifetime. Now, in his old age, he was battling the most insidious enemy of all—the slow erosion of ancient ways.

The two men met at the foot of the trail. Washakie's embrace was as firm as ever, but his aging bones, through the worn fabric of his flannel shirt, felt sharper than Morgan remembered.

"Let me look at you, my son!" The chief thrust Morgan away from him, his eyes narrowing. "Trouble. I see it in your face. Has there been no word of your younger brother?"

Morgan hadn't mentioned Ryan, but it came as no surprise that word of his disappearance had reached the Shoshone. Morgan shook his head. "We've posted a reward for news of him, but no, we've heard nothing."

"And my old friend, your father, is dying."

Washakie's words shook Morgan because he had said nothing, but then, the old chief had always seemed to possess a sixth sense about such things.

"I felt it here." Washakie touched his heart. "And when I saw you, I knew it was true."

"His spirit is still strong," Morgan said. "I can't help hoping he has some time left."

Washakie shook his head. "It will happen sooner

than you think. But enough of such sad talk. You are
here and my heart is glad. We will hunt and fish like
we used to in the old days, and smoke some of that
fine tobacco you have brought me. And we will talk
only of good things.'' His handsome brown face
brightened. ''Come on! Race an old man back to the
village!''

He kneed the pony and was off like a shot, shriek-
ing like a young warrior, his long silver hair streaming in the wind. Left hopelessly behind with the
loaded packhorse, Morgan felt the laughter bubble out
of him and break free. The sunlight was warm on his
face, and for this brief moment life was simple and
good.

Four days later, at the close of a long day's hunting,
the two of them sat cross-legged by the fire in the
solitary twilight. Washakie had shot a bull elk, and
Morgan had skinned and hung the massive animal for
him. Then they had dined like kings on fresh tender-
loin, rubbed with wild onion and roasted over a bed
of fragrant cedar coals.

Morgan watched the smoke curl upward from the
dying fire, his eyes half closed like a drowsing cat's.
An owl called from a nearby thicket, then flapped
upward to drift across the clearing, ghostlike on its
silent wings. The flutter of aspen leaves in the soft
night wind was like the sound of falling rain.

''Tomorrow you will go,'' Washakie said. ''My
heart will be sad when you ride away.''

Still lost in silence, Morgan glanced up at the old

man, then nodded. Until this moment he had not acknowledged the fact of his leaving, not even to himself. But all day he had felt the familiar stirrings that always called him back to the ranch—worries about his father; concern for the stock and the precious hayfields in the summer drought; the need to be there in case there was news about Ryan; and Cassandra. Cassandra most of all.

Morgan had made this journey to the Wind River country to escape the firestorm of desire that threatened to burn away all sense of right and wrong. But time and distance had only deepened his need for her. The peace of this temporary Eden had resolved nothing. He was as torn as ever.

Washakie prodded the coals with the tip of a green willow. "I see trouble in your face," he said. "Trouble you hide, perhaps even from yourself."

Morgan glanced up at him but did not reply. The old chief regarded him quizzically for a long moment, then burst into laughter.

"I knew it! Only one thing could make a man look so beaten. Woman trouble!"

Morgan sighed, too tired to protest as Washakie pounced on this new tidbit like a dog on a bone.

"Listen, my son. I have lived a long life, and there is one thing I have learned. The only thing worse than woman trouble is *no* woman trouble!"

He chuckled at his own joke, then sucked deeply on his pipe and blew the smoke lazily into the air. "You have been without woman trouble for too long.

That is not good for a man. It makes him as sour as old vinegar.''

''And you, I take it, are not sour yet,'' Morgan commented dryly.

Again the old man chuckled. ''It's you we're talking about, not me. Have you mounted her?'' He grinned at Morgan's startled expression. ''No, I see that you have not. What a shame. Doesn't she want you?''

''That's not the problem,'' Morgan hedged.

''If you want her, and she wants you, then there *is* no problem. Except maybe in your own stubborn head.''

Morgan groaned, knowing that Washakie would not release him to sleep until he knew the full story. ''It's more than that,'' he said wearily. ''Much more.''

The words came painfully. Morgan had always kept his inner thoughts to himself. But here, in the peace of the forest with the one man who would neither betray nor judge him, he made the effort to speak. Slowly, with the old chief prodding at every pause, the story emerged.

When the words were spent, Washakie sucked on his pipe and laughed. ''That is all? You won't take the woman because you think she might be lying? Pah! Women have been lying to men for ten thousand years! It's one of the things that makes them so much fun!''

''What if she isn't lying?'' Morgan felt drained

now that the story was out. "What would that make me?"

Washakie shrugged. "If your brother had wanted the woman, why would he have gone off and left her? Alive or dead, he has no claim. She is free to take another man." He sucked on his pipe, the wrinkles deepening around his mouth. "You and your questions about right and wrong! Your head is shouting so loudly that you cannot hear the voice of your heart."

"Maybe I don't trust my heart."

"Do you trust the wind? Do you trust the rain? The man who does not move until he is sure of everything will spend his life waiting. Do not be afraid to do a foolish thing, my son. Do not be afraid to lose, to hurt, to bleed, or you will die old and lonely, mourning all the things you have never known."

Morgan stared into the dying coals, weighing the old chief's words and knowing they were wise. Loving Cassandra loomed as the greatest gamble of his life. That he would end up wounded, bitter and sorry was a near certainty. But could he bear the alternative—to hold back and burn forever in his own solitary hell?

She had been with him every moment of this journey. He had heard her impish laughter in the rustle of aspen leaves and matched flowering lupine to the color of her eyes. Even the chickadee that scolded him from an overhanging willow had brought her lively temper to mind and made him ache with the pain of wanting her.

Cassandra would not make things easy for him. That was not her way. She would challenge and frustrate him at every turn. Claim her, and he risked never knowing another day's peace. Was that what he wanted?

Could he trust the voice of his heart?

Could he trust the wind?

Morgan stared into the dark red coals and knew that, tired as he was, he would find no refuge in sleep that night.

Cassandra shaded her eyes and peered into the blinding afternoon sunlight. Heat waves shimmered like ghost water, blurring her view of the place where the mountain trail emerged from behind the tinder-dry foothills.

How many times had she gazed toward that spot, hoping to see Morgan's erect figure appear around the bend? He had been gone for only nine days, but each hour of that time had passed in a torment of anxiety— of dreading his arrival one moment and feeling certain, in the next moment, that she could not survive another day without him.

The past week had been especially trying. A hot summer wind had struck like a blast from an open furnace, searing everything in its path. Heat had sucked the moisture from the prairie grass, leaving the blades so parched and brittle that they crumbled under the horses' hooves. Only the precious hayfields, irrigated from the reservoir, remained green.

The torrid days and sticky nights drained the energy from everyone on the ranch. Rachel was impossibly cranky, and Jacob had grown too listless to enjoy the nightly poker game. It was only the heat, Cassandra told herself, but she had developed a deep affection for the old man, and she could not help worrying about him.

Johnny Chang had made a run to the summer pasture to deliver supplies to the cowhands and check on the herd. He'd reported that the drought was less severe on the mountain. But if rain did not come soon, the thinning meadow grass would be gone.

In everyone with whom she spoke, Cassandra sensed the longing for Morgan's quiet presence. His was the strength that held the ranch together in hard times, and though he had only been gone for a little more than a week, the anxiety that threaded every moment of the day had become a palpable thing, an enemy that only Morgan's arrival could vanquish.

Cassandra felt that anxiety now as she peered up the road one last time, then lowered her hand with a sigh. What if something had happened to Morgan? What if he was not coming home at all?

Clouds were scudding in from the west, spilling across the tops of the Big Horns. But she knew better than to hope they would bring rain. For the past three afternoons the weather had been the same—wind, thick, dark clouds, even thunder and lightning, but not a drop of moisture. She could not expect today to be any different.

Thrusting her worries aside, she turned toward the corral, where her old mule waited with his head thrust over the top rail of the fence. Xavier had grown sleek and fat at the ranch and was fast becoming everyone's pet. Cassandra suspected she wasn't the only one who smuggled him tidbits from the kitchen.

"You old glutton!" She laughed as he nuzzled her hand for the buttered biscuit she'd saved him from lunch. "At least I did *you* a favor by coming here. Maybe when they throw me off the place, they'll let you stay on."

She pressed her cheek against the mule's warm neck and felt the ripple of his throat as he swallowed the biscuit. Two nights ago, unable to sleep, she had stolen down the hall to Morgan's room, opened the drawer of his writing desk and found the ex-Pinkerton agent's letter gone. Had he taken it with him? she wondered. Had he opened it and read the whole sordid story of her landlord's death and her sudden disappearance from Laramie?

Maybe she should have started packing as soon as she discovered the letter was gone. Maybe, even now, there was time to leave before Morgan's return. Xavier appeared strong enough for the journey. His harness was in the shed, along with a two-wheeled cart she had never seen anyone use. When she reached a place of safety she could always sell the cart and send Morgan the money, or leave it at some livery stable where he could have it picked up and returned.

But what was she thinking? Rachel was barely recovered from the sickness that had threatened her life. And Jacob doted on the little girl he believed to be his granddaughter. Losing her could be a fatal blow to the old man. No, Cassandra concluded, she could not possibly leave now. She had no choice except to wait for Morgan's return and face her punishment.

For a moment her arms tightened around the old mule's neck. Then she pulled herself away from the fence and turned in the direction of the barn. Heat waves shimmered before her eyes as she crossed the yard, each step raising whorls of powder-fine dust behind her. Clouds were thickening overhead. The air felt strangely heavy, as if she were walking through water. Dared she hope it would really rain this time? After so many days of disappointment it seemed almost too much to ask.

The barn's shadowy depths offered a welcome retreat from the glaring sunlight. Cassandra walked softly down the rows of stalls to where the bay mare stood guard over her foal. The little creature had been asleep in the straw, but at Cassandra's approach it scrambled upward and stood quivering on its stiltlike legs, its eyes impossibly big and soft.

The mare lifted her elegant head, her ears pricking forward as Cassandra found the small apple she had hidden in her pocket. The mare took it from her hand with a brush of her velvety lips. While her big teeth munched, Cassandra knelt in the straw and stroked the wide-eyed foal. Its body quivered beneath her hand, recalling that early morning, here in this very stall, when Morgan had brought the foal into the world. He had been so gentle, so tender, Cassandra remembered. Then she had ventured too close and he had lashed out at her with a coldness that had left her reeling.

She closed her eyes, willing away the memory of their soul-searing kisses. Morgan wanted her as much as she wanted him. There was no denying that. But he would never trust her. And Morgan was a man who needed to trust in order to love.

Fighting tears, Cassandra pressed her cheek against the foal's warm, velvety coat. Why had she come to this place, to lose her heart to a man she had betrayed even before she met him?

From outside, the first thunderclap, still distant, echoed through the walls of the barn. The foal flinched and edged closer to its mother. With a sigh, Cassandra rose to her feet. Enough of this brooding! It was time she returned to the house, before Rachel woke up and demanded her afternoon meal.

Closing the stall, she squared her shoulders and walked outside. A sultry breeze struck her face as she passed through the wide doorway of the barn. The sun had vanished behind a bank of roiling black clouds. Even as she watched, lightning leaped across the sky, followed by the shattering boom of thunder. But there was no sign of falling rain. Dry storms, Johnny Chang called them, and this would be yet another one.

The air seemed to crackle around her. Sensing the danger, Cassandra picked up her skirts and sprinted for the house.

Another flash of jagged white light streaked across the sky, striking the ground a half mile away. The deafening thunderclap seemed to shake the very earth under Cassandra's feet. Breathing hard now, she flung herself onto the porch and collapsed against one of the supporting timbers. Through the open window above the porch she could hear Rachel crying. The thunder had probably startled her awake.

Cassandra plunged across the porch, only to freeze at the door as the prairie wind carried a new scent to her nostrils. The mule began a frantic braying as the same scent reached the animals in the corral. Horses reared and stamped. Johnny Chang came racing from the back of the house, and she knew he had smelled it, too—smoke, mingled with the acrid odor of burning grass. The fear in his eyes confirmed what she already knew.

The prairie was on fire.

Chapter Thirteen

Morgan smelled the smoke as he neared the top of the last ridge. The odor of burning grass stung his eyes and nostrils, and he knew at once what was happening. Gripped by a gut-wrenching dread, he paused only a few seconds to unload the packhorse and turn it loose. Then he dug his boot heels into the mare's flanks, and together they rocketed up the slope.

From the crest of the hill, in the fading daylight, he could see the rolling foothills and the broad sweep of the prairie beyond. To the south, the fire crawled in a long, hungry line across the open grassland, leaving nothing but charred ground in its wake. The ranch buildings lay directly in the fire's path.

Mud-colored smoke billowed upward to surround him as he tore down the steep trail on the cat-footed mare. Guilt lashed at him as he rode. He should never have left the ranch. Visiting Washakie had been an act of pure selfishness. It had taken him away from home at the very time when he was needed most.

Now everything and everyone he held dear was in peril.

Animals and birds raced ahead of the flames. A pronghorn exploded out of the brush, zigzagging up the slope in blind panic. Jackrabbits bounded through the grass, fanning out before the fire. How long before the flames reached the ranch? Twenty minutes, Morgan calculated, if the west wind held. Less if it shifted to the south. He leaned forward in the saddle, urging the mare to greater speed.

Through the smoke, he could make out the people in the yard. The Chang brothers were soaking some feed sacks with water from the well. Cassandra held Rachel in her arms. The wind whipped her skirts as she gazed toward the fire.

Johnny's dog trotted back and forth across the yard, its agitation showing even at a distance. The animal's anxiety mirrored Morgan's own. The yard itself was bare of grass, but a high wind could send flames and sparks leaping to the outbuildings and even the house. It was a fear that ranchers and squatters had always lived with in this country—a fear that Morgan knew all too well.

He could hear the fire now—the crackle and pop of burning brush and the upward whoosh of air when something new and dry ignited in the summer heat. Even as he watched, the wind shifted, blowing the sparks in a new direction. A trail of flame spat upward, streaking along the foothills, straight across his path, cutting him off from the ranch.

They had spotted him now. Johnny Chang was

yelling and waving one of the sacks over his head. Cassandra was shading her eyes with one hand, straining to see him. Her hair had come unfastened to flutter like burning flame on the wind.

With a blazing wall before him, Morgan yanked his canteen from where it hung over the saddle horn. Gripping the saddle with his knees, he soaked down his neckerchief and plastered it over the mare's face, covering her eyes and her tender nose. There was barely time to splash what water remained on his own face and shirt before he felt the blistering heat and heard the roar of the fire. Pressing his face against the mare's neck, he tightened his knees and urged her to a mighty leap.

He felt the upward motion as the well-trained animal plunged straight into the wall of smoke and fire. For an instant they seemed to hang suspended in a world of blazing heat. Then, suddenly they burst through, and they were flying down the hill again. Morgan snatched the steaming cloth from the mare's face and used it to brush the sparks from her mane and coat. His own shirt was smoldering. He could feel the burning heat on his back as he galloped the mare into the yard, reined to a halt and flung himself out of the saddle. The quick-thinking Johnny Chang wrapped him in a wet sack, smothering the fire. "I'm all right, Johnny," Morgan said. "See to the mare."

The setting sun glowed like brimstone through the choking haze of smoke. In its hellish light, Cassandra's hair was the color of burning coals. She clutched Rachel in her arms, her eyes wide and frightened.

Morgan knew she was thinking of the baby and how to save her if the worst happened. He was thinking about it, too, thinking about every life on the ranch.

As a last resort, they could climb to the reservoir and go into the water to save themselves. Morgan had seen numerous fires in his twenty-five years on the ranch, but such drastic action had never been needed before. The family and hired hands had always managed to turn the flames aside before they reached the heart of the ranch. Could they do it again?

He shot Cassandra a swift, reassuring glance. "It's all right. We'll stop it," he said, but his words rang hollow. Driven by a hard wind, the fire was racing closer, threatening to engulf everything in its path. And with Jacob crippled, Ryan missing, and the cowhands in the mountain pasture with the herd, there weren't enough able-bodied people left to fight back the flames.

Glancing back toward the house, he saw his father on the porch. Mei Li stood in the doorway, half-hidden by shadows.

Jacob's gaunt face, with its prominent bones, looked like a death's head in the fiery glow. Even in the past ten days, his father had lost weight, Morgan observed. It was one more reason why he should never have left the ranch to visit the Shoshone.

As Morgan strode toward the porch, Chang came around the house and fell into hobbling step beside him. His face was grim and Morgan could guess what he was thinking. If the worst happened and they had to go into the reservoir, Jacob would need to be carried up the long, steep slope of the earthen dam. Mei Li, with her bound feet, would also have trouble making the climb, as would Cassandra and her baby. With all hands needed to get everyone to safety, there would be no one left to stay and fight the fire. The ranch buildings, the corrals, even the animals, would have to be abandoned to the flames.

Cassandra had followed him to the porch. He felt her silence behind him as his father's hand moved to beckon him close.

"Dynamite!" Jacob rasped, his voice even hoarser than Morgan remembered. "We've got to blow the dam and flood the ranch, or we'll lose everything!"

"We have dynamite," Chang said. "It's in the toolshed."

Morgan's stomach knotted as he remembered the dusty wooden boxes. "That dynamite's been in storage for at least a dozen years. We should have gotten rid of it a long time ago. If it's crystallized, even a stumble can set it off."

Chang nodded gravely. "I was a dynamiter for the railroad, remember? I can do it. I know how to be careful."

"No," Morgan said quickly. "Not you. With that bad leg, you might not get away from the blast in time. And forget about sending either of your boys. I'll do the job myself."

Chang started to protest, then sighed as he gave way to Morgan's decision. "I will show you what to do," he said. "Hurry. We don't have much time."

* * *

Cassandra stood watching as Morgan and Chang entered the toolshed. *We'll stop it,* he had told her, and she'd believed him as she had never believed anyone in her life. If anyone could stop the fire, Morgan could. But at what cost? The dynamite was old, and likely unstable. Morgan himself had said that even a stumble could set it off. And the bursting of the dam would be dangerous, too. So much water. More than enough to sweep a man away and drown him.

For a moment she stood still, clinging to that brief moment of reassurance when his eyes had met hers. The sky was the color of flowing blood, the sunset's vermilion glow deepened by clouds of smoke and flame. Smoke billowed over the top of the barn, filling the air with its bitter, choking smell. She could feel the heat in the wind that blew in from the prairie, sweeping the flames closer and closer. In the corral, horses reared and stamped. Xavier's heathen bray mingled with their shrill whinnies.

Rachel had begun to cough and fuss. Covering the baby's face with a corner of her blanket, Cassandra raced for the porch.

Mei Li reached down for the squirming baby. "Let me take her inside," she said. "I will keep her safe."

Cassandra murmured her thanks, then wheeled and raced back to the yard. Of all the ranch buildings, the barn, with its vast, shingled roof, was the most vulnerable to flying sparks. It could catch fire at any minute, trapping the animals inside.

The two milk cows had already sensed the danger.

They lowed frantically, bumping against the sides of their stalls. Swinging the doors wide, Cassandra tore off her apron and used it as a flail to drive the terrified animals outside. Then she sprinted back toward the far stall, where the bay mare stood over her wide-eyed foal.

"Come on, girl!" She tugged frantically at the mare's rope halter, but the mare only rolled her eyes, laid back her ears and swung her massive head in the opposite direction, refusing to budge. In desperation, Cassandra seized the foal around its chest and haunches and hefted it in her arms. The little creature had put on considerable weight and bulk since its birth, and it was all she could do to lift it, but she held it fast and staggered toward the door, praying the mare would follow.

As she stumbled through the barn door with the squirming foal, she managed to glance back over her shoulder. Yes, the mare was ambling along behind her, nickering anxiously as she tried to reach her baby.

Morgan had just come out of the toolshed. He was carrying a rough wooden box of a size that might be used to contain a pair of boots. He held it carefully, almost gingerly, between his two hands.

Through the dark haze of smoke, their gazes met and held. In the depths of his black eyes she read fear, concern and determination. He would risk his own life, and no one else's, to see that the ranch and everyone on it was saved.

In that one blinding instant, Cassandra knew with

soul-deep certainty that she loved him. She loved his strength, his tenderness, and the needs he masked with a gruff and solitary manner. She loved his face, his hands, his body, every part of him. She loved him as she had never loved any man in her life.

Heaven help her.

Johnny Chang hurried forward with the fresh horse he had saddled, but Morgan shook his head. "The dynamite's too unstable. Can't risk jarring it. Better to go on foot."

He glanced toward the porch where his father sat, then his gaze darted back to Cassandra and Johnny. "Get as many animals as you can to higher ground," he said. "When the dynamite's in place, I'll fire three shots. That will be the signal for everyone to get to the house before the dam blows."

"Morgan—" Cassandra was barely aware that she'd spoken until he looked directly at her, his eyes narrowing sharply.

"Be careful," she whispered.

His only answer was a curt nod. Then he turned away, moving swiftly but with great care toward the back of the house where a long, steep path led to the reservoir.

Cassandra gazed after him as he disappeared into the smoldering dusk. *Please,* she prayed silently, *let him come back safely so I can tell him.*

Tell him what? The question mocked her, scattering the words of her prayer in hopeless confusion. Tell him she loved him? Tell him she was a liar and a fraud? Tell him she had killed a man and was likely wanted for murder?

The fire was perilously close now. Dirty black smoke and crackling flame spread across the eastern horizon, reaching out hungry fingers where the wind was strongest. Cassandra lugged the foal onto the porch, using her apron strings to tie it to one of the pillars. The mare hovered nearby, staying close.

Johnny Chang had opened the corral. His surly dog was doing a masterful job of herding the horses, growling and nipping at the heels of the stragglers, driving them uphill toward the house. Cassandra felt a surge of relief as she saw her old dun mule among them. Xavier, at least, would be as safe as possible.

The chickens, however, were another matter. When she unfastened the gate to their wire pen, they exploded into the open and scattered in all directions. Cassandra gave chase, her lungs burning from the smoke-filled air. Once she managed to grab a handful of feathers, but that was all. She could only hope the flighty birds would have sense enough to save themselves when the time came.

Gasping for breath, she sagged against the fence. A flock of wild pigeons streaked across the darkening sky. Two pronghorns bounded across the yard and rocketed toward the hills. Out of the corner of her eye, she saw Thomas Chang coming through the willows, staggering under the large, lacquered Chinese chest that contained the most precious of the things Mei Li had brought from China.

Catching up her skirts, Cassandra sprinted down

the path to help him. The Chang house was on low ground and would surely be flooded by the bursting dam. She could only hope that its sturdy stone walls would hold against the rush of water.

How much time did they have? An eternity seemed to have passed since Morgan had disappeared around the back of the house. Cassandra imagined him climbing the brushy slope of the dam, cradling the rough box as if it contained the Holy Grail itself. Dear heaven, what if he stumbled? What if the crystallized dynamite was so volatile that the very motion of walking set it off?

She reached Thomas and seized one end of the heavy chest. They were nearing the house when a pistol shot, followed by two more, rang out from the direction of the dam. The dynamite was in place. Morgan would give them a few minutes to get to the house. Then he would light the fuse and blow up the dam that held back the waters of the reservoir.

What if he couldn't get out of the way in time? He could be drowned or crushed or shattered by the explosion. She would never hear his voice again or feel his arms holding her close. She would never have the chance to let him know how much she loved him.

Breathing hard, Cassandra lugged her end of the beautiful Chinese chest up the steps. *Please,* her heart pleaded silently. *Please keep him safe and bring him back.*

The high wind had blown sparks onto the roof of the barn. Cassandra could see smoke rising as the dry wooden shingles curled in the heat. She lowered the

chest to the porch and saw Jacob's hand reaching out
to her. As the roof burst into flame she caught the
gnarled fingers in her own and gripped them with all
her strength.

Heartsick, Morgan stood partway up the slope of
the and watched the barn go up in flames. His nostrils
stung. His eyes burned and watered in the glowing
darkness.

Not far from his feet, the bundle of dynamite sticks
lay in the hollow he had dug into the earthen dam.
The fuse and detonator lay in place beside them, waiting for the kiss of the match. Morgan had chosen the
spot with care. It was low enough to cause plenty of
damage to the bank of earth, but high enough that the
water would be slowed by what remained of the dam
after the blast.

Even now, his nerves quivered like bowstrings
from the strain of placing the dynamite. The oiled
paper wrappings had been dotted with crystals of pure
nitroglycerine. The mere memory of handling them
made him sweat. His shirt was already dripping.

As he watched the fire, his mind ticked off the seconds. One minute. Then two. He would allow three
minutes before lighting the fuse to make sure everyone had made it to high ground.

The sight of the burning barn sickened him, as did
the thought of the lost hayfields and the cattle that
would have to be sold off to keep them from starving
over the winter. But it was the human lives that were
the heart and soul of the ranch, he reminded himself.

His father and the Chang family—and Cassandra. She and her little daughter had become so much a part of this place that he could no longer imagine life here without them.

The moment he had ridden into the yard and seen her standing there, the smoke swirling behind her, the wind whipping her flame-colored curls, he had known he loved her. Now, as he thought of her again, Morgan ached to burn Ham Crawford's unread letter, throw all caution to the winds and make her his.

But what if she was not what she seemed? What if all the worst things he had ever imagined about her were true? Would one taste of heaven be worth a lifetime of pain and regret?

Three minutes. It was time to stop brooding and light the fuse. Morgan had already chosen his path up the slope of the dam to the higher ground that surrounded the reservoir. He would just have time to make it, he calculated, before the blast ripped the dam apart and sent a torrent of water pouring down onto the ranch.

Nerves screaming, he crouched low, struck a match against the rough side of a rock and touched it to the fuse, which had been stored in the shed with the dynamite. Could he trust it to burn steadily, or even to burn at all? Morgan held his breath as the fuse smoked and sputtered, then ignited with a hiss. His pulse leaped, pumping energy through his body as he sprang to his feet and raced up the slope.

A few yards short of the top he paused to glance over his shoulder. From where he stood he should have been able to see the burning fuse easily, but the dam lay in dark shadow below him. There was no sign of flame.

Morgan hesitated, cursing under his breath. A man would have to be crazy to go back and check that fuse. It could still be smoldering, ready to blow any second. But there were precious lives at stake, lives that could be snuffed out if the fire were allowed to engulf the ranch.

Did he dare give the fuse more time, even a few seconds? Morgan's gaze swung back through the twilight, to the ring of fire closing in on the ranch below. The barn was already ablaze. Would the house be next?

Even a delay of seconds might be too long, Morgan concluded. If the fuse had sputtered out, he would have to relight it, even at the peril of his own life.

Taking a deep breath, he turned back and started down the dam toward the spot where the dynamite lay. He had not gone four steps when a shattering blast seemed to rip the very earth apart. The dam split open with a roar of tumbling rocks and breaking water. Morgan scrambled upward, but it was too late. The edge of the bursting deluge caught him with brute force, sweeping him outward and downward, tumbling him like a broken twig.

Cassandra stifled a scream as the water came crashing down the dry bed of the creek that had been dammed to make the reservoir. Reaching level ground, the flood spread outward. For a few moments the rise of land where the ranch house stood became an island, its shore pounded by the force of a muddy sea. Where water met fire, hissing steam arose to mingle with the black billows of smoke.

The amount of water seemed huge at first, but it did not spread far before it was sucked down by the parched ground, vanishing almost as swiftly as it had come. In spite of this, it soaked a wide enough area to quench the nearest part of the fire and halt the threat to the ranch.

After the roar of the explosion and the first rush of water, the silence hung eerily on the air. One by one the watchers crept off the porch to inspect the damage. Only Mei Li, who had come outside with Rachel in her arms, remained beside Jacob's chair.

The yard was a sea of mud, but except for the ruined barn most of the buildings appeared to be standing. The chicken coop had washed loose and been carried about twenty yards before coming to rest against the timbers of the windmill. A rooster and three of the hens clung like wads of wet cotton to the top of its tin roof. At least the makings of a new flock had survived, Cassandra mused. With luck, she would find even more of the chickens.

Johnny Chang, with his brother's help, was already rounding up the cows and horses and shooing them into the corral. Behind them, the dog darted back and forth, nipping at the flanks of the stragglers. The air smelled of smoke and dampness. Rising moonlight gleamed on a score of silvery fish that were stranded in the mud. Ever the practical man, Chang picked up a bucket from the porch and gathered them for the next day's meal.

Everything would be all right, Cassandra reassured herself. But even as the thought crossed her mind, her sense of relief was wrenched aside by a clutching fear. Her frantic gaze searched the shadows for Morgan's dark face and tall rangy form. He should have returned by now. But he was nowhere to be seen.

Others had missed him, too. As she mounted the porch to take Rachel, she saw the desolate look in Jacob's hollow eyes and she knew that he, too, was counting the minutes since the explosion. Gathering Rachel into the crook of her left arm, she rested her right hand on his shoulder. Beneath her palm the ropy muscles were taut, the bones all but fleshless. This man had already lost one son, she reminded herself. To lose Morgan, too, could be a killing blow—to her own heart as well as to his.

Johnny Chang mounted the horse he'd saddled earlier. At a silent signal, his dog trotted in from the yard, keeping to his side as he swung his mount toward the broken dam.

"Find him, Johnny," Jacob said. "Bring him back."

Cassandra felt the leaden beat of her pulse, coursing like a dirge through every part of her body, as she watched the three of them—man, horse and dog—disappear into the murky darkness. Somewhere out there, Morgan lay dead, perhaps, or badly hurt. He had to be in serious trouble. Otherwise he would be here, strong and quiet, making light of the danger.

What if he didn't come back? How could she face the days ahead without him?

Cassandra knew about loss. She had lost her parents at such a young age that she could barely remember them. She had lost her grandparents, and she had lost Jake. But nothing in her life had prepared her for losing Morgan.

Embers glowed eerily in the smoke-clouded twilight. Beyond the reach of the flood, the fire still burned. But even there, cut off from new vegetation to devour, it was dying.

Once more, Jacob's bony fingers reached for Cassandra's hand, clasping it tightly. By now, full darkness had fallen. The last, distant flames of the fire seemed to float above the prairie like disembodied devil-ghosts. The moon glowed bloodred through the black haze of smoke. Rachel stirred, whimpered and settled back to sleep in the crook of her mother's arm.

Mei Li had gone to the far edge of the porch and was leaning out to peer into the darkness. "There!" she exclaimed suddenly. "Something is coming!"

Cassandra plunged across the porch to the rail, her heart in her throat. The pale shape of the gray horse Johnny had taken emerged from the darkness. The figure in the saddle was little more than an indistinct blur at first, but, straining her eyes, she could make out Johnny's light blue bandanna and the high-crowned hat he always wore. The dog trotted at his stirrup, tail high, tongue lolling.

Cassandra's knees had gone limp beneath her. She

clutched the porch rail, her stomach churning as she braced herself for the news that would crush them all.

Then, as the horse came closer, she realized it carried not one rider but two. The second, larger figure, straddling the horse behind Johnny, was all but hidden by darkness. Cassandra's throat jerked as she realized it was Morgan.

Thomas had lit a lantern and hung it from a hook on the porch. Moments later, in the circle of its light, Morgan slid off the horse's rump and dropped wearily to the ground. He was coated in mud from head to toe, and blood trickled from a gash above his eye. Judging from his movements, he was sorely bruised. But he was on his feet, in one miraculous piece. He was alive. Nothing else mattered.

The whites of his eyes glittered in his mud-blackened face as he looked up at Cassandra, where she stood on the porch. Something in those eyes caught and held her, storming her meager defenses, penetrating her to the very core of her soul. For the space of a heartbeat, it was as if the two of them stood alone, naked, with nothing hidden between them. She felt the reaching, the need that burned in him as it did in her, so intense that it left her breathless. Her throat moved, but no words would come.

Breaking the tension that threatened to shatter them both, he turned to his father. "Damned fuse," he muttered almost apologetically. "Blast knocked me out and pinned me under a timber. If it hadn't been for the dog—" He coughed into his fist, shaking his head.

Moisture gleamed in Jacob's eyes. "Never mind, son," he said. "You did what you had to. You're alive, and I'm damned proud of you."

His words were the kindest Cassandra had ever heard the old man speak to his son.

Legs braced against collapsing, Morgan slicked the mud from his face and hair. Cassandra fought the urge to fly down the steps and wrap him in her arms, to undo each button of his water-soaked shirt, peel the fabric gently off his shoulders and kiss every bruise on the battered body beneath.

"Go inside and get some rest," Jacob rasped. "We'll manage fine here."

Morgan glanced from Cassandra to his father, his eyes bloodshot in his mud-streaked face. "I'm all right," he muttered. Then, with a shake of his shoulders he strode off to help Thomas round up the stock.

Cassandra was nursing Rachel when she heard the clatter of the big copper tub being carried up the stairs and rolled down the hall to Morgan's room. She leaned back in the rocker, listening to the rapid succession of footfalls that followed, the clang of tin buckets, the splash of water. One, two, three, four, five, six, seven. She counted the buckets, knowing exactly how many it took to fill the tub.

By the time Rachel had eaten her fill and drifted into angelic slumber, the clamor had died away. The ranch house lay in darkness, its silence broken only by the wail of a distant coyote searching, perhaps, for its own kind in the wake of the fire.

As Cassandra straightened from lowering the baby into her cradle she heard the weary tread of Morgan's boots on the stairs. She stood on the circle of the braided rug, trembling beneath her ecru silk nightgown, listening to the familiar double thud of his boots dropping to the floor and the faint clink of his belt buckle as his trousers followed suit.

Morgan's low groan, as he eased himself into the water, was audible all the way down the hall. Cassandra could almost picture his tired body sinking into the steamy water, the bruised limbs, the matted hair, the gash above his eye.

She had prayed that he would return so that she could open her heart to him once and for all. Now he was here, and it was time for the lies to end. Morgan needed to know everything she had done. And he needed to know how much she loved him.

On unsteady legs, she took a step toward the door. Would Morgan despise her forever? Or would he welcome her honesty and embrace the fact that his missing brother had no claim on her? Soon she would know.

At the door she hesitated, her hand quivering on the latch. Only the memory of the look that had passed between them gave her the courage to open the door. And only the yearning in her heart gave her the strength to cross the landing and walk down the dark hallway, toward Morgan's room.

Chapter Fourteen

Nudging the door open, Cassandra stepped into Morgan's room. The high-backed tub sat a few paces from the door, facing the far wall. In the flickering candlelight, she could make out the muddy spikes of Morgan's black hair above the tub's copper lip. She could hear the trickle of water as he soaped his bruised and naked body.

For a moment she almost lost heart. Turn around and run—that would be the prudent thing to do. What kind of woman would walk into a man's room when he was taking a bath? Not a lady, certainly.

But then, Morgan already suspected her of being less than pure. There was little that could further damage her standing in his eyes. As for his own modesty—a nervous little smile tugged at the corner of her mouth. From what she knew of Morgan, it might not even occur to him that he wasn't properly dressed.

In any event, her fear had little to do with facing a naked man in his own bedroom. She was about to bare her heart and soul to Morgan Tolliver, and the thought of what she could lose tightened knots in the pit of her stomach.

Her feet padded quietly across the damp wooden floor. Morgan had not shown any sign that he'd heard her come in. But he knew she was there, no doubt of that. He was simply biding his time, waiting to see what she would do.

Say something. Anything. Cassandra's mind struggled to form words, but no words would come. She could only move closer, like a moth to a candle flame, until she stood behind him in an agony of hesitation. His nearness swam in her senses. She could smell the salty aroma of his skin and the stark, clean fragrance of homemade lye soap. Again she willed herself to speak, but she was as tongue-tied as a bashful young schoolgirl.

She could not speak, but she could move. Without her willing it, her hand stirred. Suddenly it seemed the most natural thing in the world to reach past him and take the soap bar from its dish on the stool beside the tub. Lathering her unsteady hands, she leaned close and began rubbing the soap into his muddy hair.

A shudder passed through his body. Then, as her strong fingers massaged his scalp, he gave a long sigh of surrender. A little moan of pleasure escaped his lips.

Now would be the time to speak to him, Cassandra thought. But the moment was so precious that she could not bear to break it. Taking care not to reopen the gash above his eye, she slicked the soap suds from his hair. Then she reached for the pitcher of clean rinse water and poured it, in a slow trickle, over his head. His golden skin glistened in the candlelight, luminous with drops of water.

As Cassandra leaned forward to replace the pitcher on the stool, her breast brushed Morgan's shoulder. The brief contact flooded her body with a rush of liquid heat. Startled, she drew away from him.

"Don't stop." His voice was thick and husky.

Forcing herself to move, she retrieved the soap and began to lather her hands once more. "I shouldn't be here," she whispered.

"Then go. I can't force you to stay, Cassandra. But I want you to."

"Johnny and Thomas will be coming for the tub soon. They mustn't find me here."

"I sent them home to get some sleep. They won't be back for the tub till morning."

The implication of his words dizzied her. She could feel the pounding of her own heart as she placed her soapy hands on his shoulders, her thumbs pressing small circles over the tight muscles at the nape of his neck. He sighed as her strong fingers worked their magic, loosening the taut cords, easing the cramped and weary muscles.

Cassandra's hands could not get enough of him. Unbidden, her slippery palms slid lower, cradling the bruises, nicks and scars. In another life he would have been a Shoshone warrior, a slayer of enemies, streaked with war paint and adorned with eagle feathers. Even here, in his chosen place, he had a warrior's body, proud and strong and beautiful. She ached to touch every part of him.

But she had come here to talk, she reminded herself. She had resolved to lay all her cards on the table, sparing him nothing; but in the sweetness of this moment there was no place for words. There was only the warmth of Morgan's skin and the deep, hypnotic cadence of his breathing.

He leaned forward as she soaped his back from shoulders to tapering hips. When her fingers touched the hard, flat diamond that separated his buttocks, Cassandra paused, sensing that she had entered forbidden territory. When her hand moved away, he made an impatient little sound, reached back and caught her wrist. Gently but forcefully he drew her around to the front of the tub. His lips were wet, his obsidian eyes hot and hungry. The damp white silk clung to her body like a transparent skin, hiding nothing.

Morgan's thumb stroked the spot where the pulse fluttered at the base of her wrist. The sensuality of that simple gesture drained the strength from her legs and released a freshet of moisture between her thighs. If she did not stop him now, they would both be lost.

"We need to talk, Morgan," she whispered. "There are things you need to know…things I have to tell you."

His fingers continued the stroking, heightening the sensations that sang through her body. "This doesn't strike me as a good time for talking," he muttered, drawing her in against him until his face rested in the hollow below her breasts. His mouth tasted her flesh through the sheer, wet silk, tongue skimming upward to circle one puckered and aching nipple.

A sharp little groan escaped Cassandra's throat. No, she didn't want to talk. She didn't want to do anything that was correct or wise or sensible. All she wanted was to love this man, to feel his strength inside her, filling the emptiness that had been there even when she was married.

Her free hand caught the back of his neck, pressing him closer. She felt her nipple slip inside his mouth. He sucked her softly, so that her milk would not come. She moaned again as the liquid throbbing grew inside her, aching for more. "Don't..."

"Don't?" he whispered against her breast.

"Don't...stop. Oh, please don't stop, Morgan."

Releasing his grip on her wrist, he slid his hands around to cup her buttocks and pull her hips in against him. Lowering his head, he pressed his face into the hollow between her thighs. The pressure ignited heat flares through the wet silk. She curled around him, her hand groping downward, slipping into the water to find him. Sweet heaven, how hard he was, how smooth and perfect, like tempered steel cloaked in the velvety softness of rose petals.

With a rough little laugh he rose to his feet in the tub, holding her against him, kissing her mouth, her throat. "You're wet," she murmured against his hair. "Let me dry you."

Her groping hand found a towel on the back of a chair. She blotted the moisture from his skin, kissing each spot as she dried it. "I love you, Morgan," she whispered, the words bursting out of her like birds from an opened cage. "I've loved you from that first awful day when you thought I was a boy, and I fainted, and you caught me in your arms..."

"And I've wanted to make love to you from that very first night—round little belly and all." He had taken the towel away and was peeling the wet nightgown off her shoulders. "I've never looked at you without wanting to love you...all the ways a man can love a woman."

The nightgown dropped to the floor, leaving her damp and trembling. Without a word he lifted her in his arms and strode to the bed, which was turned down and waiting for them.

"Morgan..." The last vestige of conscience stirred in her. She had not kept her promise. She had not said the things she'd come to say. But it was no use. She was already a lost soul, drowning in need. She wanted him more than she wanted air, more than she wanted life.

Cassandra was ready for him, wet and welcoming as he entered her. She sobbed with joy as he filled her, hips arching high, hands clasping his buttocks to pull him deeper. She felt his need as he thrust into her, loving her with the hunger of lonely years, and with the wild sweetness of new discovery.

When the singing began inside her, she knew that he felt it as she did. They moved as one now, soaring like twin hawks as their spirits joined, touched the sky and spiraled slowly back to rest on the earth.

She gazed up at him in wonder, her finger tracing the edge of a shadow that fell across his face.

"Again," she whispered. "Please..."

The dawn sky gleamed like black opal as Cassandra eased herself away from Morgan's naked warmth and lowered her bare feet to the floor. Finding her damp nightgown where it had fallen beside the tub, she pulled it over her tousled head and stood for a moment, looking down at him.

He slumbered as sweetly as a child, a glimmer of pale morning light falling across his face. One arm curled around the empty spot where she had nestled beside him. The hair she had tangled in her frenzied fingers spilled blue-black against the muslin pillowcase. His broad golden chest rose and fell with the rhythm of his breathing.

Aching with love, she battled the urge to slip back beneath the covers, to mold her warmth to his and awaken him with little nibbling kisses. But no, the ranch would soon be stirring with activity. It would not do for the Chang brothers to come for the tub and find her in Morgan's bed.

As she turned away, Cassandra felt a raw twinge between her thighs. She and Morgan had made love again and again, with a hunger so deep that each shattering peak had only left them wanting more. Nothing had mattered last night except that burning need to possess and to be possessed, to have him, to love him, to give him every part of her. Now the night was over, and a new day, fraught with consequences, was about to begin.

For the space of a breath she gazed down at him, burning his image into her memory. Then, on tiptoe, she stole out of the room and closed the door softly behind her.

Only when she was back in her own room, with the door safely closed, did she give way to the tremors that had racked her all the way down the hall. Last night, in the heat of desire, she had put aside the awful burden of what she'd done. But this morning, with gray dawn gleaming above the fire-blackened prairie, Cassandra knew that it was time to face up to her crimes.

She should have told Morgan the truth last night— every word of it, from beginning to end, without so much as coming near him. True, he would have hated her for it, but not as much as he was certain to hate her now.

Her spirits plummeted even deeper as she remembered the letter from the ex-Pinkerton agent. Had Morgan read it? Destroyed it? And what of her own future, and Rachel's? When Morgan heard her story, would he throw them off the ranch at once, or would he keep them here for Jacob's sake and save her punishment for later?

Never mind. It was time for the lies to end. She owed Morgan the truth, and she would give it to him now, this very morning.

Rachel's little waking-up sounds broke into Cassandra's thoughts. She reached down into the crib, lifted up her warm, sleepy daughter and cradled her in the hollow of her shoulder.

"What a fine pickle I've gotten us into, sweetness," she murmured, her lips brushing the damp, coppery curls. "But there's no need for you to worry your little head about it. Whatever happens, you're going to have a beautiful life, with pretty dresses and ribbons in your hair, and all the things a little girl could want! I'll see to that, Rachel, if I have to work my fingers to the bone! I promise you on my life!"

Cassandra's arms tightened protectively around her baby. She would keep that promise, she vowed. If Morgan sent her away, she would change her name and find a new place to live, where no one had ever heard of Cassandra Riley. Perhaps, in time, she could even remarry—some kind, hardworking man who would be a good provider and a good father. He wouldn't have to be handsome or dashing. She wouldn't even have to love him, not the way she loved Morgan. Affection and respect could go a long way toward making a marriage tolerable.

Fully awake and hungry now, Rachel began to gum at her mother's bare shoulder. With a little sigh, Cassandra settled herself in the rocker and opened the front of her nightgown for the baby to nurse. From the other end of the hallway, she could hear the muffled sounds of Morgan getting out of bed, moving about the room as he pulled on fresh clothes and boots. He would have his hands full today, dealing with the damage from the fire and the flood. It wouldn't be easy, finding a quiet time to talk with him. But never mind, she had already made too many excuses. If an opportunity did not present itself, she would make one.

As she was changing Rachel's soiled diaper, she heard Morgan come out of his room and walk somewhat painfully down the stairs. A moment later the front door opened and closed, and she heard his footsteps moving across the planks of the front porch.

Tucking the baby back into her cradle, Cassandra chose a fresh gown, yanked on her boots, splashed her face and ran a hasty brush through her tangled curls. If she wanted to catch Morgan alone, now would be her best chance. Delaying the confrontation would only make things more difficult.

She came out onto the porch as the sun was rising over the prairie. The first rays of morning glittered on a broad expanse of charred earth that stretched to the eastern horizon. Vultures circled above the plain, searching for the burned carcasses of trapped animals.

The sight left Cassandra heartsick. But when she looked for them, she found signs of hope. To the west of the ranch the rocky foothills, aided by water from the bursting dam, had halted the fire before it could sweep into the mountain forests. Above the black line of destruction, the grassy slopes teemed with birds and animals that had escaped the flames.

The barn had burned to the ground, but the other buildings on the ranch had been spared. Horses and cows, crowded but safe, milled in the corral. Cassandra's spirits rose as she saw her old dun mule among them, munching placidly on a wisp of hay.

The air still smelled of smoke, but the songs of meadowlarks rang out across the clear distance, a poignant reminder that nature was resilient and life would continue.

Morgan stood alone beside the ruined barn, gazing morosely at the soaked and blackened timbers. Cassandra's stomach clenched as she saw him and, for the space of a heartbeat, her courage threatened to take wing. But no, she had to tell him now. If she waited another hour, she would lose her resolve altogether.

Gulping back the tight knot in her throat, she walked down the steps and across the yard. The mud's surface, already dry, crumbled where she stepped.

Morgan did not turn around as she came up behind him, but when she spoke his name, he reached back, caught her waist and pulled her to his side. Cassandra pressed her head against his shoulder, sensing how much he needed her. Last night, in his loving, he had held nothing back. He had joined with her in complete trust. But all that was about to change. After hearing what she had resolved to say, Morgan would never trust her again.

Oh, why hadn't she told him sooner, before her words had the power to crush his heart?

Steeling herself, she took a sharp breath. "Morgan, there's something I need to—"

"Mr. Morgan!" Thomas Chang had burst out onto the porch, his pigtail flying as he sprinted toward them. His voice, so seldom heard, rang with panic.

"It's Mr. Jacob!" he panted, reaching them. "Something's wrong! I can't wake him up!"

Jacob Tolliver lingered near death for nearly nine days, drifting in and out of consciousness in the massive four-poster bed he had shared with Ryan's mother. With Morgan and the Chang men needed for the rebuilding of the dam, it was Cassandra who most often sat by his bedside, gripping his hands when he was in pain, reading or sewing while he slept.

Sometimes she brought Rachel with her, cradling the baby in the crook of her arm to keep one hand free for Jacob. If he happened to be awake, he would gaze up at the tiny girl, eyes glimmering with pleasure in his pain-ravaged face.

"Dyin's not so bad, Red, long as a man knows he's left a piece of himself behind," he told her as she sat beside him on the ninth day. "Little Red, here, she's not just a piece of me, she's a piece of my Anna Claire and a piece of Ryan. That's what counts in the long view of things."

Cassandra masked a spasm of self-disgust with a gentle smile. The burden of her secret had become almost unbearable, but she was not about to shatter the peace of a dying man.

"You're quite a woman yourself, Red," he gasped, reaching out to capture Cassandra's hand in his knotted fingers. "My son is a lucky man. Hell, if I was a few years younger I might give him a run for his money!"

Once again, Cassandra willed her expression to

freeze. Was the old man talking about Ryan, confused in his illness between past and present? Or had he somehow guessed that she spent her nights in Morgan's bed, loving him when their need burned hot and sweet, or simply holding him when the burdens of the day were so heavy that he could not put them aside, holding him as a woman holds her man when he is weary and wounded and needing the comfort of her arms?

She had not told Morgan her terrible secret. How could she, when he was so beset with concerns about his father and the ranch? How could she shatter his trust when he needed her almost as much as she needed him?

"Red?" The hoarse croak of Jacob's voice broke into her reverie. Cassandra felt the strain in him as he gripped her hand.

"Are you hurting?" she whispered.

Jacob's head rolled from side to side on the pillow, but his pain-glazed eyes told her the truth. "Listen, Red, there's somethin' I need to tell you." He paused to clear his throat. "That night of the party, I had a lawyer fellow here. Took him inside and changed my will, so it's all legal. Little Red, here, will get a fifth of my estate, and the two of you will always have a home here, for the rest of your lives if you want."

All this for cheating you! Cassandra could not muster enough resolve to hold back her tears. She gripped Jacob's hand, feeling trapped. She had everything she had ever wanted—security for herself and her child, and the love of a man who stopped her heart every time she looked at him. But at what price? And when would payment be due? She felt as if she had made a deal with the devil, who would show up shortly to demand her eternal soul.

Would telling Jacob the truth now be an act of redemption, or would it only cause a dying man needless pain? Cassandra gazed down at her sleeping daughter, struggling against the voice of her own conscience.

"So, what d'you say, Red?" Jacob was waiting for her response. His sunken eyes glowed like embers in the light of the fading sunset.

"Thank you." Cassandra forced the words she knew he wanted to hear. "You've been so good to me, Jacob. So much better than I deserve."

"You've made an old man happy," he said. "Now I can die in peace, knowing I've done my best for Ryan's little girl."

Cassandra lifted her gaze to the window, unable to meet his eyes. A tiny sob escaped her throat.

"Tell Morgan I said to give Little Red anything she needs," he rasped. "Anything…" His voice trailed off as he lapsed back into unconsciousness. Cassandra remained at his side, clasping the gnarled hand, lifting it now and again to press against her damp cheek.

Jacob did not speak again. Late that night, with Morgan and Thomas at his bedside, the old mountain man breathed his last and slipped silently away.

Raw and drained of tears, Morgan closed his father's eyes and pulled the top of the sheet up to cover the craggy face he knew so well. Thomas was weeping openly, the tears streaming down his broad ivory face. His broken sobs echoed in the stillness of the lamplit room.

Morgan walked softly out of the room and made his way through the parlor, past the stairs and out onto the porch. Leaning against the railing, he gazed across the yard to where the charred timbers of the barn jutted against the cloudy sky. The air was thick and muggy, flowing around him like water. The scent of rain tantalized his nostrils. But it was only ghost rain, he told himself. It had fooled him before, but he would not let himself be drawn in by its siren's call tonight.

Turning, he glanced up at the dark window of Cassandra's room. She had scarcely left Jacob's side over the past few days, and tonight she had looked dead on her feet. When she'd fallen asleep in the armchair, Morgan had carried her upstairs and laid her gently on her bed.

Had she remained there, he wondered, or would he find her waiting when he dragged himself into his own bed, her arms ready to cradle and soothe him? Over the past nine difficult days, Cassandra's love had renewed and sustained him. She had become his anchor. It was almost frightening how much he needed her.

But what they had was an illusion, like the ghost rain, Morgan reminded himself. The two of them had been living in a state of truce, a truce that was not

meant to endure past the end of Jacob's fragile life.
Now that his father was gone, the old demons of distrust and antagonism were bound to rear their heads
again. This time he would have no choice except to
deal with them.

Morgan mounted the stairs, one hand rubbing the
strained muscles at the back of his neck. Thomas,
devoted to Jacob in death as in life, would prepare
the body for burial and place it in the pine coffin that
lay across two sawhorses in the coolness of the spring
house. The grave would be dug tomorrow, and the
funeral service would be held as soon as they could
summon a few close friends and neighbors. But nothing on the ranch would be the same without Jacob
Tolliver. The old mountain man had built this place
from raw prairie, and his had always been the vital
spirit behind it. Now Jacob was gone. Ryan was gone.
And Morgan had come to realize in the past nine days
that it wasn't the land, the stock and the buildings
that made the Tolliver Ranch home. It was the bonds
of family.

His bedroom lay in darkness, the bed an indistinct
block of shadow against the far wall. Exhausted, Morgan dropped his clothes where he stood, lifted the
bedcovers and tumbled wearily between the sheets.

She was there, sweet and fragrant, drawing him
close to bury his face between her breasts. "I'm
sorry," she whispered. "Oh, Morgan, I loved him,
too. I'm so sorry."

He pressed against her, seeking the warmth and
comfort that only she could give him. Her eyelashes

were wet against his cheek, and suddenly he knew that he wanted nothing more than to spend every night of his life holding this woman in his arms, loving her, giving her his children. What did her past—or his—matter, as long as they could start clean and go on from here?

There would be no more games between them, Morgan resolved. No more distrust. No more deception. When Jacob was buried and the worst of the grieving was done, he would ask her to be his wife.

As for the letter from Hamilton Crawford, he would take it from the safe first thing tomorrow and burn it, unopened. Cassandra's past no longer mattered. Nothing mattered except their love.

Thunder echoed through the open window, rumbling like cannon fire across the charred prairie. A cool night breeze ruffled the gingham curtains, filling the room with fresh, moist air. There was a second thunderclap, so close that it rattled the glass panes. Then, as if the night sky had split open, the rain began to fall—not a fleeting shower, but a life-giving downpour that went on and on for much of the night. Morgan lay with his arms around Cassandra, listening to the drone of water on the roof. The rain was a gift from Jacob's departing spirit, he thought. A gift and a blessing.

Chapter Fifteen

Two days later Jacob Tolliver was laid to rest beside his beloved Anna Claire on a knoll overlooking what was left of the reservoir. The ground was damp with rain, the grass already greening in the clear morning sunlight. Meadowlark songs sparkled on the crystal-line air.

Morgan stood gazing down at the long mound of earth that Cassandra had decorated with the few wild-flowers she could find. It was a peaceful spot, he mused. If Ryan's remains were ever found he would bring them home and bury them here, next to those of his parents. If nothing else, that would provide a sense of closure—for Cassandra as well as for himself.

Glancing around, he caught sight of her a few yards away, chatting with a neighbor couple who'd come for the funeral service. Word of Jacob's passing had traveled fast. Friends had come from as far as fifty miles to pay their respects to one of the true pioneers of ranching in the territory. The gathering was a somber echo of last month's party. Chang had outdone himself once more in preparing a feast of barbecued beef and beans, with his incomparable biscuits and, for dessert, tiny jam tarts that melted on the tongue. The aromas of meat, onions, spices and fresh-baked pastry floated up to the solemn gathering on the knoll, calling hungry guests to put aside their mourning and troop back down the path to feed their bellies.

Morgan's eyes rested briefly on a small mound in a lonely corner of the family graveyard. Had things turned out differently, his stillborn son would have been six years old now—bright and quick, big enough to sit his own pony and lasso a fence post from the saddle. He would be learning to read and write and to do a man's chores on the ranch.

Could anything have been done to save his baby boy? That question would haunt Morgan to the end of his days.

A flash of blue caught his eye, and he saw that Cassandra had laid a fresh bouquet of gentians across the tiny grave. Glancing up, Morgan caught her watching him. Her eyes were warm with understanding and love. Yes, he had made the right decision last night. The past no longer mattered. Only the future was important, the future he wanted to build with her as his wife.

From the top of the knoll he could see the broad sweep of the prairie below. The seared landscape was already dotted with patches of green. By next spring, there would be few signs the fire had even occurred.

The grass would grow again. The hayfields would recover. The barn would be rebuilt and the reservoir would fill. Life would go on, and he would do his best to see that it was good.

The crowd was milling toward the downward path now. Among them he noticed a gaunt man wearing the dusty uniform of an army captain. Morgan had seen the man at Fort Caspar, but the two of them had never spoken. Strange that he would be here now, especially since there would not have been time for the commander of the fort to get word of the funeral and dispatch someone to represent the garrison.

The captain had moved off to one side of the trail, fidgeting impatiently as if he had some business to finish. Catching his eye, Morgan delayed until most of the crowd had left the knoll. Then he walked over to where the officer stood waiting.

"Have you come to pay your respects, Captain?" he asked.

The captain shook his head. He had close-cropped, graying hair and a face so lean and narrow that it reminded Morgan of an ax head, viewed blade-on. "You have my condolences, of course, Mr. Tolliver," he said. "But I didn't know about the funeral. I'm being transferred north, so Colonel Craig gave me something to deliver to you on the way. He said it might be important."

He reached into his military tunic and drew out a cigar-sized roll of tanned buckskin. It was tightly bound with a rawhide thong, the long edge of it carefully sealed with tallow. "An old trapper who stopped for supplies brought it in,'' he told Morgan. ''Said a party of Arapaho gave it to him. I would guess it might be some kind of message, since it has the name of your ranch on the outside.''

Morgan's fingers closed around the tightly rolled leather. At first he'd thought it might be from Washakie. But the captain had said it was the Cheyenne who'd given it to the old trapper. The Shoshone and the Cheyenne had never been friends.

Then there was the writing on the outside. Only a white man would have added the name of the ranch, in English.

The bundle was stained and curled at the ends, as if it had been dropped into water or soaked in the rain. Morgan turned it until he could make out the weathered lettering that ran along the sealed edge of the buckskin.

The name, Tolliver Ranch, was printed in faded reddish brown, as if the writer, lacking pen and ink, had dipped a sharpened quill in berry juice, or even in blood. Each block letter was formed in classic schoolboy fashion, exactly the way Anna Claire Tolliver, who'd counted good penmanship as golden, had taught her young son.

Morgan's mouth went dry as reason confirmed what his heart had known at once.

He was holding a message from Ryan.

Morgan's first impulse was to slash the rawhide thong and read the message here and now. But the captain was watching him with curious dishwater eyes, and he realized that whatever was inside, he wanted to open the rolled buckskin alone, where his own responses could not betray him.

The mourners were trailing down the hill, with Cassandra in their midst. Looking demure in a hastily altered gray silk bombazine gown, she was going out of her way to be gracious, making sure each guest was introduced to the others and made to feel comfortable. She might have noticed the captain's presence, but she had left the graveside before his encounter with Morgan. She would not have heard their conversation or seen the mysterious bundle change hands.

Morgan glanced down the path, to where the coiled braid of her fiery hair shone like a beacon in the sunlight. The leather missive felt unnaturally heavy in his hand. By rights, he should share it with her, he thought. What it contained could be as vital to Cassandra as it was to him.

But he did not trust his own emotions at a time like this. The message could be months old, written before the accident, or whatever it had been, that separated Ryan from his dory on the upper Yellowstone. To fill her with false hope before he knew what the message contained would be cruel.

"I'll be taking my leave," the captain said. "I'm due at Fort Kearny in two days' time, and it's a long ride."

"We can't send you on your way hungry," Morgan said, remembering his manners. "You'll need to eat sooner or later, and there's a good meal waiting down below."

"Can't refuse an offer like that," the captain responded. "I've heard that Chinese cook of yours makes the best beef and biscuits in the territory."

"I'll see that Chang gives you an extra portion to take along. But it tastes best while it's hot. Go on. Tell them I'll be coming in a few minutes."

Morgan was relieved when the captain took his cue and strode off down the path. He forced himself to bide his time, waiting to be sure the blue uniform had disappeared from sight. Then he walked back to his father's grave, where he stood staring down at the freshly shoveled earth, thinking how much it would have meant to Jacob to get word of his adored younger son before he died. Swallowing the ache in his throat, he opened his pocket knife and slashed through the rawhide thong that bound the rolled bundle. It peeled away, leaving its shrunken imprint in the softer buckskin.

Morgan's hands quivered as he ran his index finger under the tallow seal. Stiffened by time and moisture, the thin leather rustled as he unrolled it, threatening to crack and break apart. Smoothing it gently against his vest, he held the weathered surface to the most favorable light.

The message was brief, and there was no date, but the water-blurred writing was unmistakably Ryan's. Morgan strained his eyes to make out each word.

Broke leg and lost boat in rapids. Now on upper Big Horn, resting with Arapaho who found me.

Great fishing and hunting here. Will be back before first snow. Don't worry about me.
Ryan

Morgan's legs refused to support him. He dropped to his knees beside the grave, seized by such a storm of relief and fury that it was all he could do to contain it.

Damn fool boy! The family had all but given him up for lost, his father had died grieving, a young woman had probably given birth to his child, and here he was, off having himself a grand adventure without a care in the world! If the two of them had been face-to-face, Morgan would not have known whether to embrace his brother or shake the teeth out of his reckless young head!

Only when a drop of moisture spattered the leather surface did Morgan realize he was weeping. For the space of a long breath he let the scalding tears flow down his windburned cheeks. Then, grateful to be alone, he rose to his feet, rolled up the message and tucked it into the inner pocket of his vest.

Sooner or later, he knew, Cassandra would have to see it. And then what? He reeled as the implications struck him.

He and Cassandra had become lovers. He had been looking forward eagerly to putting the past aside, making her his wife and raising her daughter as his own. But all of this had been premised on the belief that Ryan was gone for good. Now, suddenly, everything had changed.

Cassandra had claimed to be in love with Ryan. Would she love him still? Would he love her? And, love aside, wouldn't Ryan have the obligation—and the right—to marry the mother of his own child?

Churning, Morgan gazed out over the burned prairie. Only one thing was rock solid in this mess of uncertainty. He loved Cassandra to the depths of his dark and lonely soul. And he loved his hot-blooded young brother almost as much. If he did not do the right thing by both of them, and by little Rachel, he would regret it to the end of his days.

One more thing became certain as he mulled it over in his mind. He could not wait months for Ryan to come home on his own. He would have to go and find him, tell him about Jacob's death and bring him back to resolve matters with Cassandra. If a shotgun wedding was the only solution, so be it. Morgan would see things made right, whatever the cost.

How much to tell Cassandra was the one remaining question. Tell her everything, his conscience argued. She had the right to see Ryan's letter and to know that he, Morgan, was leaving to bring his brother home.

But what if the worst had happened and Ryan was no longer alive? Or what if the young whelp refused to come back to the ranch and face his manly responsibilities? The more Cassandra knew at the outset, the more she would worry, and the more she could be hurt in the end. No, he could not risk telling her anything. Not until he found Ryan and made certain the truth was served.

He would leave at once, Morgan resolved, before

she could demand to know where he was going, or even insist on going with him. He would leave before her arms and kisses and pleas could hold him back, before the temptation to lie to her beautiful face became too strong to resist.

From the edge of the knoll he could see the long plank tables and benches that had been set up in the yard below. He could see Cassandra among the guests. Her duties would keep her there long enough for him to circle to the back door of the house, grab a few essentials and speak briefly with Chang. One of the boys could saddle a horse and bring it to a secluded spot farther up the creek, where he would be waiting, ready to ride.

His best chance of finding Ryan lay in picking up the course of the Big Horn River and following it north, toward the Montana border. The distance was not great. If Ryan was still with the Arapaho, and if they had not moved their camp, it could take as little as a week's time to reach him. The two of them could be back at the ranch in a fortnight.

But that estimate was based on the best possible conditions. In reality, a list of things that could go wrong would be almost endless. By now, Ryan could be anywhere in the vast wilderness of forest, mountains, streams and canyons that stretched all the way to Canada and beyond. Finding him—assuming it was even possible—could take weeks, even months. But he would not give up, Morgan vowed. No matter how long it took, dead or alive, he would bring his brother home.

He could only hope Cassandra would understand and forgive him.

"Have we met before, Captain?" Cassandra seated herself across the table from the blade-thin army officer, who was digging into the mountain of food on his plate.

"Not likely, ma'am. I'd have remembered." He took a hefty mouthful of buttered biscuit, his manner suggesting that food was more important to him than conversation.

"You're a friend of Morgan's then? Or Mr. Tolliver's?" she persisted, determined to be a good hostess.

He shook his head, his stubbled jaw working as he chewed. Cassandra's gaze darted hastily around the yard, searching for Morgan, but there was no sign of him. Perhaps he had remained on the knoll to mourn beside his father's grave.

"You must have known Ryan then!" Cassandra could hear the artificial brightness in her own voice. "How kind of you to come all this way for the burial service!"

Again he shook his head, taking a moment to gulp down the food in his mouth. "Didn't come for the funeral. I was passing this way and stopped by to deliver a message from the fort. But thank you right kindly for the meal. That Chinaman of yours is one fine cook."

"Message?" Cassandra stared at him, apprehension crawling like a spider up the back of her neck.

"Yes'm." The captain seized a fresh biscuit from a tray on the table, split it open and slathered on a generous dollop of butter. "Some old-timer brought it to the fort. Not much to it—just a rolled-up piece of leather with the name of the ranch written on the outside. Looked like it might have come a long way."

"Who was it from?" Cassandra felt as if a cold hand were tightening around her throat. "Did you see what it said?"

"Didn't think it was my place to look." The captain dipped a piece of biscuit into the spicy bean gravy and held it poised between his plate and his mouth. "Anyhow, it was sealed shut. I gave it to Mr. Tolliver up there by the grave. If you want to know more, you'll have to ask him about it."

"Yes…yes, I'll do that." Cassandra forced her face to freeze in its polite smile. Surely Morgan had many acquaintances—trappers, prospectors, rivermen, even Indians—who might have sent such a message. There could be any one of a dozen explanations behind it, none of them having anything to do with her or with Ryan.

But all her instincts shrilled that she was wrong. The message had to be from Ryan, or from someone who had found him. Nothing else would have kept Morgan alone on the knoll for so long. And nothing else would trigger the gut-clenching premonition that her life was about to change forever.

"Enjoy your lunch, Captain." She forced herself to stand, turn and walk back toward the house. She needed to find Morgan. She needed to tell him everything while she still had the chance.

For the past ten days she had been living a stolen dream of love, pretending that it would never end. If Ryan Tolliver was alive—and she prayed for Morgan's sake that it might be so—her dream was about to shatter into a thousand pieces.

She rounded the house, startling a red hen that was pecking for crumbs outside the kitchen door. Maybe she was wrong about the message. Maybe it meant nothing. But that made no difference. She had lied to the man she loved and to his family. Now, once and for all, it was time for the lies to end.

Beyond the backyard she could see the lower end of the path that wound to the crest of the knoll. *Let him still be there,* she prayed, catching up her skirts for the climb. *Oh, please let him be there!*

As she broke into a run, she saw Chang's stocky figure hobbling toward her from the direction of the creek. "Chang!" she exclaimed, wheeling toward him. "Have you seen Morgan? Someone told me he was—"

The worried expression on his face brought her up short.

"Mr. Morgan is gone, missy," Chang said. "He told me to say that he might be gone many days, but not to worry."

She stared at him, feeling strangely numb. "But where was he going, Chang? And why? Surely you must know something!"

Chang shook his head, his face furrowed with concern. ''I know only what I told you, missy. Nothing more.''

Morgan gave the mare her head, letting her pick her own path through the tall, thick willows. Ahead, he could hear the musical splash of a waterfall. The sound was cool and inviting in the midday heat.

Pity he couldn't give in to the temptation to stop for a swim. After ten solid days of riding, he was sweat-crusted, mosquito-bitten, saddle sore and as cross as a grizzly bear. Nothing would have felt better than a plunge into clean, cold water. But he had been seeing signs of Arapaho all morning—tracks, signs of harvested game, even occasional flickers of movement on the bluffs above the Big Horn River. The Arapaho were not at war, but he would be vulnerable in the water, and he had lived too long as a Shoshone not to be wary.

Drifting from the north, the breeze carried the blended aromas of alder smoke and roasting venison. All Morgan's senses told him he was nearing the camp of the Arapaho band Ryan had mentioned in his letter.

Would he find his brother here, safe and well? Or had this long, rough ride been a waste of time? Ryan had always been as unpredictable and elusive as the wind. Aside from his comment on the good hunting and fishing, there was no reason to believe he would have stayed here with the Indians. But Morgan was not sorry he had made the journey. Given one chance in a hundred of finding Ryan alive, he would have taken it.

The sounds of the waterfall were closer now. Mingled with the splash of falling water, Morgan could hear high-pitched peals of feminine laughter. He hesitated, then decided to remain on his horse. If he ran into trouble, a swift retreat would serve him better than a stealthy approach.

With one hand resting lightly on his pistol, he nudged the mare forward. The willows were tall and thick enough to hide him, but they also blocked his view. He would have to venture dangerously close to the falls to see what might be happening there.

Now, through the screen of willows, he could see the waterfall, a sheer white cascade falling over a series of rocky ledges to splash into a rock-lined pool. For the first few seconds, Morgan could see no one. Then, suddenly, three heads broke the surface of the water, two of them dark and sleek, one as tawny as the pelt of a cougar.

Ryan Tolliver had never looked more alive.

Morgan cursed under his breath as he realized he had come upon a spirited game of tag. The two giggling Indian girls, who looked to be about seventeen, were as naked as newborn babies. They splashed Ryan with water, then laughed hysterically as he plunged after them. It was a game all three participants seemed to be enjoying.

Not trusting himself to speak, Morgan pushed through the screen of willows into plain sight. The two girls shrieked and scrambled onto the rocks at the far side of the pool. Their wet buttocks flashed as they vanished into the alder thicket, leaving Ryan alone in the water.

"Hey, brother." Ryan grinned up at Morgan, his cat-colored eyes sparkling with merriment. "Come on in! The water's not too cold once you get used to it. Maybe I can even talk the girls into coming back!"

Burdened by the full weight of an elder brother's responsibilities, Morgan glowered down at him. Just looking at Ryan, tanned, laughing and heedless of the world that was crumbling around him, made him feel old and tired.

Wearily he dropped the reins and climbed down from the saddle. "Get out of the water," he said. "We need to talk."

"If you say so." Ryan dog-paddled to the near side of the pool and stretched out his open hand, a clear sign that he wanted to be helped onto the bank. Morgan reached out and clasped his brother's strong fingers, only to be caught off guard as Ryan, his feet braced against an underwater rock, gave a hard pull and, with a raucous war whoop, jerked him headfirst into the pool.

Morgan hit the ice-cold water with a splash, went under and came up fighting mad. All the months of worry and mourning, all the turmoil that had befallen the family, and this featherbrained young scapegrace was as unconcerned as a summer breeze!

Raging, Morgan lunged for his brother. Ryan met the force of his attack with a whoop of laughter. In the next instant the two of them were wrestling wildly in the water, each struggling to subdue the other.

Morgan had the advantage in strength and experience, but he was weighed down by his soggy clothes, and Ryan was as agile and slippery as an otter. Again and again, he slid out of reach, only to duck under the water, seize Morgan's legs and yank him off balance.

Ryan's spirit, however, was infectious. As the melee continued, ending in a draw, Morgan felt his rage evaporating. By the time they heaved themselves out onto the bank, laughing and exhausted, his anger was gone. It was simply good to be with his wild young brother again.

Side by side they stretched out on the grass to let the sun warm their chilled bodies. Morgan cleared the laughter from his throat and mind, knowing the news from home could not wait any longer.

"Now we talk," he said.

"All right." Ryan, to his credit, knew when to be serious. "Tell me what's happening."

Morgan told him about the fire and about Jacob's death. Ryan's throat moved as he swallowed tears.

"I should have been there," he said. "Damn it, Morgan, I should have been there for the old man. I'm sorry."

"There's one thing more." Morgan girded himself to speak the words. "A few months ago, it seems, you became a father."

"What?" Ryan sat bolt upright. His golden eyes had taken on a wild, hunted look. "But I al-

ways…take precautions. I swear it, Morgan. I don't know how anything like this could happen.'' He swallowed hard. ''All right, who's the girl?''

Morgan willed his voice to sound flat and expressionless. ''Her name's Cassandra. Cassandra Riley. She and her baby are waiting for you back at the ranch.''

Ryan stared at him blankly. He shook his head. ''I'm sorry, I—''

''Is your memory that short? Spunky little redhead, about as tall as your vest pocket? Curly mop of hair? Blue eyes?'' Morgan's gaze narrowed as he forced himself to continue. ''According to her story, she met you in Cheyenne and the two of you fell in love. She's seen the scar on your leg and knows how you came by it. And her little girl's the spitting image of your baby picture, dimpled chin and all.''

Ryan looked as if he were about to be sick. ''Tell me this is a joke,'' he said weakly. ''Morgan, I've never heard of Cassandra Riley, or any other Cassandra. I've never even met the woman, let alone slept with her. I swear it on a stack of Bibles. I swear it on my mother's grave. She's lying. That's all there is to it.''

Chapter Sixteen

Abandoning the river course, Morgan and Ryan cut across the mountains, shortening the journey home by three days. They rode hard, mounting at first light and collapsing into their blankets only after it became too dark to see their way.

Much of the trail was too narrow for them to ride abreast, which was just as well, since Morgan was in no mood for conversation. He sat grimly in the saddle, his emotions churning as he remembered the heaven of Cassandra in his arms, her kisses, her whispered words of love.

So many lies. And he had come to believe them all. What was he going to say to her when he saw her again?

He had burned Hamilton Crawford's letter unread, telling himself Cassandra's past didn't matter. But he should have known better. Past mistakes could be buried and forgotten. But how could love survive without honesty and trust?

Had Cassandra's love been a lie, like the rest of her story? Soon he would confront her and demand the full truth. He was not looking forward to hearing what she had to say.

"What are you going to do about her?" Ryan had come alongside him where the trail crossed a high meadow, dotted with late summer pasqueflowers that matched the deep blue of Cassandra's eyes. "There are laws against what she's done to our family. She could go to prison for a long time."

Morgan shifted his weight to ease the soreness of too many hours in the saddle. "She was good to Jacob," he said. "It made his last days easier, having her there. And if he died happier, believing her little girl was his grandchild, what harm did it do?"

"What harm? Bloody hell, Morgan, she took him in! Just like she took you in, and everybody else!" Ryan's golden eyes narrowed sharply. "That plan would have set her up for life, wouldn't it? I don't come back, so she marries you. She gets a father for her bastard baby, a fine home with servants, the Tolliver name, the whole package! I can't wait to meet the scheming little redheaded Jezebel and give her a piece of my mind before we haul her off to jail! She deserves to—"

"That's enough!" Morgan snapped. "Can't you just be quiet for a while?"

Ryan stared at him. Then his eyes twitched at the corners, and he burst out laughing. "By heaven, she really *has* taken you in! You were ready to play right into her dainty little hands and give her everything she wanted! Then my message arrived, so you decided you had to find me and do the right thing. Only it didn't turn out that way, did it? Morgan, you big, noble Shoshone fool, I salute you! Under that stodgy exterior beats the heart of a true romantic!''

Morgan was saved from the temptation to throttle his brother by the sudden narrowing of the trail. Ryan's laughter echoed behind him as they fell into single file. He nudged the mare to a trot, his face burning below the brim of his Stetson. Was he really that transparent? Was it so evident that he'd fallen in love with the woman Ryan described as a scheming little redheaded Jezebel?

The shadows were deepening into twilight when they topped the last hill and emerged from the trees above the reservoir. Ryan gave a low whistle as he saw the broken dam and the charred remains of the barn below. "I'm sorry I wasn't here to help," he said.

"There wasn't much you could have done," Morgan replied. "But we could use your help with the rebuilding. I hope you plan to stick around for a while."

"You can count on it," Ryan said. "I can swing a hammer with the best of them."

For a few minutes they paused to pay their respects at Jacob's grave. Then, leading their tired horses, they followed the trail that wound down the knoll and along the creek. Morgan braced himself for the reunion with Cassandra. Whatever happened next was bound to be painful for her and wrenching for him.

In the gathering dusk, they almost missed the small, silent figure standing where the path branched off toward the Chang house. Only when she spoke, startling them both, did Morgan realize it was Mei Li.

"We saw you coming," she said, beaming at Ryan. "Our hearts are happy that you have returned to us. My husband is preparing your supper in the kitchen." She turned to Morgan, her smile fading. "This is for you."

The envelope she handed him was unsealed, with the flap tucked neatly inside. In the darkness, he could not make out the writing on the envelope's face, but he recognized the weight and texture of the paper he kept in his own desk.

He felt the plummeting of his heart. "Where's Cassandra?" he forced himself to ask.

"She and her little one are gone." Mei Li's voice was like the tolling of a sad, small bell. "Very early, the morning after you left, she hitched her mule to that old cart in the shed. Then she took her baby and some supplies, and she drove away."

"You didn't try to stop her?" Morgan demanded.

"Stop her how? She is a free woman. She took time only to say goodbye and to give me this letter for you." She glanced back over her shoulder, where a lantern was bobbing toward them from the direction of the Chang house. "My younger son is coming to put your horses away. You can use his light to read, if you wish."

Morgan would have preferred to open the letter in private, but that would have meant refusing Mei Li's

offer and causing her to lose face. Forcing his features
into an impassive mask, he slid the single folded page
from the envelope and opened its face to the light of
Johnny Chang's lantern. Calming his emotions, he began a silent reading of her plain but graceful script.

My dearest Morgan,
If you have spoken with your brother, you already know that I lied to you. And even if
you've returned without finding him, it's time I
told you the truth. All of it. I've been wanting
to tell you for many weeks, now. But time after
time, my courage has failed me. I cannot let it
fail me now.

Morgan glanced up from the letter to find three
pairs of eyes fixed on his face. Johnny Chang's gaze
was bright and curious, his mother's brimmed with
compassion. Ryan's golden eyes blazed with angry
impatience.
Ignoring them all, Morgan read on.

Rachel is not your brother's child. She was
fathered by my late husband, Jake Logan, who
died last winter in a saloon brawl, leaving me
alone, friendless and destitute. It was seeing
Ryan's picture and noticing his close resemblance to Jake that first suggested this terrible
scheme to me. The details of how I carried it out
no longer matter.
I know you will never forgive me, Morgan.

But try, at least, to understand the desperation that drove me to deceive you. I was close to giving birth, with no means to provide for myself and my child. We were about to lose the roof over our heads and be thrown out into the street. Even then I resisted the plan that the very devil seemed to have put into my head. I had been raised to be honest and fair. Taking advantage of a family's grief was, to me, an unthinkable wrong.

It was not until my landlord, a man named Seamus Hawkins, lay dead at my feet, killed in a fall as I fought off his advances, that I realized I had no choice. If I stayed in Laramie I would surely be arrested. I had to leave town, and I had only one chance of refuge for myself and my baby. I took that chance. You know the rest of the story.

I knew from the beginning that one day I would pay for my sin. But I failed to anticipate the goodness, friendship and generosity I would find here. I certainly didn't expect to fall in love, but it happened. I lied to you about many things, Morgan, but when I said I loved you, it was no lie. I love you still, with all my heart. Whatever happens in the days ahead, that will never change.

Forget me, my dearest. And please don't let what I have done leave a stain on your life. Find a good woman to love, and be happy with her. You have so much to give...

The last lines of the letter were blurred by splattered tears. There was no signature at the end.

Paralyzed by his own emotions, Morgan gazed down at the page in his hands. Cassandra had lied to him. She had lied to his father, and taken advantage of their grief in the cruelest possible way.

Why couldn't he find it in his heart to hate her?

He thought of Hamilton Crawford's letter, the letter he had burned in the dark morning hours while she slept in his bed. What if he had opened it and learned the truth? Would it have made any difference? Would it have kept him from falling in love with her?

"I think I have the right to see that letter." Ryan snatched the page from Morgan's hands. Morgan bit back the protest that the message was too personal to share. Ryan had been a vital part of Cassandra's scheme. He deserved to know what she had written.

From babyhood, Ryan had possessed an open countenance that mirrored whatever he was thinking. Now, as he read Cassandra's letter, his face was a kaleidoscope of changing emotions. Rage. Anger. Dismay. Disbelief. Amusement. Suddenly, with no warning at all, he burst into unbridled laughter.

Morgan stared at him, dumbfounded. "What the devil?"

Ryan was still laughing. He shook his head as he struggled to bring himself under control. "I'm sorry. It just struck me, Morgan. There's no problem here. You love her. She loves you. And for all her scheming, she hasn't done any of us a lick of harm!"

He shoved the letter back into Morgan's hand.

"Don't be a proud fool, brother! Go and find the woman! Marry her, bring her back here and start having babies, before you go sour on life and turn into a cranky, bitter old man!"

Cassandra dunked the scrub brush in the wooden bucket, splashing soapy water on the grimy floor. It had been a another busy day at the Cheyenne Star Hotel. The dining room staff had been on the run since breakfast, splattering the kitchen with maple syrup, coffee, pan gravy, meat drippings and bacon grease. Now that the place was finally closed, it was her job to make everything spick-and-span for the next day's work.

Pausing to rest, she sank back onto her heels and massaged the soreness at the small of her back. Above her, on the countertop, the plates, glasses, pans and utensils she had washed gleamed in orderly rows. She'd been lucky to find this job, Cassandra reminded herself. And she'd been luckier still to get her meals and a spare room right above the kitchen, from which Rachel could be heard if she happened to wake in the night.

She'd even managed to find a corner in a nearby livery stable for Xavier. The money for his keep was dear, but the surly old mule had been a true friend, and Cassandra could not bear the thought of abandoning him to the glue works.

All in all, she'd not done badly for herself. But Cheyenne was only a two-hour train ride from Laramie, and she lived in a state of constant fear that she would be seen and reported to the law. As soon as she saved a little money, she planned to move to Omaha, or even Saint Louis. But the meager change she'd managed to put aside so far would not get her ten miles out of town.

Yawning, she pushed her hair back from her face with a dripping hand. Her puckered fingers came away stained with cheap, black dye.

The new hair color was not flattering on her. It washed out her eyes and made her skin look like stale flour paste. But it was survival that mattered now. And no one looking for her would expect to find a brunette.

Cassandra had changed her name and her appearance and taken this night job, where she wasn't likely to be seen by strangers. Still, she jumped at every passing shadow. As the woman who had killed Seamus Hawkins and plotted to cheat the Tollivers, she was branded for life. No matter how far or fast she ran, she would never stop looking over her shoulder.

As she bent to her scrubbing, images crept in, unbidden, from the shadows of her memory. Mornings on the ranch; the rising sun chasing shadows across the windswept prairie; meadowlark songs, the smell of fresh coffee and the heavenly aroma of Chang's biscuits, and the sight of Morgan standing straight and tall beside the corral fence, the breeze ruffling his raven hair.

Cassandra willed the images to disappear. Her life on the ranch had been a beautiful dream. But like all dreams, it was over. This was reality—bleeding knuckles, grimy floors and the dark, smelly room where she spent her days with Rachel, afraid to venture out into the sunlight. Remembering only made things worse, especially when the memory of Morgan's lovemaking swept over her, leaving her hollow and aching in her bed. She had hurt Morgan, she knew, and he would never forgive her. But she would never be sorry for having loved him. Whatever happened in the years to come, she would hold him in the deepest part of her heart as the one true love of her life.

A sudden noise outside the back window startled her, causing her to glance up. The shadow on the other side of the glass vanished so quickly that Cassandra could not be sure whether she had seen it at all. It was nothing, she told herself, or at worst, it might be some homeless drifter rummaging through the trash for scraps of food. The door was locked. She was safe here.

But even as she returned to her work, she felt the danger sense, as if something cold and reptilian had just slithered up her arm.

Hamilton Crawford leaned back in his leather armchair, one hand toying with his well-trimmed silver-gray mustache. Morgan watched him anxiously as he read the letter Cassandra had written. Sharing that letter, even with a friend, had not been an easy thing for Morgan. But he was willing to do anything that might help him find Cassandra.

"Do you really think you can track her down?" Ham glanced up, scowling.

"That's what I'm asking you," Morgan said. "I've been through Laramie with a fine-tooth comb and found no trace of her. There's a chance she could be here in Cheyenne, but every day I'm losing time. If you know of someplace she might have gone, or someone who might have taken her in—" He thrust his hands into his pockets. "She said her people were from Nebraska. I've got a ticket to Omaha, but I wanted to stop and check with you on the way."

"Everything I discovered about the woman was in that letter you burned," Ham said. "If you'd chosen to open it, you'd have learned that when her baby was conceived, she was working at the Union Pacific Hotel in Laramie and married to a ne'er-do-well named Jake Logan, who got himself shot in some whore's bedroom. She stuck around Laramie until she was too far along to work, and then, one night, she disappeared. A week later she showed up at your ranch."

"That bears out what she told me in her letter." Morgan stared out the window of Ham's upstairs study, his eyes on the quiet street below. "But it's not enough. Not when she's afraid of being arrested and doesn't want to be found."

"That's the one thing that puzzles me." Ham rose to his feet. He was nearly as tall as Morgan, lean, leathery and a dead shot with a pistol. But an arthritic hip had ended his sterling career with Pinkerton. Now he supplemented his pension by hiring himself out as a private investigator.

"I don't understand the part about her having killed a man," Ham muttered as if to himself. "This is the first I've heard of it. When I looked into her disappearance from Laramie, no one mentioned a death. And I always check the local papers. Nothing there, either."

His frown deepened as he stared down at the letter in his hand. "Seamus Hawkins. Why does that name sound so familiar?" He rubbed the back of his neck, then suddenly his hand froze. "Good Lord! Now I remember!"

Morgan stared at him.

"It would've been a couple of months ago. He came here to see me, a big, dirty fellow with an awful-looking gash on the back of his head. Looked like he'd dressed it himself and taken the wrappings off too soon."

Morgan grappled with the weight of what he'd just heard. Hawkins was alive. Cassandra hadn't killed anyone. But she thought she had, and that in itself was a danger to her.

"What did Hawkins want?" he asked.

"To hire me. He said he was looking for a female tenant who'd skipped out in the night, owing him rent. Offered me a fair sum to find her. But something about him struck me as wrong. Maybe it was the way he talked about her, as if he owned her. I found myself sympathizing more with the woman than with him."

''So what did you do?''

''Sent him on his way. Suggested he try somebody else. Blast it, I must be getting old! By the time your letter arrived, a few days later, I'd forgotten all about the man!''

Morgan stood on the platform with his travel-worn leather valise, waiting for the eastbound Union Pacific to pull into the station. He had mixed feelings about traveling to Omaha. But after three days of searching, he had found no trace of Cassandra here in Cheyenne. It was time to move on.

What would he do if he couldn't find her? The trail was getting colder each day. Sooner or later, Morgan knew, he would have to give up and go home. But where was home now? Not on the ranch. Not without Cassandra.

The melancholy shriek of a steam whistle, still distant, broke into his thoughts. He stood apart from the clutch of waiting passengers, watching the train's long approach as it grew from a black dot on the western horizon to a hissing behemoth, terrible in its beauty.

Clouds of steam rose from the wheels as the locomotive glided to a stop. Passengers from as far away as California tottered onto the platform to stretch their legs. Morgan hung back, biding his time, reluctant to admit defeat and leave Cheyenne behind him. Something, he sensed, was here. And he had failed to find it.

As he watched, a husky, unkempt man ambled out

of the second car onto the platform. His grimy collar was unfastened, his stained felt hat askew, and even at a distance he smelled of garlic and cheap whiskey. But it was the expression on his face—the eager half smile of a predator on the scent of a victim—that sent a chill rippling over the surface of Morgan's skin.

An undersized, ratlike man in a brown plaid suit sprang off a bench and scurried across the platform to meet him. The two of them shook hands, then turned and walked side by side toward the latrines that flanked the Union Pacific depot.

The afternoon was hot, the air filled with the buzzing of flies from the stockyards beyond the tracks. Morgan had taken no more than a passing interest in the strange pair. It was purely by chance that he happened to glance around as the big man took off his hat to wipe his sweating head and neck with a dirty white handkerchief.

Morgan's pulse lurched as he saw it—an ugly red scar, flowing like wax from a guttered candle, all the way down the back of the man's large, greasy head.

Cassandra was sitting up in bed, nursing Rachel, when she heard the thud of a heavy fist on her door. Still drowsy, she glanced up at the clock on the wall. Four-fifteen in the afternoon. It was far too early to be summoned to the kitchen for her night's work.

The pounding came again, more insistently this time. Cassandra kept silent, a knot of fear tightening in the pit of her stomach. The hotel staff knew she was here. But they also knew she worked nights and slept days. If they bothered her at all, they would knock softly and probably call out her name. Maybe some guest had wandered down the wrong hallway. Maybe—

''I know you're in there, girlie! Come on, now, open the door!''

The sound of the asthmatic, whiskey-laced voice galvanized Cassandra with stark terror. She went rigid in her white cotton nightgown, her sleep-fogged mind groping for a way out of what had to be a nightmare.

But everything in the shabby room was real, as real as her crawling flesh and exploding heart. This was no nightmare. Somehow Seamus was alive. Somehow he had found her. And this time she had no weapon or means of escape.

Sensing her mother's panic, Rachel spat out the nipple and started to cry. Spurred to action, Cassandra flew from her bed, laid the baby in the empty dresser drawer that served as her cradle and covered her with a light blanket. Then she flung her weight against the heavy wardrobe that stood against the wall, straining to shove it in front of the door. But it was no use. She could not move it more than an inch at a time.

She heard the rattle of a key—Seamus could have gotten one easily enough by slipping a few dollars to the desk clerk. The lightweight bolt that secured the door from inside splintered off the frame as the big man shoved his way through.

His odiferous bulk seemed to fill the room as he closed the door behind him. Cassandra shrank against the far wall as his gaze crawled over her body. She could hear Rachel screaming beneath the blanket. Whatever it cost her, she had to protect her daughter.

He grinned, showing rotten teeth in his loose-lipped mouth. "Thought you could hide from me, didn't you? But you were wrong. You owe me, you little redheaded bitch, and ol' Seamus is here to collect."

Morgan had lost his quarry. He cursed aloud as he stared down the long, branching corridor lined with closed doors that all looked exactly the same. What now?

He had kept a careful distance, hoping the man he believed to be Seamus Hawkins would lead him to Cassandra. Things had gone all right until the big fellow had left his ratlike companion, cut down an alley and entered the back of the new three-story Cheyenne Star Hotel. Morgan had stayed out of sight as Hawkins panted his way up the indoor service stairway, turned left at the second-floor landing, and disappeared. Once he was out of sight, Morgan had raced after him, taking the stairs two at a time.

He had emerged from the stairwell to find that Hawkins—assuming the man really was Cassandra's former landlord—was nowhere in sight.

How could such an ungainly fellow have disappeared so quickly? Morgan strode to the first intersecting hallway. He saw more doors, all the same, and no one in sight except one elderly couple just leaving their room. Frustrated, Morgan turned in the opposite direction. Nothing. The place was a nightmare maze.

And if his hunch was right, Cassandra was some-where inside, trapped and in danger.

He stiffened as his ears caught a dim but familiar sound—the crying of a baby. For a moment he shrugged it off. After all, the world was full of babies. But there was something in this cry that touched him. He had heard that a mother could always recognize the cry of her own infant. Was that also true for a father or for a man who'd loved and nurtured a child as he had nurtured Cassandra's daughter?

But this was no time for questions. Not when all Morgan's instincts told him it was Rachel's cry he was hearing. Trusting those instincts now, he raced toward the sound.

"Can't you shut that little bastard up?" Seamus had backed Cassandra against the bed and was fum-bling with his belt buckle. But Rachel's full-bodied screams were clearly affecting his manhood. He glared down at his own crotch, cursing.

"Shut her up!" he growled, "or I'll shut her up for you!"

Sick with terror, Cassandra made a move to go to her baby, but he seized her arm and flung her back on the bed. "No, you don't. I don't trust you, you little slut! I'll take care of the brat myself!" He snatched up a pillow from the unmade bed and stum-bled toward the dresser drawer where Rachel lay kicking and squalling. "I'll shut her up once and for all—"

His words ended in a bellow as Cassandra leaped

on him, kicking, scratching, gouging and biting like a tigress. Her fingers went for his eyes, her feet for his groin. He was strong enough to kill her with his two hands, but she would die protecting her baby.

"You hellcat! I'll show you!" He tossed her against the wall and swung back toward Rachel. But Cassandra was on him again, attacking with a mother's desperate fury. His hands worked upward to close around her throat. Little by little he began to squeeze the life out of her. She fought for breath, eyes bulging with the strain.

"That's enough, Hawkins!" The door crashed open and Morgan lunged into the room. Dropping Cassandra, Seamus wheeled to face him. But the struggle was over before it could begin. Coward that he was, the big man weighed the odds, shoved past Morgan and staggered down the hallway, trailing blood from a torn ear.

Morgan let him go. There was no way Hawkins would get far before the law caught up with him. With luck, the judge would put him away where he could never threaten a woman again.

Rachel was still crying. Cassandra stumbled to the corner of the room and lifted her out of the makeshift cradle. Crooning softly, she settled the small head in the hollow of her shoulder. Her strained features softened as she stroked and rocked the small, jerking body. She looked like a battered Madonna, Morgan thought, her nightgown torn, her face bruised, her strange black hair a wild tumble around her face. But to him she had never looked more beautiful.

Morgan gathered them both into his arms, holding them tightly, feeling the warmth of their precious bodies against his own. He would love and protect them for the rest of his life, he vowed. This fiery woman and the tiny girl who had been his from the first moment he cradled her in his hands.

His family.

Forever.

Epilogue

April 17, 1880

"They're coming!"

Johnny Chang raced down the path from the knoll, gripping Morgan's binoculars in one hand. The dog bounded behind its master, tail high, tongue lolling.

Thomas, who was steadying the ladder for Cassandra, said nothing, but his eyes gleamed with anticipation. He looked like a prince in his traditional embroidered silk tunic and trousers. Johnny had insisted on dressing as the cowboy he was, but his plaid shirt was brand-new, his hair washed and freshly slicked back from his face. Both young men wanted to look their best for their brides.

Cassandra stood on a low rung of the ladder, hanging a garland of flowers above the moon gate. She laughed down at their excitement. Thomas, Johnny and Mei Li had been counting the days since Chang and Morgan had left for San Francisco to fetch the two Chinese sisters. Cassandra had been counting the days, too, but not for the same reason. She could hardly wait to see Morgan again and tell him her happy secret.

"Do you think they'll be pretty?" Johnny asked anxiously.

"Pretty doesn't matter as long as they're good girls." Mei Lei shifted the squirming Rachel against her hip. "Oof, she's getting heavy, this one! What are you going to do when you have two of them to manage?"

Cassandra stared down at her friend. "But, how did you know? I haven't told anyone yet, not even Morgan!"

Mei Li laughed. "How could I not know? You are blooming like a spring meadow! If heaven is kind, this ranch will soon be swarming with little ones!"

"Let's hope so!" Cassandra climbed carefully down from the ladder and gathered Rachel into her arms. "Come on, let's go and meet the wagon!"

Johnny and Thomas had already darted ahead, but Cassandra walked slowly to keep pace with her friend's tiny, tottering steps. "What a pity Ryan's not here," she said. "No one enjoys a good celebration more than he does."

"Ryan is like the wind, never happy to stay in one place," Mei Li said. "Maybe you should find him a good wife."

Now it was Cassandra's turn to laugh. "When Ryan's ready, he'll find his own wife, but something tells me she won't be an ordinary woman. Not for him!''

By the time they reached the ranch house, the loaded wagon, with Morgan driving the team, was rolling through the gate. The two Chinese girls sat on a box behind the seat. Their eyes were modestly lowered, a sign of good manners. They were indeed pretty, and when Chang helped them down from the wagon, Cassandra saw that their feet were not bound. As wives, they would be able to work alongside their husbands and run with their children across the open prairie.

Mei Li, flanked by her sons, walked forward to meet her two new daughters-in-law. Cassandra stayed back, sensing that this was an auspicious moment, a private time for the Chang family.

Her eyes met Morgan's across the distance. She felt the love in his gaze, and she sensed that even he had already guessed her wonderful secret.

You are blooming like a spring meadow! Mei Li's words came back to her as she waited, half-breathless, for the moment when he would climb down from the wagon seat and she would fly across the yard to his open arms.

She had learned that life was never easy on this raw, rough and splendid land. But now and then there were moments of heart-stopping beauty and unbridled joy. This was one of those moments.

* * * * *

Travel back in time to the British and Scottish Isles with Harlequin Historicals

On Sale July 2003

BEAUCHAMP BESIEGED by Elaine Knighton
(England, 1206-1210)
*A feisty Welshwoman and a fierce English knight
are used as political pawns—and discover
the passion of a lifetime!*

THE BETRAYAL by Ruth Langan
(Scotland, 1500s)
*When a highland laird fights his way into the
Mystical Kingdom to prevent a grave injustice,
will he become spellbound by an enchanting witch?*

On Sale August 2003

A DANGEROUS SEDUCTION
by Patricia Frances Rowell
(England, 1816)
*An earl hell-bent on revenge discovers the fine
line between hate and love when he falls for
the wife of his mortal enemy!*

A MOMENT'S MADNESS by Helen Kirkman
(England, 917 A.D.)
*With danger swirling around them, will a
courageous Danish woman and a fearless Saxon
warrior find their heart's desire in each other's arms?*

Visit us at www.eHarlequin.com

HARLEQUIN HISTORICALS®

Can't get enough of
our riveting Regencies
and evocative Victorians?
Then check out these enchanting
tales from Harlequin Historicals®

On sale May 2003

BEAUTY AND THE BARON by Deborah Hale

Will a former ugly duckling and an embittered
Waterloo war hero defy the odds in the name of love?

SCOUNDREL'S DAUGHTER by Margo Maguire

A feisty beauty encounters a ruggedly handsome
archaeologist who is intent on whisking her away
on the adventure of a lifetime!

On sale June 2003

THE NOTORIOUS MARRIAGE by Nicola Cornick
(sequel to LADY ALLERTON'S WAGER)

Eleanor Trevithick's hasty marriage to Kit Mostyn
is scandalous in itself. But then her husband
mysteriously disappears the next day....

SAVING SARAH by Gail Ranstrom

Can a jaded hero accused of treason and a
privileged lady hiding a dark secret save
each other—and discover everlasting love?

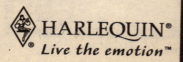

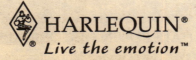

LOOKIN' FOR RIVETING TALES ABOUT RUGGED MEN AND THE FEISTY LADIES WHO TRY TO TAME THEM?

From Harlequin Historicals

July 2003

TEXAS GOLD by Carolyn Davidson

A fiercely independent farmer's past catches
up with her when the husband she left behind
turns up on her doorstep!

OF MEN AND ANGELS by Victoria Bylin

Can a hard-edged outlaw find redemption—and
true love—in the arms of an angelic young woman?

On sale August 2003

BLACKSTONE'S BRIDE by Bronwyn Williams

Will a beleaguered gold miner's widow and
a wounded half-breed ignite a searing passion
when they form a united front?

HIGH PLAINS WIFE by Jillian Hart

A taciturn rancher proposes a marriage
of convenience to a secretly smitten spinster
who has designs on his heart!

Visit us at www.eHarlequin.com

HARLEQUIN HISTORICALS®

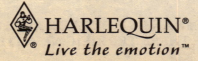

COMING NEXT MONTH FROM

HARLEQUIN HISTORICALS®

- **THE NOTORIOUS MARRIAGE**
  by **Nicola Cornick**, author of LADY ALLERTON'S WAGER
  Eleanor Trevithick's hasty marriage to Kit, Lord Mostyn, was
  enough to have the gossips in an uproar. But then it was heard that
  her new husband had disappeared a day after the wedding, not to
  return for five months…and their marriage became the most notorious in town!
      HH #659 ISBN# 29259-7 $5.25 U.S./$6.25 CAN.

- **SAVING SARAH**
  by **Gail Ranstrom**, author of A WILD JUSTICE
  Lady Sarah Hunter prowled London after dark to investigate the disappearance of her friend's children and unwittingly found herself
  engaging in a dangerous game of double identities with dishonored
  nobleman Ethan Travis. Now, would Ethan's love be enough to heal
  the wounds of Sarah's past?
      HH #660 ISBN# 29260-0 $5.25 U.S./$6.25 CAN.

- **BLISSFUL, TEXAS**
  by **Liz Ireland**, author of TROUBLE IN PARADISE
  Prim and proper Lacy Calhoun's world was turned upside
  down when she returned to her hometown and discovered that her
  mother was running the local bordello! And even more surprising
  were Lacy's *im*proper thoughts about the infuriating and oh-so-handsome Lucas Burns!
      HH #661 ISBN# 29261-9 $5.25 U.S./$6.25 CAN.

- **WINNING JENNA'S HEART**
  by **Charlene Sands**, author of CHASE WHEELER'S WOMAN
  Jenna Duncan was sure the handsome amnesiac found on her property
  was her longtime correspondent who had finally come to marry her.
  But when Jenna learned his true identity, would she be willing to risk
  her heart?
      HH #662 ISBN# 29262-7 $5.25 U.S./$6.25 CAN.

KEEP AN EYE OUT FOR ALL FOUR OF THESE TERRIFIC NEW TITLES

HHCNM0503